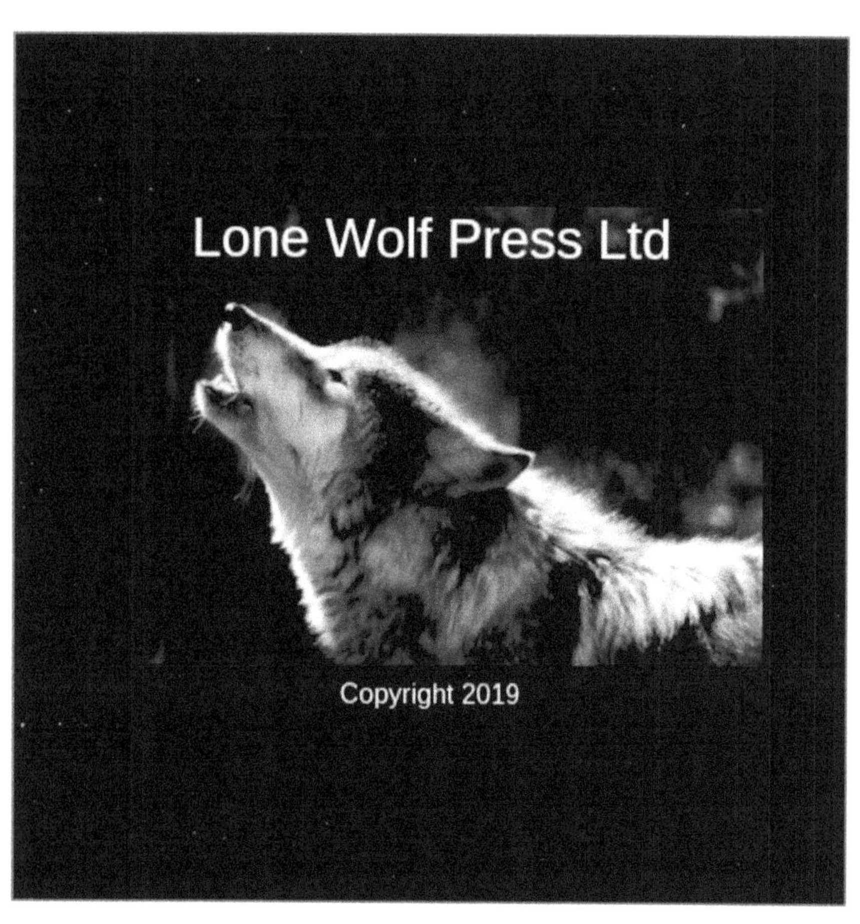

A publication of Lone Wolf Press, Ltd.

A Woman of the Road

By Amy Wolf

Book I of the Honest Thieves Trilogy

Books by Amy Wolf

Don't Let Me Die in a Motel 6: or One Woman's Struggle Through the Great Recession

L.A. Knight

The Misses Brontës' Establishment

The Cavernis Trilogy

Book I: A School for Dragons

Book II: A War for Dragons

Book III: A Hero for Dragons

Upcoming:

A Woman of the Road and Sea, Book II of the Honest Thieves Trilogy

The Twelve Labors of Nick

A WOMAN OF THE ROAD

Published: October 12, 2019

Paperback edition

ISBN: **9781696293563**

Find out more about the author and upcoming books online at:

https://amy-wolf.com & @AmyWolf_Author on Twitter

Find out more about this trilogy at

https://www.facebook.com/amywolfauthor/

To download a FREE BOOK, go to:

https://amy-wolf.com/landing

Special Acknowledgements

Rachel (R.E.) Carr – beta reader extraordinaire

Jorden Pritchard – firearms expert

Dr. Mark R. Levy – medical advisor

Theresa Mudrock – University of Washington Historical Librarian

This book is dedicated to the memory of Vonda N. McIntyre

Author, Mentor, Friend

. . .it was a liberal profession. . . which required more accomplishments than either the Bar or the pulpit. . . The finest men of England. . .the very noblest specimens of man. . .were beyond a doubt the mounted robbers who cultivated their profession on the great leading roads. . .

Thomas de Quincey

Table of Contents

Initiation

I confess I froze as Captain Jeffries pointed his pistol at *me.*

"Now," he said, "heed me, and you will live. Wield your weapon with menace but do not fire lest *you* are fired upon. We have enough grief as is without being hanged for murder."

"But captain," I said, shifting in my saddle, "I wonder how it matters? Is not the penalty for our trade death?"

Jeffries, astride his mount, winced beneath the black crepe that covered most of his face. His eyes narrowed, and I thought he would breech his own code by sending a lead ball through *me.*

"Let us not dwell on unhappy thoughts," he said. "For the moment, let us be merry. Your first adventure must be thrilling and—" he winked. "—most important, lucrative!"

Jeffries chuckled beneath his mask as I tried not to stare. In truth, he *was* dashingly handsome in his all-black breeches, silk stockings to match, and leather boots which reached to his thighs. Over his grey doublet, he wore a long dark cloak, and to add to a sense of menace brandished not one but two pistols, with a sheathed sword at his hip. Indeed, this was a captain ready to ride to battle.

To my amazement, so was I! I wore much the same raiment (for my costume belonged to Jeffries), though I bore but one pistol, and my doublet was green. To distinguish us further, I felt the strange discomfort of wearing another's clothes. I could feel the cuffs of my sleeves brushing past my fingertips; while my hat, festooned with feathers, fell nearly over my eyes. Since I was not yet half Jeffries's age, nor nearly as tall and bulky, I must have looked like a comical child.

"It is time," said Jeffries, spurring his horse forward while reaching to grab my reins. We rode across a road pitted with rocks and the wheel marks of many coaches.

As our horses trotted up a hill, nearly sending me out of my stirrups, Jeffries delivered a final word: "Remember—your task is to show swagger even if you feel fear."

"But I have no actual skill," I said, sharp pains striking my thighs as they pressed into hard leather. At that moment, I felt I could have crawled home and begged Father for forgiveness.

"Megs," Jeffries said, "recall—*you* were the one who sought me out. It was your wish to join me, and surely you comprehend this is not like serving beer. You must be *bold*. You must be *quick*. But most of all, be merry!"

He let loose a raucous laugh that shook his powerful body. I had observed through the years that despite his love of good wine, he had never put on an ounce. But I had no time for further thought as a dreaded clatter—iron wheels scattering pebbles—sounded around a bend.

"Your deflowering!" Jeffries crowed, letting loose my reins and handing them up to me. "Do not disappoint, dear Megs, or tarnish my name as a 'parfit, gentil' thief."

With that, he slapped my horse full on the rear, causing it to plummet like a chick thrown from its nest.

Beneath my own black mask, I tried to recall Jeffries's words: *Always search the coach*—for *weapons and hidden treasure. Be courteous to ladies, and a gentleman to gentlemen.*

My limbs shaking, I fought to keep my seat.

"Halt!" I cried, swooping upon a coach bearing a gold crest on its door. It was manned by a crusty old driver seated beside a shooter. The four harnessed horses obeyed (or at least the coachman did), and I boldly halted their progress on the Road to Bath. So boldly, in fact, that the coach's glass window shook.

My next words might be familiar, but for my first time, they thrilled:

"Stand and deliver!" I cried. "Your money or your life!"

Thank the blessèd Lord, that poor "shooter" was armed with a sword, while *I* had a flintlock pistol. I watched as his steel blade clanked to the road and lay silent.

"Whom do you carry?" I asked, motioning with my pistol that both men were to descend.

"Lady Castlemaine," the driver growled.

I snickered beneath my mask.

"Old Rowley's mistress?" I asked.

I was answered by a dark-eyed lady who stepped gracefully out of her coach. God's blood, she was hardly older than me, and I was but eighteen!

"If you mean the king, then yes," she said, as unruffled at being in the road as she would have been at Whitehall. I marveled at her calm, not to mention her dress: so much gold fabric encased her that she looked less gowned than minted!

Next, what drew my eye was of course her ornaments: she wore three strands of pearls and a brooch worth more than most earn in a lifetime. With caution, I leaned from my mount.

"Your keepsakes, madam," I said, pointing to them with my black glove.

"Very well," she sighed, "but know they are gifts from the king."

"Lady," I told her, gesturing at the road, "in this place, *I* am king."

I was rewarded with a laugh and even a small curtsy.

"How glad I am," she said, "that gallantry still exists in our high tobys. So many are lowborn now."

"Rest assured, Lady Castlemaine, that though I do not dance like the famed outlaw Du Vall, still, I strive to be courteous."

I inclined my hat, red feathers and all, to her, then rapidly pulled up the brim which had fallen over my eyes.

"Well, I must admit," she said, "I don't mind the infrequent robbery. Such a tale it will make in court!"

I knew that Jeffries would rage if I did not search the coach, but my victim was so good-humored that I did not have the heart.

"Good day to you," I said, with another tug of my hat. "Pray give my regards to the king."

"And who shall I say they are from?" she asked, as the waiting coachman and guard looked on with open mouths.

"I am called Megs," I said.

"What a curious name."

"And what a curious creature," said I. "The king, though married to a staunch Catholic, has more mistresses than you have pearls!" I dangled her strands from my glove.

"Ha! I love a good wit. I will pass your good wishes to Charles. He will be greatly amused."

"As one would expect from our merry monarch," I said.

With a final half bow, I spurred my mount a few paces until it thankfully brought me to Jeffries's side.

"Well done, young Megs!" said the captain, giving me such a clap on the back that I nearly hit the rough heath. "There's no doubt my London fence can get us sixty pounds for the pearls and two-hundred for the brooch. It is well that our dear Charles gifts his harem so richly."

"Queen Catherine will not share your joy," I said, "but I can affirm that *I* do."

"With this bounty," said Jeffries, lifting up the brooch so that its gold glinted in the sun, "there's no sleeping rough tonight! After I conduct my business, let us make for my favorite inn—I can almost taste the wine now!"

As my horse trotted beside him, jolting my innards until I felt they would burst, I tried my best to be merry. Yet, despite my smile, I felt a sense of foreboding. It was one thing to escape one's prison—quite another to return.

The Whale

As the sun arced west, we two road north toward London. Jeffries stopped at a Tudor shop on the outskirts while I contemplated dismounting to save my aching rear. I looked around this block, known for its disrepute: nothing but shoddy pawn shops, ale houses, and barely cobbled roads. Happily, Jeffries soon emerged, looking for all the world like a satisfied bridegroom. He displayed the lumpy object of his affection: a leather pouch so fat its cord could not be tied.

"Is it not lovely?" he cried.

"More so than Lady Castlemaine," I said.

The captain spilled a sea of guineas into my waiting glove. Any misgivings I'd had about my new trade disappeared with the gold I pocketed.

My horse followed Jeffries's as he headed southwest for Middlesex. This, I well knew, was where his favorite inn lay. Before it was even in sight, I could envision its old white stones and welcoming candles. When we at last stopped, I saw its distinctive sign graced by a carved leviathan caught in the crest of two words: *The Whale.*

"Time to unmask," said Jeffries, removing the crepe from his face. With great reluctance, I followed suit.

I felt my stomach rise as I handed my reins to the ostler, but, for Jeffries's sake, I displayed no outward sign. After I alighted from my saddle, I tried to ignore the pains shooting from back to legs. In my whole life, I had never ridden so much: in fact, before today, I had never ridden at all!

Be bold, I told myself, as I moved away from the ostler. *Show swagger despite your fear.*

It was thus with a firm step that I entered the Whale with Jeffries. We were both playing a part and I was determined to see mine through.

That is why I did not flinch when Richard "Dick" Tanner, the proprietor, skipped over to Jeffries with a grin and an open palm. He was rewarded with several guineas: not just for his "service," but his ability to keep silent.

"It's the cpt'n his'self!" Tanner cried.

I stared at this familiar figure with its tufts of grey hair protruding from under a cap. I knew without looking that his mouth bore precious few teeth, and that he wore a white grease-stained apron. I determined to keep a close eye, for I also knew he stole from his guests as surely as *I* had on the road.

"Wine, cpt'n?" Tanner grinned.

"Yes, and for my young friend," said Jeffries. "We two have ridden hard and are practically starving, so bring your best bread and cheese, a brace of pigeons, and a dozen scotch collops. We shall consider a fruit pie later."

Tanner nodded, waddling back to the kitchen. For the first time since I had entered, I let out my breath. It was clear the man did not know me. That was good for him, for had he uttered a word, I would have skewered him like an eel.

Jeffries, sensing my unease, said, "Ah! The comfort of a warm fire."

Indeed, it crackled merrily behind its brick façade. This main room could be comforting if you were a paying patron: what with its even wood floor and bar made of pewter, the latter polished to a high gleam.

I nodded to the captain, unwilling to speak. I needn't have troubled myself, for, consumed with thoughts of guineas, Tanner made himself our servant, scraping back two sturdy chairs at the captain's usual table. Naturally, this was the one in the farthest corner.

"Sir, 'ho's the young 'un?" asked Tanner.

"This is Megs, a new recruit. He has so far proved invaluable."

"Glad to 'ear it, cpt'n. Never seen you with nobody else."

Jeffries grinned.

"There is no one else like Megs."

Thankfully, our meal arrived, and my companion and I stabbed at it with knives we carried with us. I sought to purge from my mind the thought of the cook in the kitchen: unclean, dripping with sweat, and not above serving meats that had long ago lived their time. Still, *this* fare was excellent, as befit a man likes Jeffries.

When we'd done and wiped our knives clean, Jeffries asked for gooseberry pie. He was none the worse for having gone through two jugs of wine, while I merely too a few sips. I knew that while at the Whale, I must keep a clear head.

As we put away our pudding, other diners at a long center table started a game of Hazard.

"Say there, gents, care to join us?" asked a boisterous drover. "Only a ha'penny a hand."

"No, thank you," said Jeffries from his corner. "My friend and I are tired from a long, but fruitful, day."

"Suit yerself, sir," said the drover. He turned to the other players. "Not pertic'u'lar'y friendly, is 'e?"

Jeffries gave a rueful smile. This gave way to a groan as, an hour on, the drover grabbed a lute, and sang (rather badly, I thought) "Two Maids Went Milking":

Two maidens went milking one day
Two maidens went milking one day
And the wind it did blow high
And the wind it did blow low
And it toss-ed their pails to and fro, la, la, la
And it toss-ed their pails to and fro.

They met with a man they did know
They met with a man they did know
And they said, "Have you the will?"
And they said, "Have you the skill
For to catch us a small bird or two, la, la, la
For to catch us a small bird or two".

"Yes, I have an excellent good skill
Yes, I have an excellent good skill
If you'll come along with me
Un-der yonder flowering tree
I might catch you a small bird or two, la, la, la
I might catch you a small bird or two".

So they went and they sat 'neath a tree
So they went and they sat 'neath a tree
And the birds flew round about
Pret-ty birds flew in and out
And he caught them by one and by two, la, la, la
And he caught them by one and by two

Now my boys, let us drink down the sun
Now my boys let us drink down the moon
Take your lady to the wood
If you really think you should
You might catch her a small bird or two, la, la, la
You might catch her a small bird or two

As the drover finished to shouts and claps, undoubtedly "milked" by drink, Jeffries rose and tapped me on the shoulder.

"Come, Megs. We should retire."

His words sent a chill through me which no fire could dispel. I, above all, knew the inn's accommodations, and was not at all surprised when Tanner led us to a goodly sized chamber containing but *one* large bed.

"Fare you well," the innkeeper bid, then eyed us both. "I can provide a doxy or two if that be the gentlemen's wish." He winked like a comic actor at the newly reopened Globe.

"It is not," I said icily, being sure to deepen my voice. "We are weary and in need of rest."

Jeffries sighed but nodded.

"My young friend speaks true."

"Very well," said Tanner, displaying his gap-toothed grin. "If ye change yer mind, ye knows where to find me."

As he shut the door, I muttered, "Abed with your *own* doxy."

Jeffries chuckled.

"Well," he said, "that went better than expected. He has no idea who you are."

"It took all my resolve not to kick him downstairs."

"Come, Megs," said Jeffries. "This hideout is perfection: good wine and a crooked innkeep. What more can a tobyman ask for?"

I sighed.

Jeffries came over, removed my hat, and ruffled my long, dark hair.

"Do not despair, Megs," he said. "If you wish it, revenge will come. That depends on your desire to keep the flame of hatred alive."

I started. *What could he possibly mean?* My hatred of Tanner would outlast even England's for the dam'd Dutch!

Jeffries removed his cloak and unfastened his doublet's laces. Though I tried to forestall the feeling, I felt myself color.

"Come, come, dear Megs," Jeffries laughed, "you needn't blush before me. We are men of the road, are we not?"

I drew myself up to my full five-foot-five height.

"Indeed, we are, sir," I said.

"And sworn merry companions, with no need to stand on ceremony."

He proceeded to throw off his collar, breeches, stockings, and boots until he stood before me in only his long white shirt. Tiptoeing against the cold, he eased onto the feather mattress, making sure to slide to one side.

"As much as I love the Heath," he said, "a *real* bed wins by at least a Newmarket nose."

I knew this as the course where the Charles I had held races. Now that Cromwell was dead, perhaps the new king would resume them.

"Don't be shy, Megs," Jeffries entreated, "climb in before you catch cold."

He gestured to the wide berth on the other side of the bed. Still, I did not move. In truth, I had never slept with another, only rats and fleas on a filthy bundle of straw.

"Perhaps I should sleep on the floor," I said. "Or on that sturdy chair."

"Nonsense!" cried Jeffries. "I have plans for the morrow, and they require you be well-rested."

I wanted to join him but could not.

"Am I not your captain?" asked Jeffries.

"Yes, sir."

"And do you think . . . that even in light of your circumstances, I would ever harm you?"

His question hung in the air as I considered our long acquaintance.

"No, sir," I said. "I know that you would not."

"Then get in before I reverse myself and give you a good thrashing!"

The laughter in his voice told me he was not serious.

Shaking slightly, I shed as much clothing as I thought proper—I admit, it wasn't much. I still wore my doublet and breeches but made what I thought was a real concession by casting off my coat.

At last, I crept in the bed, then heard a low laugh beside me.

"Lord, Megs," said Jeffries, "thanks to your bright green doublet, I shall no doubt dream of the forest."

Soon, the captain's deep snores told me of his state. All the sounds of the inn, each of which I knew by heart: the walls groaning and settling as if to protest old age; the laughter of the wine-fueled game downstairs; Tanner's heavy step he jingled a handful of guineas; seemed to heighten like those of a cave.

When I woke with the sun the next morning, I found Jeffries's left arm draped across my shoulders. Still, I was not alarmed. He had proved his fealty during the night and had earned my trust. It was not an easy object to secure.

Learning the Trade

After we both had dressed (it did not take me long), we descended the stairs and sat at "the Captain's table." There, we breakfasted well on pickled oysters and anchovies washed down by swallows of beer. I had never known such luxury and frankly felt cowed in front of the serving girl. *Poor Sally.*

Tanner soon took her place. Since his breath stank of onions, I fought to keep my seat.

"All is well, sir?" he asked me, standing with hands forming a steeple. Ha! As if he'd ever been to church.

"Quite," I muttered.

"No complaints?" His grin told me he expected none.

I grunted in response. *Oh, I have them,* I thought, *a full eighteen years' worth.* But I vowed to listen to Jeffries: save my revenge for future.

Tanner scuttled off like a greasy crab.

"We shall change our lodgings tonight," Jeffries said.

"Pity," I replied, as he ruffled the feathers of my hat.

I was never so glad to leave a place (again) as I trailed Jeffries into the yard. There, we found our mounts in readiness, held by the same ostler as on the prior eve. He grinned over at me, nearly making me shudder, but I managed to steel my limbs. Hoisting myself into my saddle, I was even glad to trot off. Though I tried to mimic Jeffries, whose rear never rose from his saddle, *mine* spent most of the ride suspended in the free air . . .

I must have made an ungainly companion as Jeffries rode up a small rise fronted by scrabbly heath. This country stretched mostly flat to every horizon. Though it was in Middlesex and not one league from the Whale, I had seldom ventured here, for I knew the local legend: this place, Hounslow Heath, was a nest of robbers and thieves.

"Come, Megs!" Jeffries cried, as we entered a narrow valley hidden by gentle hills.

"Dismount," Jeffries ordered, and I did so . . . gladly. On the ground, I was as awkward as Lady Castlemaine was graceful, and, for some reason, this brought a lump to my throat. *Stop,* I told myself, watching Jeffries unharness our horses so they could graze where they might.

"We commence now," said Jeffries, which caused me to groan. I did not know to what he referred, but suspected it involved training. "Yesterday, you did well," he said, "but you only *brandished* your pistol—now, you must learn to use it."

"I do not wish to!" I cried. "I would rather go before the assize."

"Then you will be hanged," he said.

This made me lower my head.

"By no means do I say become another Prince Rupert," he chuckled. "God's blood, how that man loved his pistols!"

I started, for I'd heard of Rupert. He was the old king's nephew who had led the royals against Cromwell. Curious, I wanted to ask Jeffries if he had ever met the prince, but something in his eyes caused me to close my lips.

"Now," said Jeffries, "as far as pistols go, I have cautioned restraint. But if some puffed-up earl or duke fancies himself a marksman, we must respond in kind."

"Oh."

I suppose I had been swayed by romantic tales of tobys, their weapon being their wit and not a gun.

"Pay attention!" barked Jeffries, noting my glazed visage. As he strode toward me, I saw that his dark, shoulder-hair length—his own, as opposed to a wig—made him that much more handsome. I could well imagine a doxy waiting in every town.

"Megs!"

"Yes, sir," I said, blinking to clear my mind. *Back to business,* I thought, *bad though it might be.*

Jeffries seized my pistol from where it hung at my belt and held it up to my nose.

"This fine gun," he said, "is a flintlock. D'you know what that means?"

"Not really, sir."

"God's legs," he said softly. "It is called a flintlock since flint strikes steel and creates a spark, which in turn ignites your gunpowder."

I nodded, though these were just words to me.

"This is your cartridge," he went on, dangling a cone of paper. It smelled decidedly acrid. "Inside lies the correct measure of powder, *plus* a lead ball. Now."

Opening the pistol from the center, he poured in the cone's contents, then snapped the weapon shut.

"Breech loading," he said proudly. "Unusual, but effective."

"Yes, sir."

I tried to sound enthused.

"Ready?" Jeffries placed the gun in my hand and gestured toward a tree some thirty paces off. "Aim for the trunk," he said.

I gulped, setting my feet in what I hoped was a shooting position. This whole matter of "aiming" was completely foreign to me. Still, I closed one eye, steadied my right hand with my left, cocked the pistol, and fired. The white flash and noise caused me to fling away the gun as if it were a viper.

"Ha ha!" Jeffries laughed, holding his stomach. "*That* will surely impress! At least the birds will fly off."

He gestured to three winging sparrows.

"Captain Jeffries," I said, my ears still ringing, "I do not think . . . at this time . . . I am worthy of a gun. Perhaps I can be the highwayman who wields only a blade?"

"That would have done before the war," he said, bending to retrieve my gun. "These days, there are many old soldiers about who have shot their fair share of men."

I sighed.

"Very well, *you* load," he said, handing me the hated firearm.

I fumbled with paper and powder, wasting a good three cartridges. I tried time and again to dislodge just a splinter from that tree, but it merely stood there in mockery. Indeed, with each successive shot, my aim seemed not to improve, but worsen!

Jeffries put a hand up to his forehead.

"I do not like defeat, but . . . " he muttered.

This set my cheeks aflame: just two days into my career, and I was about to be sacked!

"Please—" I began.

"Watch me."

Jeffries withdrew one of his pistols, stepped back, and hit a twig from fifty paces . . . five times in a row.

I let out a low whistle.

"I would not wish to face you in a duel."

"No man would," he said. "Now, try to steady your arm and keep it perfectly still. Do not flinch when you fire."

He took a position behind me and I could feel his chest against my upper back. He pulled my shoulders straight.

"Ere squeezing the trigger, draw in your breath and hold it," he said.

I did.

"Very well. Proceed."

I aped his stance, legs spread apart, intent on holding my breath and keeping that barrel steady. A great *flash-bang*, and then a sliver of bark tearing from that tree.

"Better," said Jeffries. "Again."

From the nearby road, I heard coaches, riders, even a likely robbery, yet I willed my mind to focus. With each lead ball that flew, I grew in skill, so that first, I hit the broad trunk; then an adjoining branch, and finally, a high limb which came arcing out of the sun. Though my arms now ached along with my horseman's legs, I could not help but smile.

"Just so!" Jeffries cried. "You'll make a highwayman yet."

I puffed out my chest beneath my coat as I seized another cartridge and poured its contents into the breech. Yet before I could cock the gun, the thing went off in my hand, burning through my glove and emitting a shower of sparks.

"Ahhh," I groaned, hurling away the pistol as I doubled over in pain.

"Megs, are you all right?"

Jeffries gently brought me upright, tearing off the rest of my glove and lifting my poor right hand. I could see an unnatural redness spreading over my palm, accompanied by a throbbing.

"Here."

Jeffries reached under his cloak and drew out a small vial, from which he extracted an ointment. As he rubbed it over my palm, the relief was almost instant.

"What is that?" I asked.

"Crushed Alder leaves."

"For all I care," I said, "it could be a crushed alderman."

Jeffries smiled as he wrapped my hand with his handkerchief.

"You'll recover soon, Megs, but know this to be a danger—an ember must have hid in your barrel. There is naught we can do on the road, for there's no time to clean between rounds. Like soldiers, we take our chances."

"Is this a war?" I asked, my dreams of dancing on the Heath, getting off a good bon mot, and bowing to a chorus of laughter revealed as the nonsense they were.

"It is not a game," said Jeffries, a pistol in each hand. "We might be 'knights of the road,' but even knights in their armor were slain. Our aim is to rob the rich, and they and those that serve them are usually armed. That is why when we shoot, we must see not a traveler but an enemy on the field."

I bit my lower lip. When I'd first asked to join him, I knew my life would be filled with adventure—and possibly quite short. As I looked at Jeffries, I could not fathom how he'd lasted this long. Most highwaymen met their end at an age less than half of his—and not much more than my own.

"One more thing," said Jeffries.

Sighing, I bent to retrieve my gun.

"In stature, you are small," he said, "so, when you approach your quarry, swing your arms wide and square your shoulders."

I nodded, affecting what I thought was a suitably tall swagger.

"Good," said the captain. "Also, use your voice to instill fear. DROP YOUR WEAPON!" he shouted.

Mine flew from my hand as if in a second misfire.

"Now *you* say it," he ordered.

"Drop your weapon!" I yelled, like a squeaking mouse.

"Lower your register," said Jeffries. His voice took on basso tones. "Like thisss . . ."

"Drop your weapon!" I yelled, now sounding like a bigger animal. A pointer, perhaps.

"Better," he nodded. "Work on that every day."

I clutched my throat. "Yes, sir."

"On the morrow, we sleep in Epping Forest," said Jeffries. "Let us slay one of Charles's deer and increase the bounty on our heads."

My eyes widened, and not just at the thought of bounty.

"But that is a distance of sixteen leagues!" I cried.

"So long as no highwaymen strike, we should arrive before breakfast."

Journey to Epping

Yet, with each of those leagues, I found myself fading. As we loped northeast, my thighs felt heavy as lead while Jeffries's borrowed clothes seemed to grow even larger. How I longed to stop and rest! Still, the captain maintained a killing pace, refusing to stop at villages or the stone farmhouses with their prospect of nourishment. My breath began coming in gasps, as did my poor horse's, but I had come to learn that when Jeffries made up his mind, he made Cromwell look soft!

Just when I felt I could not set eyes on another cathedral, we came to a place of great greenery. Jeffries slowed his lathered mount and made for a small dirt path which wound between the trees. I could hear the sweet call of birds as we arrived at last at a cave covered with brambles. Thankfully, Jeffries halted, while I not so much dismounted as tumbled to the ground.

The captain unburdened the horses, who set off for a fresh green pasture.

"Water," I croaked. Damn the highwayman's habit of always traveling light!

Jeffries chuckled, then leaned into the cave to retrieve a big pewter jug. He crashed off through beeches and birch which gave me a chance to rest. I threw myself down and smelled the scents of the woodland: bark, spring flowers, even the fertile soil. What a change for me, used to London and its environs! Here, one could sit back and almost sink into Nature: appreciate her gifts without rushing to and fro. I felt as content as the horses, sprigs hanging from their mouths, as I basked in the cold morning sun which fought to shed its rays between copses of trees.

"Look alive, Megs!" Jeffries cried, stomping gentle as a bull through the Epping undergrowth. On his shoulder he hoisted his jug, now spilling over with water.

I drank my fill, marveling at its cleanness. To me, the usually spurned drink was as precious as the finest French wine.

"Thank you, sir," I said.

He grunted and proceeded to pick up some branches. After amassing a pile, he removed some implements from his coat: a small quartz stone and fire striker. Under his hand, the dry wood had no chance, and we soon had a cheerful blaze.

I leaned back on my elbows, my lips forming a question I had wanted to ask since Middlesex.

"Captain, why are we come?"

"Best not to linger," he said. "Especially on the Heath. Promotes our continued existence."

"Ah."

"I shall now search for game," he said. "I am no Carnatus, but we can at least thank the king for staying away from these parts."

He crashed back through the trees.

I confess that when he departed, I must have fallen asleep, for I was jolted upright by the report of a pistol. There followed the heavy tramp of boots, and then Jeffries himself, holding a fat rabbit by the ears. Despite my fearsome exterior, I had to look away as Jeffries prepared it for stew. I had never hunted and felt sorry for the poor beast but knew it had given its life to ensure our survival. *Good Christ,* I thought, *the sheer arrogance of man! We think ourselves better than all creatures on earth . . . which, the Church tells us, do not even have souls . . .*

While I brooded, Jeffries stomped back to the cave, and I heard his echoed, "We're in luck; it's still here!"

He emerged bearing a large silver jug and two chalices. What a robbery *that* must have been! He sat next to me on the grass as he poured a ruby liquid and handed me a cup which itself was inlaid with rubies!

"Enjoy this Latour," he said, quaffing a mouthful and stabbing some meat with his knife.

I took a small sip, followed by several others. "Nice fruit," I said, "tastes of plum."

Jeffries roared with laughter.

"Aye," he said, "far better to *drink* fine wine than to *serve* it."

"The Whale's is none too fine," I said. "Except for *your* stock, captain."

"By God, you speak the truth!"

Jeffries laid down, enjoying the warmth of the fire like a satisfied cat.

"This life's not too bad, eh?" he said. "There are others which exceed it in comfort

but . . ." He trailed off, staring into the flames. I wondered what life he'd led prior. He was so well-spoken . . . and an intimate of Price Rupert, so . . . I closed my eyes, seeing him as a lord overlooking his lands.

"What do you think thus far?" Jeffries asked, leaning to refill our cups. "Do you wish to continue? Most who join me do not last long."

I mimed his physical attitude, putting my hands behind my neck.

"Well . . . in the main, I s'pose I like it. Despite the riding of horses."

"Would you wish to be a lowly footpad?" I heard the horror in his voice.

"Oh no, sir. I *like* being a highwayman. We surpass all outlaws."

"I'll be dam'd if you're wrong!" said Jeffries, draining his cup again.

"I still fear guns," I said. "But I like going where I please, and of course there's the guineas. And . . . the fear in their eyes when you first ride upon then. Then the relief when they see you're a gentleman."

"Just so" Jeffries nodded, taking out a clay pipe and lighting some fragrant tobacco. He offered it to me, but I merely coughed at the smoke.

"Megs," he said, half-jokingly, "you must learn to acquire the vices of a respectable thief."

I smiled. "Aye, sir. All but smoking and one other."

"Hmph. Yes."

We could hear the stirrings of beasts beyond our cover of trees: deer, perhaps, or game birds—all serving at the pleasure of Charles II. *What would it be like,* I thought, *to own a forest so vast you could journey for days on end without reaching its border?* Yet, Jeffries had told me the king rarely came here. Perhaps Epping was just a small prize which came with a reclaimed crown. Thinking of the chasm between me and royalty, I soon fell into a sleep aided by the hoot of an owl. That was good luck, wasn't it?

Another Merry Companion

Jeffries and I rested for the remainder of the day, dining on a fat partridge which he'd brought down with a single shot.

"Let us say grace," said the captain before we sat down to our dinner.

This left me puzzled: he had never observed such niceties.

"Dear God," he began, bowing his head. I hastily followed suit. "Thank you for this bountiful meal which we found in the wilderness. But mostly—" he gave me a wink, "thanks to our precious new monarch, who taketh away that which his father hath giveth. Amen."

"Amen," I said, still confused.

After our fill of fowl and wine, we set about sleeping "rough," though there was nothing unpleasant about this fine spring night. The trees stood sentinel over us until we woke with the sun.

Jeffries was quick to warm some leftovers, but I must confess I was growing tired of game. What I would not give for a good shoulder of lamb, or even an oatmeal pudding!

I sighed as I splashed my face with water while Jeffries loaded his pistols.

"We've a busy day before us," he said.

I was unsure whether to be glad or not. Sensing my apprehension, the captain clapped me on the back before harnessing our mounts.

"Where to, sir?" I asked.

"Newmarket Road!" he said. "Usually fresh pickings this time of day."

I swung aboard my mount, ignoring the pain in my legs.

"Aye, aye, captain," I said. "But isn't the present hour a bit early for thieving?"

From his saddle, Jeffries laughed.

"Daylight is the *best* time. Night provides cover, of course, but few travel after sunset, for the 'hundreds' will not reimburse them."

"What does that signify?" I asked. He might as well have been speaking Latin.

Jeffries urged his horse forward.

"Travelers avoid the night for they are perceived as rascals—those bent on evil. But . . . if we meet them during the day, they are entitled to half the cost of what we steal. An admirable system all round."

"Yes, sir."

"Ah, there is Harlow."

Not far from Epping, Jeffries pointed out a small village which housed an ancient church. I saw what must have been the Newmarket Road, for Jeffries led us away from it toward a small path hidden by trees.

"Ho," he told his mount. He gestured toward the road. "Megs. Have a look!"

I saw some clustered riders and the poor on foot, but these did not catch my gaze. What did: a fat bishop, alone on a mule laden with packs.

"The fool," Jeffries whispered. "Does he think his vestments protect him?"

Before I could answer, he pulled up his mask and plunged from our hideout, forcing me to follow suit.

"Hey ho, friar," Jeffries called, "where to so early in the morn? Off to harry some Catholics? Or is it Dissenters today?"

"Blasphemer," said the bishop, looking up to heaven. "Continue your depravity, and you will suffer hellfire!"

"As will you," said Jeffries, leaning down to seize the bishop's reins. "Is not the Church of England, founded on Henry's whim, as fully corrupt as our court? Do you not jail Quakers? And adopt every Papist ritual? I expect that shortly, you'll answer to direct to Rome."

"I-I will see you tried before the Court of High Commission!" the bishop sputtered.

"Not the vice court!" Jeffries cried in mock-horror. "Yet I am about to *commit* an act which will bring you *low*."

Despite the bishop's rich silks and elaborate ruff, I could not help but laugh.

"Impudent whelp!" cried the bishop. "Do you wish to be cast in the Pit along with your friend?"

"It is better than going alone," I said.

"Enough," said Jeffries. "Let us see what this overfed churchman bears."

I was sure to unloose my pistol as the captain dismounted and approached the trembling cleric.

"Now. This ass must alight from his ass," Jeffries said.

I could barely hold onto my weapon as I shook with laughter.

Jeffries kindly helped the bishop to the ground and was rewarded with oaths unfit for a drover. Pushing his prey aside, Jeffries unsheathed his blade and ripped open the mule's packs. What spilled forth were two golden candlesticks, an enormous gold Cross, and a torrent of coin!

"Well met!" Jeffries crowed, bending to scoop up the guineas. "Keep 'im in your sights, Megs." He straightened and turned to the bishop. "Is

His Holiness advancing to supply an altar, or in retreat, having just robbed one?"

The bishop glowered as Jeffries proceeded to strip his rich raiment. Soon, a shirt with billowing sleeves, joined by a long black robe, sat at the side of the road. I had to avert my eyes, for the bishop was now exactly as God made him.

"This is an outrage!" he shouted, while attempting to cover his privates. "Are you not aware that King Charles heads our Church?"

"I am," said Jeffries, motioning with a pistol for the bishop to remount his ass—but with the churchman's head facing its tail!

"Since Charles is so rich, he will surely not miss these trifles," I said, pointing to our gold bounty.

"We would not wish you to fall ere you reach the next town," said Jeffries, tying the bishop to his saddle with the man's own reins!

"You will hang for this!" cried the bishop. "I will see to—"

"Ha!" Jeffries slapped the mule's rear, causing it to take off. The sight of the naked bishop turned wrong-way-round on his ass brought tears of laughter to my eyes.

Jeffries seemed similarly incapacitated.

"There will indeed be a tale told in the taverns tonight!"

"No doubt," I said, smiling under my mask. "You have reformed the Reformation."

"And restored *these* from the Restoration."

He held up the two giant candlestick. I must confess, we laughed the entire way to Waltham.

I left Jeffries there with a "friend," who, in an act of alchemy, could change gold straight into guineas. Dreaming of future riches, I felt so lighthearted that on my way back to Epping I sang a snatch of "The Three Butchers":

> With that, came out ten swaggering blades,
> With their rapiers in their hand.
> They rode up to bold Johnson,
> And boldly bid him stand.
> Oh, I cannot fight; says Gibson,
> I am sure that I shall die!
> No more won't I," cries Wilson,
> For I will sooner fly!
> *With my hey, ding, ding, with my ho, ding, ding,*
> *With my high, ding, ding, high dey!*
> *May God keep all good people from such bad company!*

With the realization that *I* was now bad company, I headed for our camp and slid to the ground in relief. Would that the pain in my thighs might dispel! My horse, at least, seemed pleased as I released him. I searched our cave but did not find what I was after: namely, something to eat. Just as I resigned myself to wait 'till Jeffries's return, I felt a sharp object between my shoulder blades. Was this the captain bent on some kind of jest? But, as the object tore through my coat, I knew it for what it was: the hard, pointed tip of steel.

Since I was facing the cave, my hands hidden from my assailant, I attempted to free my pistol.

From behind came the sound of laughter. This, more than anything, made me whirl around.

"What do you want?" I growled. I tried to lower my voice as Jeffries had instructed.

"Your purse, of course, dear fellow!"

My masked attacker soon freed me of the guineas on my person.

"You do not know whom you accost," I said. "*I* am a feared highwayman who rides with Captain Jeffries. He shall hear of this."

"Oh, I can assure that," said the man. "For now, feared highwayman, I challenge you to a duel."

I looked up at him with concern. He was tall and gaunt, dressed all in black down to his sleeves. His long dark hair cascaded from beneath his hat and his eyes were so dark I could swear they were black too. Like most Cavaliers, he sported a mustache and small beard.

"Stand and deliver!" he cried, and, at hearing this phrase from his lips, my blood flamed. With a hesitant hand, I accepted from him a sword which he unloosed from his belt. In truth, I had never held such a weapon and feared this foe who raised his like a master. Though I tried to mimic his stance, I could see my own blade quaver.

In my defense, I did not run, though the thought stayed with me. My opponent could hardly contain his glee as he smote the steel from my hand time and time again. He whirled and feinted so gracefully, using arms and legs with equal skill, that at last I collapsed on the ground like a shaky pudding.

"Take all I have, blackguard! How dare you attack without warning?" In a fit of pique, I added, "May God damn your soul to hell!"

He surprised me by growing reflective.

"Who amongst us will dwell in eternal fire?" he asked. "As for your query, the Bible tells us: 'If the master of the house had known the hour of night when the thief was coming, he would have stayed awake and not let his house be broken into.'"

"God's legs!" I cried. "What are you, a priest? We have just dealt with one of you. When he returns to Harlow, he will tell his tale as God brought him into the world: without a stitch of clothing."

The tall man chuckled as he resheathed his weapon and with his other hand ripped off his mask.

"Insomuch as that priest was likely not of my faith, it troubles me not at all," he said.

I wanted to ask *and what faith is that?* but, knowing his skill as a swordsman, I wisely held my tongue. When I regained my breath, I rolled to my feet, brushing the grass from my breeches.

"You may wonder who I am," he said.

"It did cross my mind," I said sharply.

"My name is Aventis. And you are he who answers to 'Megs.'"

"How do you know?" I asked, eyeing my fallen blade.

"Captain Jeffries. You see, young Megs, I too am a member of his band. I am newly returned from France."

"Oh."

This took me aback. I had never seen anyone else with Jeffries, and hadn't he told me that those who joined him failed?

"Here." Aventis gave back my guineas. "In future, you will *not* be taken unawares. Your blade will not master you: *you* will become its master."

"That seems unlikely," I told him.

His face remained impassive as he threw that hated steel at me. I caught the hilt in one gloved hand as I strove to keep the blade steady.

"Now," said Aventis, "when I do *this*—" he thrust his blade toward me, "—you do *this*—" In one motion, he showed me how to parry. For the first time that day, steel struck steel more than once before it was swatted away. *Still,* I thought, surprising myself, *I prefer a pistol*: it was quicker, more deadly, and did not seem as old-fashioned as this ancient art. We lived in a modern age and it required a new form of fighting if it were ever to last.

"Good," said Aventis, as I roused myself to meet his sword by springing onto a tree stump.

"I see you have the instinct to use all around you—rocks, walls, men—to hold the high ground. That is where victory lies."

He slashed beneath my blade, and for once, I maintained my grip. The sun's rays on our crossed steel nearly dazzled my sight.

"Very well," said Aventis. "That will suffice for the present."

He sheathed his sword in a narrow black scabbard while I made a move to hand back mine.

"No, no" he said, holding up a black-gloved hand. "That blade belongs to you. It is my gift."

"I-I thank you," I said, touching my hat. I was such a stranger to kindness I did not know how to respond. "I . . . I take it Jeffries sent you?" I finally came up with.

"Of course."

As the sun shone down on his face, I saw how handsome Aventis was: even his moustache had grown on me. His features were fine and even, and, unlike most of my countrymen, his teeth gleamed with perfection. Realizing that I stared, I directed my gaze to the trees, then tried to master my thoughts so I did not appear mad.

"I . . . I must be a dreadful burden," I said. "Both to Jeffries and you. What I mean is I know so little, in truth, actually nothing."

"Nonsense," said Aventis. "A good man is worth fifty guineas. A loyal one—a hundred. And Jeffries tells me you are loyal." His black eyes scanned my face. "That you have a reason to be."

I broke from his gaze. Had he been apprised of my circumstance?

"Do not fret, young Megs," he said. "I only know what I must. Jeffries would not have endured this long had he not the power of silence."

I nodded, feeling better.

"As long as we are here," said Aventis, "what say you to a Lafite?"

"If it is as good as the Latour, then let us be friends forever!" I cried.

Aventis strode to the cave and removed a gold jug, along with three matching cups. He filled them with precious red liquor, the finest that France could provide . . .

What I remember from that night is Aventis, joined by Jeffries, making toasts to each other and singing a verse from "The Three Butchers":

> Out sprang ten bold highwaymen with weapons in their hands.
> They strode up to young Johnson and boldly bid him stand.
> "Stand I will" said Johnson "as long as ever I can.
> For I was never in all my life afraid of any man".
> Then Johnson being a valiant man he made those bullets fly,
> 'Til nine of them bold highwaymen all on the ground did lie.

This wicked woman standing by young Johnson did not mind,
She took a knife all from his side and stabbed him from behind.

Curious, I thought, as I lay sprawled on the grass. Those two sing of betrayal, but I have never seen such companions. Indeed, by the light of our campfire (and aided, it must be said, by my wine-soaked vision), they seemed more like congenial brothers than cutthroat men of the road.

Our Third Merry Companion

I awoke to the chirping of birds as I lay by the spitting fire. During the night, someone had taken care to cover me with a blanket.

"Today," said Jeffries, standing over me, "we seek our third and final companion."

"Beg pardon?" I asked.

Though both he and Aventis seemed sober as saints, I found that *my* head rang as with the bells of St. Paul's. I struggled to throw off my covering, groaning like the worst drunk at the Whale.. Now what was all this about a *third member of our band?*

"I wish to find him as much as you do," Aventis was saying to Jeffries. "But where? He could be near his seat in York, or at any gaming house anywhere."

"I have received a report," said Jeffries, "that he is to be found in Harlow. As Gad was seen there last week, his master will not be far."

"Ah, *that* narrows our range." Aventis nodded. "The village is not great, so he should be discovered with ease."

"It is nigh impossible to hide a man of his girth," said Jeffries.

"And foppery," added Aventis.

The two men erupted in laughter. I had no notion of whom they spoke: only that his appearance must be that of a stout peacock.

"Let us go," Jeffries ordered. Happily, I was still dressed. I snuck off for a moment to "conduct my own affairs," then mounted alongside the others.

Once we reached the Newmarket Road, I saw it was heavily trafficked: mainly by those on foot. They must have learned the ways of our kind, for they did not clump in a bunch; rather, they spread out so if we set upon them, those the most distant from us could raise a hue-and-cry. Yet after his triumph with the bishop, Jeffries had no need to ply his trade and even raised his hat to passersby.

As we entered Harlow, we passed the old stone church, a block of shops in the Tudor style, and crossed a fine stone bridge.

At the end of one narrow street, we stopped at an alehouse for a bite of bread and ale. I was glad, for I had not breakfasted and my supper the prior eve had mainly consisted of liquid. I noted Aventis ate little and even bowed his head before commencing his meal. Unlike Jeffries's farcical grace, *his* seemed to be genuine.

"Still the devout?" Jeffries asked him.

Aventis gave a thin smile.

"What harm can it do?"

I thought it somewhat curious that a man who rode with Jeffries showed such signs of piety. Still, I shrugged my shoulders. Let him recite all the Gospels if he wielded a sword like he did!

Once we were sated, we sauntered out, where I saw villagers cross the road. Either Jeffries was known in Essex, or our costumes gave us away. Perhaps a bit of both.

Harlow was pleasant enough, though rather dull compared to London. As we strode down a dusty thoroughfare, we saw a woman mumbling to herself, carrying on as lively a discourse as if she had a companion.

Jeffries shook his head.

"Pray that the Witchhunter General does not track her," he said.

"Hopkins is gone," said Aventis. "Have you not heard?"

"Good riddance," said Jeffries. "It is amazing what some folk believe."

"About us, too," said Aventis.

I nodded, thinking he referred to our band. After we'd passed a few shops: a tailor's, a smithy, and a shoemaker's, I saw Jeffries and Aventis freeze.

"Look!" the captain cried, pointing to a broad bay Shire tied by a small cookhouse.

"I know that mount as I know myself," said Aventis.

I half ran to keep up with their strides until we entered the place. But what a melee awaited us!

A lad clad all in blue was threatening a cook with a whip, while *that* flour-coated fellow brandished an upraised pan. A person who must have been the lad's master bellowed at the cookhouse owner, all the while taking bites from *two* roast chickens he held up in each hand!

"—and *I* must insist that one shilling apiece for these fowl is . . . I so *hate* to use the term, but . . . it is no more highway robbery! I'll pay no more than 10d!"

"Sir," the proprietor begged, his bald head shiny with sweat, "I think you'll find that a shilling is the going rate in London—"

"Are we in London, sir?" his enraged customer asked. This man was more mountain than flesh, as wide as he was tall. On his head was a long blond periwig spilling past features which included a thick nose now red with anger. The overturned jug before him told of his recent exploits.

"Gad, strike him!" he ordered his liveried lad.

This Gad drew back his whip prior to cracking it at the cook, but the latter deflected it nicely with a quick turn of his pan.

"Am I to be thus insulted?!" the master roared. "A fine gentleman like myself, freshly returned from my manor."

He straightened his wide lace collar which matched his patterned sleeves, his coat of so many colors it might have belonged to Joseph. He stomped his enormous boots against the floorboards, then surprised me by withdrawing two dice from his doublet.

"Let us play for the bill," he said. "If I throw two sixes, you win. Anything less than eleven, I win. If the left die shows more than the right, the victory is mine. If opposite, it goes to you."

"I—" said the proprietor, scratching his head. "I do not comprehend the rules."

"Simple if one's not a simpleton," the man said with a shrug.

"Enough of yer nonsense!" shouted the cook from beneath his small white cap. "Pay up or we'll have the law on ye!"

"Friends!" The giant shouted over my head to my two companions. "Will you stand there unmoving while my honor is impinged?"

"Of course not, Carnatus," said Jeffries.

"Unthinkable," said Aventis.

I stood there uncertain until Carnatus glared down at me.

"I'faith, I am with you!" I cried, and we five, including Gad, proceeded to stand against the owner, two cooks, a serving maid, and even a diner or two.

I spent the next few minutes ducking as these objects flew past my head: a leg of mutton, a side of beef, a tart oozing with pear, and a line of pewter plates. When I could, I withdrew my new blade, seeing through flying foodstuffs that my friends were likewise assailed. Gad, poor devil, took on such a quantity of flour he looked fit for the roasting pan!

"Pinion him!" cried a patron, pointing at Carnatus. "He disturbed my bread and cheese!"

"He is a thief in gentlemen's clothing!" said another, with a toss of his sharp eating knife. Carnatus deflected this easily, sending the blade flying into a jug of wine. This naturally shattered, spewing its contents like blood across a table.

I, to my shame, held the poor serving girl at bay.

"I am truly sorry," I told her.

"It is not your fault," she said. "Only that horrible giant's."

We both watched as Jeffries threw a roast ox head at a cook. Even this fellow recoiled at the sight of his flying fare.

"You will pay what you owe!" cried the owner, moving toward Carnatus with a knife that could carve the rest of that ox.

"Perhaps not," said Aventis, unsheathing his sword and holding the angry mob back.

"Best that we go!" cried Jeffries. His hat, formerly topped with feathers, now bore a fat pear on its crown.

I needed no more encouragement: I fled, followed by Jeffries and Aventis, where townsfolk, having heard the ruckus, had assembled in the street.

"Let us quit this place!" cried Aventis, shaking the remains of pie from his cloak.

"Not without *these!"* said Carnatus, bolting out of the cookhouse with Gad at his heels and a chicken in each hand.

Gad untied our horses, then leapt behind Carnatus as we galloped off as one. I scraped some soup from my cheek as I leaned forward like a jockey.

"Scofflaws!" I heard from behind us. *"Thieves! Divers!* After them!"

But no clatter of hooves pursued us.

"Ha!" said Aventis to me, "who will they send—the watch? Those doddering fools can barely walk, much less ride."

I smiled as we thundered through Essex county, passing a good-sized town on the way back to our cave. We all dismounted.

"What an adventure!" crowed Jeffries. He removed the pear from his hat and bit into it, content.

"Carnatus has been avenged," said Aventis, bowing toward our new companion.

"I thank you all," said Carnatus, taking a mouthful of fowl. After he swallowed, he cried, "For this, I did not pay a single shilling!"

"Nor should you," Jeffries nodded. "Are we not 'knights of the road'?"

I merely grinned, but this seemed to inspire something among the others. With no words spoken, they gathered in a tight circle, unsheathing their swords and raising them.

"In the spirit of Claude du Vall," said Jeffries, "greatest tobyman of all, we vow to stand together, companions to the last."

Their three blades met with the heavy clank of steel. As Gad and I watched, I felt more the outsider than he.

Once blades were put away, Aventis strode toward the cave, emerging with that silver jug and five dangling gold cups.

"To honest thieves everywhere!" he cried, filling the cups to the brim and handing them round.

"I'll drink to that!" said Jeffries.

"As will I!" said Carnatus.

"I'll be dam'd if I don't!" said Gad.

I spoke up sheepishly.

"Don't mind if I do," I said, staring up at Carnatus: he had so many ribbons and laces that he looked out of place in Epping, and would have fit in far better at Charles's Whitehall court.

Jeffries noticed my awe.

"Carnatus, this is Megs," he said. "Though young, he has already proved himself by robbing Lady Castlemaine."

"A bold feat!" the giant roared, his wig settling under his hat.

He is a true high tobyman," said Aventis. "Quite skilled with pistol and sword."

"Well, I would not—" I began.

"Pfft!" Carnatus cried. "How can you object? There is no praise greater than flattery!"

He clinked his cup against mine.

"Ah, how foolish of me," cried Jeffries, clapping a hand to his forehead. "What kind of captain am I? I have a friend in Waltham who prayed at the foot of holy relics. Or, I should say, 'preyed,' eh Megs?"

I smiled as Jeffries removed one . . . two . . . then a *third* heavy bag from the cave.

"Now that we are all present," he said, "let us divide the spoils."

I could see the gleam of avarice in Carnatus's eye.

After slicing open the bags, Jeffries revealed a cascade of treasure.

"Aventis, Carnatus, Gad, and Megs," he said, slapping a mound of guineas into each of our outstretched palms. "Now Megs gets double since he was present."

I looked down at my two gloved hands. How the coins glistened in the sun, each calling to me with the promise of a new life.

"Thank you, captain," I said, my voice shaking.

"You earned it, lad," said Jeffries, clapping me on the shoulder.

"Let us have a big huzzah for Megs!" cried Aventis.

"HUZZAH!" the company shouted. "Huzzah and huzzah for Megs!"

I bowed deep in gratitude . . . I, who was so unused to praise.

"I will just put these away."

I nodded toward the cave, gesturing with my guineas, but truth to tell, I sought a place to hide my tears. I knew it might be fleeting and perhaps a fool's dream, but for the first time in my life, I felt a part of something—something bigger than me. I took out a handkerchief and made sure to wipe my eyes, then rejoined my new friends, where Carnatus was in the midst of telling a tale of Hazard.

Throwing a Main

The next morning, I made sure to rise early and walk to the edge of the woods. Unbuttoning my breeches and sliding them down, I squatted low and prepared to empty my bladder.

"What a damn'd strange stance," a voice cried from behind me.

With more speed than a startled bird, I vaulted upright, pulled up my breeches, and endeavored to close them. I was relieved not to feel damp, but aghast lest Carnatus had blundered upon what he should not. Happily, the giant was occupied, for *he* had unbuttoned his breeches and let loose a powerful stream.

"Pray, do not let me stop you!" he roared, slapping me on the back. "We are all men here."

"I-I confess to being ashamed," I said.

"In God's name, why?"

"Well . . . you are so … endowed . . . that I fear my own member pales beside your own."

"Of course." Carnatus smiled. "I *perfectly* understand."

He buttoned his costume and strode, whistling, back toward our camp.

My muscles untensed with such haste that I nearly fell to the ground. I leaned on a tree for support. I must never, I determined, be caught in this way again!

As I walked back to the others, I fought to calm my expression.

"Men," said Jeffries, addressing us all. "It is my humble opinion that our health will benefit, after the uh—" he looked at Carnatus, "—'incident' in Harlow, if we, to be short, get the hell out of Epping."

"Aye," said Aventis.

Carnatus rolled his eyes as the rest of us nodded. Gad proved a welcome addition, for he worked to prepare the horses. After a breakfast of wild-caught berries, and two leagues at a brisk pace, I found that the more time I spent in the saddle, the less pain assaulted my thighs. Twelve-and-a-half leagues later, when we arrived at Hounslow, I felt mere pangs in my legs as opposed to the stabbings of daggers.

"Lads," Jeffries whispered, as he led us into a hollow at the bend of a wide road. "Though we are rich enough, if some prey wanders into our path, what kind of thieves would we be not to pounce?"

"Damn'd bad ones," said Carnatus.

"Unworthy of the name," said Aventis.

"Shameful," said Gad. "Especially on the Great Western."

As we watched, waited, and listened, I found myself shaking in the cold spring afternoon. Indeed, some massed grey clouds seemed to threaten rain. Before the deluge could fall, we heard a distant rumble—not of thunder, but iron wheels. Peering over my horse's head, I could just discern eight, belonging to two now-close coaches! The first was crafted of gilt and bore a large seal—along with *four* standing shooters. The second trundled behind, looking poor and plain by comparison.

"On them!" Jeffries cried, leading the charge. As his horse wheeled into their path, Aventis shouted:

"No! Stop!"

Still, Carnatus and Gad leapt to what must be their work, binding the guards and driver with cleverly tied rope. While Aventis, eyes closed, remained behind in the hollow, I trotted my mount up to Jeffries's.

"Good day to you, missus," he bid an old woman in the first coach. She was fiercely shielding a boy, aged perhaps eleven. "And who is this fine fellow?" He smiled down at the lad.

"Only the son of your king," the woman growled.

Jeffries lowered his pistols, while Carnatus and Gad scrambled to undo their work.

"My good woman," said Jeffries, doffing his hat from the saddle, "I deeply beg your pardon. May God shed his light on this child and see that his life is fruitful and long."

The boy, dressed in opulent blue, stuck his head with its long curly hair out the coach window.

"And who would *you* be?" he asked Jeffries.

"I-I am a captain, late of service to your father."

The boy arched his dark brows.

"How do you do him a service by holding up his relations?"

This was, I can swear, the first time I saw Jeffries blush.

But the boy wasn't finished.

"*My* name is James Scott," he said, "but you may address me as duke. For I will be so two years hence. The very first Duke of Monmouth."

"God's wounds!" I heard Carnatus groan.

Jeffries regained his composure.

"Duke James," he said, "since your grandfather's terrible death, men like me have done what we must. Alas, war and treason consumed all that we had."

Jeffries bowed his head in a rare show of sorrow.

"I do not condone your profession," said Scott. "But at least you are a gentleman." He gave Jeffries a hard stare: then turned to me, Gad, and

Carnatus. "I trust we shall meet again," said the boy, "and you will bow to me as your lord."

The driver and guards took up their posts as he gave an imperious wave. Out of habit, my friends raised their pistols to ensure a quiet departure.

Aventis rode up to join us, his face white as he threw off his mask.

"Good Lord," he said, "did you not recognize the seal? Let us desist in future from robbing the king's issue."

"But he has so many!" Carnatus shouted.

"And not a one legitimate," added Jeffries.

"The last thing we should do is offend His Majesty," said Aventis. "He is no tyrant like Louis but hates to be made a fool."

"Which 'e is," said Gad.

The rest of us looked at him with amazement.

"Ain't ya heard the latest? 'He never said a foolish thing, Nor ever did a wise one.'"

"That is unfair," said Jeffries. "Did he not return from Breda to take the throne?"

"And free us from all things Cromwell?" asked Carnatus. "Gad, come here directly. I've a notion to box your ears."

Gad approached his master, head drooping, but Carnatus, after raising his arm, merely tousled the lad's hair.

Still, Aventis did not smile. His black eyes stern, he resumed his speech.

"We *must* avoid all things royal, for—" he glanced at Jeffries, "His Majesty might be merry but esteems his mistresses and children."

"That is so," said the captain. "We must aim for lesser gentry."

"Perhaps an errant earl!" called Carnatus.

"Or a doddering duke," I suggested.

"In truth, lads," said Jeffries, "we should rob from the middle: the merchants with their fat purses, and the Church. The poor we do not disturb, for they have suffered enough."

"Why not lessen their plight?" I asked, "and give them a bit of coin?"

"Megs wants to be Robin Hood!" Carnatus shouted at Gad.

"'E wants ter give to the poor!" Gad laughed, as if I already wore Lincoln green.

"Enough." Aventis leaned over his saddle. "Megs has a laudable notion. Did not Jesus say, "'Blessed are you who are poor, for yours is the kingdom of God.'?"

"And look what happened to Him," said Carnatus.

"I for one applaud Megs," said Jeffries. "Let us gift some gold—not a great deal, mind you—to the next set of paupers we see."

I had to stifle a laugh as I watched Carnatus's face: the poor fellow looked like he'd swallowed his sword.

"There are some likelies," called Jeffries, trotting onto the road. I saw him exchange a handful of guineas for a series of bows and thanks.

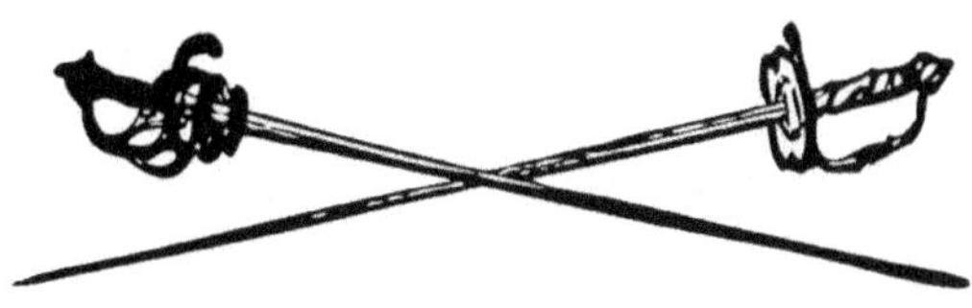

After a meal at Jeffries's old hideout, we galloped back to the Heath. I suspected the captain was anxious to replace what he'd given away. As I breathed in the scent of scrub, I had to admit that Hounslow was handsome with its high yellow grasses and occasional stand of trees. To be sure, it was no Epping, but neither was it a desert.

Once our band reached the Road to Bath, Jeffries gave me a smile. I knew that many sought a "cure" in Bath: unfortunately for them, at our hands, we cured them of being rich!

"All right, lads—come quick."

We followed Jeffries up a slight rise where we surveyed the road below. Poor pickings, to be sure: just a drover herding his cattle. But wait! Now came a sole black coach trundling over the rocky expanse. Even better, it had no seal, and was manned by a coachman and a single shooter.

"Megs and Carnatus—go to!" Jeffries cried.

"Heigh ho!" yelled Carnatus, now clad in yellow and looking for all the world like that new fruit, the banana. Despite his bulk, he was a skilled horseman, and outpaced me by several lengths as we both galloped downhill.

"*You* give the cry, Megs," he said, and I did, wheeling before two matched Cleveland Bays. The crack of the coachman's whip did nothing to halt my progress.

"*Stand and deliver!*" I cried in my best deep voice. "Your money is not worth your life!"

My pleasure at this turn of phrase was cut short by a pistol's report.

"Hullo?" said Carnatus. "Did that fellow shoot at *us?*"

He sounded as offended as if someone had touched his wig.

"At least he did not hit—" I began, but the rest of my words were lost as another blast rang out. I looked down at the white cuff now dangling from my long shirt sleeve. Carnatus and I stared in wonder at the shredded lace.

"This means war!" he bellowed, aiming his own loaded pistol at the shaking guard's head.

"Peace. Peace," the man called, hurling his gun to the ground with such speed that it skidded across the pebbles.

"Dog!" Carnatus roared, "bastard son of a Frenchman! You are fierce enough unopposed, but cry 'Peace' the moment you see a gun."

"Stay," I counseled, putting out a hand. "Why compound our crimes?"

"What matter when we still swing for them?" he groused, but his face lost its redness. He motioned for Gad to dismount and bind the two men on the coach.

"Well," I said, vaulting from my saddle and swaggering like a lord up to the near door. "What have we here?'

When I peered inside, I saw a nicely dressed woman—happily, not *too* nice.

"You wouldn't be a mistress to the king?" I asked, pulling up my mask.

Her response was a musical laugh. As I continued to survey her, I saw she was quite pretty, and young: perhaps the same age as I.

"I am not grand enough for a king," she said, lifting her skirts as she stepped onto the road. "I am merely Barbara, the daughter of a London merchant."

She gave a nice curtsy, and I bowed in turn.

"Sweet," growled Carnatus, "but we haven't time to play Du Vall. Mistress, we will not keep you, but I fear we must search your coach."

He gave a cursory bow, appearing for all the world like a giant royal canary.

"You both speak well," said Barbara, giving *me* a flirtatious glance. "What would suffice for you not to rob me? A kiss?"

She gave me a closed-mouth smile, causing me to step back.

"Hmm," said Carnatus, considering her offer. "I've had kisses enough, but what would you say to throwing a main? With each toss of the dice, the low-scorer must remove an item of clothing. At the last, he or she who bears no raiment shall be declared the loser."

"If I win, may keep my purse?" asked Barbara.

"Indeed, ms," said Carnatus.

To me, his scheme was inventive if not downright alarming. Though a dread coursed through me at the thought of Carnatus unclothed, I might withstand the sight if only I looked away.

"Young Megs, you cast the first throw."

Carnatus turned to me, placing two small dice in my glove.

"I beg your pardon?" I asked. "This is *your* sport, is it not?"

Carnatus laughed, standing with hands on hips.

"If I know one thing," he said, "besides ale and gaming, it's women, and this one fancies you. Will it cost you so dear to see her naked? I should think a man of your age would charge to the sight like a bull!"

"He is shy," said Barbara.

From the gleam in her eye to her seductive posture—back bent to show off her breasts—I could tell she was delighted.

"Very well," I mumbled. "May we at least retreat from the road?"

"Your modesty becomes you," said Barbara, leading me to a hollow which could not be spied by passersby: or Carnatus and Gad. She took a seat on the heath, her skirts tucked beneath her. "Your play."

With reluctance, I knelt and took up the dice, scoring a five and three. She then threw two sixes!

"Your hat, sir," she said demurely.

I groaned as I placed it beside me. Was there no way out of his contest? I wanted to get up and run but thought of the taunts I would endure from Carnatus.

And so, the game progressed. This Barbara must be an adept for she threw so many high rolls! Was she a secret gamester? Did the goddess of Luck favor her? I only knew that before a half-hour was up, I had lost my falling band, coat, collar, doublet, and boots. She, however, was minus but one brooch!

"Shall we halt?" I asked with hope. "It is clear you are the winner."

"Oh no," she protested, "we must continue to the end."

What she could not know is that would be the end of me! A mounting fear seized me as I discarded more articles: silk stockings and breeches. In inverse to my missing apparel, Barbara's smile grew wider.

"I shall have you yet," she said merrily, and I well knew her meaning.

Alas, at that moment, there wasn't much left to shed, and—damn those dice!—it quickly came off: all but my mask, long white shirt, and what lay beneath it: the thought of which caused me to sweat.

"A three and a four!" Barbara squealed, removing her lace collar and pulling down the neck of her gown. I actually felt faint as my limbs began to shake.

"Do not worry yourself," she breathed, "*I* will show you how."

Now it was *my* turn to hurl those cursed bones: alas, my bad luck held: *two deuces!*

As I crouched without moving like one of the Heath's scrubs, I vaguely saw Barbara approach and seize the end of my shirt. She pulled the garment over my head, leaving me naked: except for a narrow white band wrapped round my chest.

"Dear Lord!" Barbara shrieked, running back toward the road. "You're a—"

"Here."

Aventis stepped into the hollow and threw his cloak at me, which I quickly put on.

"Well, Megs," he said, calm as when we'd first met, "it seems the game is over."

Meg's Tale

As the import of his words hit me, I crumpled to the rough heath. In the near distance, I could hear voices and the wheels of a coach, then the rhythm of hooves as Jeffries and Carnatus fled. I hoped that Barbara at least had been allowed to keep her purse.

I tore off my mask and stared up at Aventis, who leaned carelessly against the tree. His countenance revealed nothing.

"What is your name?" he asked.

"What is *yours?"* I spat. "Jeffries said that in Latin, 'Aventis' means 'cheerful,' but that hardly describes you."

Beneath his thin moustache, his lips formed a slight smile.

"It is an opposite, you see. My real name you will learn in time."

"Margaret," I whispered.

"Beg pardon?" he asked.

"*My* real name is Margaret, Meg for short."

"Ah."

Aventis took out his sword and began to swing it idly.

"Excuse my queries, Margaret, but after what I have witnessed, I feel I have a right to know."

I sighed. Perhaps he had a point.

"First, from where do you hail?" he asked. "And how did you come to meet Jeffries?"

Beneath his cloak, I exhaled. When the words tumbled out, it was almost a relief.

"I am from here, Middlesex, and my father, Richard Tanner, operates the Whale."

"One of Jeffries's haunts," he said.

"Yes. That is where I first met the captain."

"I see," he said. "And your mother?"

"My coming into the world was accompanied by her leaving it."

"Alas," he said, "it is common enough."

"Before I went off with Jeffries, I wished to have gone with *her.*"

Aventis gave me a searching glance with those sharp black eyes.

"That bad?"

"My father is a man who cares only for guineas. And he is not particular about his manner of getting them."

"Like us," he remarked.

I nodded.

"From the age of five," I said, "I knew nothing but toil and the bark of commands: fetch this, knead that, wash all the stone floors. I learned to stave off all manner of pests—biting insects, rats, and the hands of male customers."

I could see disgust eclipse Aventis's face.

"It is also common," he said. "Even in the sacred church." He shook his head. "Pray, continue."

"As I grew, the hands became more frequent, especially when I served as tapstress and barmaid."

"You could not free yourself?" he asked.

"I thought of nothing else," I said, picking at the neck of his cloak. "How to rise to a better life. But there is no option for a poor girl—"

"—lest she be indentured or kept. That is the way of things."

"It should not be."

I met his eye with defiance.

"I agree," he said.

Now that we had this understanding, I did not hold back.

"There was a man," I said. "His name is Claude and he runs the stable."

"He is no Du Vall, I take it?"

"Hardly. He is a great brute of a man, filthy in appearance and manner. The more I tried to hide from him, the more he would paw—and kiss—me."

"A shame you were not a swordsman then."

"If I had been, I would have skewered him. Him and father both."

He did not display alarm.

"They were in league in?" he asked.

"Yes. Claude had a notion to wed me, not out of love, of course, but a desire to gain the inn. His final persuasion to father was that *he* would pay a groom's dowry."

"An offer the old fellow jumped at?"

I nodded, closing my eyes, a familiar rage swelling inside me. Just *thinking* of the past made me want to kill . . .

"Father knew of my hatred for Claude, and so to speed the wedding, he kept me prisoner. In my room, there was one small window, and he took care to bar it. It was, you might say, my personal Newgate."

Aventis started at the infamous gaol's name.

"How did you escape?" he asked.

"Father came for me the morning of this 'sacred union,' a smile upon his face.

'Now, m'girl,' he said, 'at last, I will see some profit from ye.'

'And a full thirteen years' labor does not enter into your reckoning?'

'Now I will have guineas—*and* your labor besides.'

I shuddered, for this was true.

'I will never marry Claude!' I cried. "You shall have to kill me!'

'I don' mind,' he said, walking up and slapping me hard in the face.

I barely flinched, so accustomed was I to his beatings. But on *this* particular morning, something inside me came loose.

'This wedding will never be!' I yelled, and I don't know what overcame me, but I leapt at him like a stag. I seized a small white basin which rested beside my bed, and hurled it at him full force, just missing his skull.

'Damn your blood!' he hissed, coming at me with closed fists.

'Then you damn your own,' I said, and using what fingernails I had after a lifetime of scrubbing, I raked him across the face, drawing thin lines of blood.

'She-wolf!' he screamed, putting his hands to his face.

'If I were, I'd tear you from limb to limb!'

I tried to make good on my promise. Taking a few steps back, I hurled my whole self at him, and, recalling the pain of his thrashings with wooden spoons and leather belts, put my hands round his neck and squeezed with all my might.

'Cl-laude!' he tried to wheeze but was unheard by all save me.

'That devil cannot help you,' I growled.

Even as my knuckles reddened with the force of my grip, I would not desist until his head fell back, his tongue hanging from his mouth.

'Farewell, father,' I said, throwing my things in a sack and hastening down the stairs. Claude, fool that he was, was already deep in his cups, so

I was able to speed past him. That was my last appearance at the Whale. As Margaret, anyway.'"

"Merciful Heaven!" cried Aventis, placing his arms over his breast. "I should have taken care when I first met you! But how did you come to join Jeffries? Was he a friend?"

"Oh yes," I said, brightening. "I would see the captain often, and I knew what he was: that was not a secret so long as he bribed father. But since I can first remember, whenever I served the captain, he was always so kind to me—almost fatherly, in a way. Then, at the end of his stays, he would slip me a shilling or two." I turned away, blushing. "I confess I thought him quite dashing, and I dare I say it . . . handsome."

Aventis laughed.

"Pray, do not tell him that. His head will swell to the size of Carnatus's!"

I smiled.

"In any case, after I fled the Whale, I made for the nearest crossing to catch the public coach."

"Where were you headed?" asked Aventis.

"I thought I might get a post in some quiet farmhouse."

"Yet a quiet life is not yours," he said, pointing to my costume which was still strewn on the Heath.

"No. And for that, I thank Captain Jeffries."

Aventis raised an eyebrow.

"How so?"

"He rode down the Great Western and robbed the public coach!"

"Ha!" Aventis laughed for a full minute.

"Of course," I went on, "*I* well knew who he was, even with his mask. And he recognized *me* and let me to keep my purse. Yet he did something curious: he said that since he took none of my money, I must ply my trade instead."

Aventis looked puzzled. "Did you then draw him an ale?"

"No. He had on his person a private bottle of wine and made me serve it to him."

Aventis laughed again.

"So that's when you joined him?" he asked.

"Oh no, there were too many persons about. So, I contrived to meet him again."

"Not at the Whale?"

"Of course not," I said. "That afternoon, I took care to walk down the road by myself . . . slowly. I made sure to take a fake gold necklace and twirl it in the air. It took less than an hour before the captain appeared."

"What delayed him?" asked Aventis.

"When he came charging up on his horse, he saw that it was me, and thought I had played a good trick on him. But as we were now alone, I begged him to take me on."

"Whatever for?" asked Aventis. "Did you not seek a life of quietude?"

"I thought I did. But when I saw Jeffries on the road, so bold, so gallant, so . . . so *rich*, I changed my mind.

"As to moral qualms?"

Aventis folded his arms.

I started, thinking this odd coming from *him*.

"Not a one," I said, "so long as no one got hurt. After my constrained life, I desired companions . . . adventure . . . and, and—"

"—gold," Aventis finished, then recited: "'And I will give thee the treasures of darkness, and hidden riches of secret places.'"

I looked into his eyes. *How could a man of piety fall as low as I?* But before I could ask, he preceded me with, "Your sex did not dissuade you?"

"No." I stood up, taking care to cover myself. "There have been women tobys before—"

"Moll Cutpurse."

"Her *name* was Mary Frith."

"And Lady Katherine Ferrers," he said.

"I understand she was merely bored."

"Still," said Aventis, "God rest her thieving soul."

"Amen."

"Well," he said, resheathing his sword, "if Jeffries has accepted you, that's as good as the king's seal to me. You have proved yourself one of us a full four times."

"Five, if you count the cookhouse," I said.

Aventis sighed, then gritted his teeth.

"That brings up a rather prickly matter," he said.

I waited as he approached until we stood just inches apart. I blushed as I recalled that only his cloak covered me.

"Do not let Carnatus know," he said. "If he should find you out, he will shoot you dead. Likewise, be cautious of Gad."

"*You* will not betray me?" I asked. Just because he was handsome didn't mean he could be trusted.

"Why would I?" he countered. "You are an excellent highwayman, and they hardly grow on trees. Other men couldn't take the road, but you seem to thrive on it, and have a mighty incentive: you've no place else to go."

"Thank you," I whispered, allowing a strange emotion—gratitude—to sweep through me.

"Here."

Aventis bent to gather my things, then threw them at me in a bundle. Before he turned his back, he did something unexpected: dropping to one knee, he took my hand and kissed it.

"Margaret—Megs—you are a credit to our company. Just be sure not to part with your shirt whenever you are *in company*."

Four "Men" In a Bed

I dressed unseen by his eyes. When I'd finished, we both took our mounts and went in search of the others. It did not take long, for from a hill came the sound of hooves.

When Carnatus came into view, his grin was so wide that his teeth gleamed in the sun.

"What of fair Barbara?" he cried. "I'truth, lad, you've been gone for hours!"

He clapped me hard on the back while Gad threw me a smirk.

"A gentleman never tells," said Aventis, "and we are all gentlemen."

"True," Carnatus sighed, then turned back to me. "Did you get something from her beside her virtue?"

"Alas," I said, "she won."

"Tell me," said Gad, leaning from the back of Carnatus's saddle. "Was she uncommon shapely? Did she have magnificent breasts?"

"You heard your master," I told him. The last thing I wanted to do was discuss the female form!

"I'm gut-foundered," Carnatus proclaimed. "Jeffries, find us a place to dine before I eat your horse."

"There is a small inn nearby, the Crown," Jeffries said with a wink at me. "I believe their ale will sate even *you*, Carnatus."

The giant licked his lips.

"I can almost taste it now!"

Jeffries led us from the Great Western onto a smaller path. It was but the matter of an hour before the Crown's man held our horses. At least he was not Claude!

"Ah, Captain Jeffries!" the innkeeper cried as our company traipsed through his door. "So glad to see you've brought friends."

Unlike father, this man was small, and still had most of his teeth. I looked around: it was much like the Whale, with its fire and mismatch of chairs. I did note that their ale selection seemed especially good. *Always the tapster,* I thought.

"Thank you, Goulding," said Jeffries, as the man led us to a corner table. "Let us have some spitted oysters, one or two steamed carp, five legs of mutton, and a mess of buttered eel!"

"Throw in some fowl," said Carnatus. "And two tankards of ale for me."

"*Plus* your finest wine," said both Aventis and Jeffries.

Goulding bowed and departed. This gave me a chance to realize just how famished I was. I smiled at Aventis, who sat across from me, the boots on his long legs nearly touching mine. Though he might seem gaunt and ascetic, to me, he exuded warmth.

When our dinner arrived, we set upon it like starving wolves. I smiled at the young serving girl, knowing full well her cares.

I was glad that we lingered downstairs before the cheerful brick hearth. One could learn much at an inn, and what *I* learned was this: never play cards with Carnatus! He made a small fortune winning at Spoil Five. I did not comprehend the game, but Carnatus grinned widely every time he "robbed" the trump. Aventis and I shared a glance. It was a comfort to know we had the same turn of mind.

At last, the church bells outside struck midnight, and Goulding led us up to what I hoped would be our chambers. Of course, it was *a chamber,* and, like the one at the Whale, contained but one large bed!

"I apologize," said the innkeeper, bowing his head. "As you see, we are full up, with nary an extra bed. However, with your large party, you will *not* have to host strangers."

"A comfort," I growled. *Present company was bad enough!*

"I am spent," declared Carnatus, as Goulding bowed his way out. The former put up his weapons, stripping down to his long shirt. He crashed down to the bed with such force that it actually leaked a few feathers.

"Easy," said Jeffries. "That bed must accommodate all."

Carnatus nodded from his pillow.

"Gad, fetch me some brandy."

"Yes, sir."

The lad scurried out the door.

"I confess I could sleep," said Jeffries, placing his doublet and breeches onto a small iron trunk. "I imagine that you, Megs, are weary, after this morning's exercise."

"Just watching Megs 'in the saddle' has made me tired," said Aventis. "That lad could teach us a thing or two."

"Doubtful," Carnatus grunted. "He says his blade is rather small." Before Gad could return with his drink, he was fast asleep.

Aventis listened for his snores.

"I know," he whispered to Jeffries.

"Ah," said the captain, "I thought there might be a chance. You will say nothing, of course."

"Naturally," said Aventis. "Our friend still regards women as either wives or whores."

"Sometimes both," said Jeffries.

I felt an anger rise.

"There must be a median," I said, "where we are simply allowed to *be.*"

"Pay no mind to Carnatus," said Jeffries. "So long as he remains ignorant, all will be well."

"And if he were not ignorant, all would be well," I said.

"We cannot change him," said Jeffries. "For now, let us rest."

Using all his strength, he pushed Carnatus over and settled by his side.

"Aventis," said Jeffries, "keep a close eye on Megs. If Carnatus rolls onto her, she will be crushed like a shell underfoot."

"Yes, sir," said Aventis, bedding down to Jeffries's left. There remained a small space for me—just to the right of Carnatus. I sought to switch my position, but there was no more room.

"You're in no danger," Aventis said. "Carnatus sleeps like the dead."

I nodded as Gad returned. Hearing his master snore, he dispensed with the brandy himself, then lay down on the floor.

I glanced over my shoulder at the sleeping giant beside me, praying that twelve pints of ale were enough to keep him still . . .

Yet sometime during the night, I felt him twitch.

"Jus' one more throw," he muttered, half-asleep. "Three to one I win."

My eyes flew open. I lay there stiffly, praying he would pay me no mind.

"Ho," he said.

In horror, I felt his arm go round my shoulder, then fall down to my breast!

"How 'bout a go?" he said.

"Carnatus!" I hissed. "It is I, Megs."

Now *his* eyes opened. Once he focused, he looked abashed.

"Megs, beg pardon. Dreaming of some doxy."

"Back to it," I said.

He removed his arm and rolled over.

By now, I was sweating so hard my shirt stuck to my flesh. Though Carnatus didn't stir again, I kept a careful watch for the rest of the night.

Aventis Meets His Match

My shirt dried out by morning—as did Carnatus from his ale. Still, I could not stop yawning and my eyes drooped with fatigue. *Damn that fool!* I thought. How could such a wide man possess so narrow a mind? If he could but set aside his prejudice, I could do the same with my pretense.

Fat chance! I thought, dressing after the others had left. Might as well hope to be crowned queen. I went down to breakfast and joined my friends, my mood lightening with swallows of bread, cheese, and beer.

"Where are your plans?" Carnatus asked Jeffries, spearing a loaf with his knife. In truth, he could have consumed the whole, along with a wheel of cheddar, as easily as he breathed.

"The Road to Bath," said Jeffries. "Let us try again." He gave me a playful nudge. "Today, let us ensure that as robbers, we rob."

"And are not shot at," said Carnatus.

I looked down at my still ripped cuff.

"I'truth, I could not agree more."

"Goulding, make sure to ready the horses," Jeffries ordered.

"Yes sir."

The tiny innkeeper slammed out the door, yelling. Just after the church bells tolled ten, we were back on the Heath.

"It seems endless," I said to Jeffries.

"Yes. Though I have plied this trade for years, even *I* have not seen it all. I hear tell it is twenty-five miles square."

I whistled. As big as all that! Though the landscape was monochrome, yellow to every horizon, it gave me a strange sense of comfort.

But all was not tranquil. Rounding a bend, we came to a stark landmark, the first of its kind I had seen: it was a highwayman, or more exact what was left of him, his skeleton wrapped in chains and hanging from a high wood gibbet.

Though I had long heard of these "cautions," seeing one made my throat seize.

We all looked up as the bones creaked in their irons. Jeffries halted his horse.

"I knew him," he said sadly. "John Hind. He was one of the best but was betrayed by a woman."

"Figures," growled Carnatus.

"Men betray women too," I said. I had to restrain an impulse to slap him.

"Ha! Give me an instance."

"They force women to wed!" I cried. "Or marry them for money. They treat them like chattel—to be beaten and abused—and it's all allowed by law."

"Megs—" said Aventis, giving me a shake of his head.

"A reg'lar firebrand, eh?" said Gad.

I took a deep breath, composing myself.

"I beg your pardon," I told Carnatus. "Perhaps I had too much to drink. But I think we can all agree that betrayal is more or less equal."

"Very well," Carnatus shrugged, turning from the sight of Hind. Then I saw his back stiffen as if he heard a sound. "Shhh," he said.

We all obeyed, then heard wheels crunching rock just a few yards down the road. This was soon succeeded by the sight of a fine golden coach. The seal upon this one was curious: that of a crowned lion and a horse with a single horn. The gilt overlay of the coach was topped by sharp gold insignias, while *five soldiers* rode on its box. The coachman, in wig and stiff livery, sat upon a red cushion. While I whistled in admiration, Aventis's eyes widened.

"Here lie our hopes!" cried Carnatus, pulling up his black mask. He swept upon the coach like a falcon, causing its team of six to come to a jumbled halt.

"*Carnatus!*" Aventis shouted, *"did we not all agree—?"*

"Too late," said Jeffries. "We must save him from disaster!"

The two of them galloped forth, and, by the coach, I heard some words exchanged. Puzzled, I too affixed my mask and loped to the side of my friends.

Then I saw Aventis do something best reserved for a fool: he actually *took off his mask! What could he be thinking? Did he* wish *to end up like Hind?*

While my mouth froze in a stifled yell, I saw him dismount and approach the coach's draped window.

"Madam," he said.

As the draperies opened, they revealed the head and shoulders of a woman. She was young, and while her eyes were dark and pretty, her teeth protruded slightly. If her beauty did not captivate, her ornaments certainly did: from her ears hung two pearl pendants each in the shape of a teardrop; and around her neck were *four* fat strands of pearls. There were yet more white gems entwined like halos in her hair. It seemed a whole bed of oysters had given their lives for this woman!

After a moment, she spoke.

"Conde del Castillo," she said, addressing Aventis, and I could tell from her accent that she was not English-born.

"My apologies, Your Majesty," he said, kneeling in the dirt of the road.

"I am not yet queen, my friend. I merely visit the country where I will soon preside. *Por favor,* Bernardino, do not grovel to me."

"Thank you, madam," he said, getting up and wiping his breeches.

"So, this is what you have come to," she said with a kind of sorrow. "*You*, of an ancient family, "become a—how do you say?—*homem de estrada.*"

I well knew, as did everyone else, that this woman, Catherine, was betrothed to Charles. I also knew that she was Portuguese and a Catholic, and therefore not to be trusted.

"It is already hard for our people," she told Aventis. "Wherever we go, we are persecuted."

So, I thought, *Aventis must be from Portugal.*

He nodded sadly as he looked in her face. I saw Carnatus squirm in his saddle, impatient to lay his large hands on that bounty of pearls.

Propelled by some mad impulse, I kicked my own horse forward.

"I beg pardon, ma'am," I said from behind my mask, "but you must go at once. Your enemies will report that you consort with outlaws."

"Thank you, sir," said Catherine in her soft accent. As she turned again to Aventis, she gave him a rueful smile. "I miss our days in Lisbon when you used to visit me daily."

The rest of our company froze. Jeffries's eyes went wide while Carnatus grinned.

"God's legs!" Gad exclaimed from behind his master, "as sure as I'm alive, the queen and Aventis have danced the Paphian Jig!"

A silence descended on the road, broken only by the creak of leather.

"Hmph," said Catherine, tossing her ringleted hair, "as I assume you wish to live, you will not repeat this tale." She gave us all a stare. "Are we agreed?"

Her manner, at once imperious and womanly, could only have come from . . . well, I suppose, a future queen.

"You have our word, ma'am," said Jeffries. "Of this meeting, no man shall speak." He looked at me. "Or woman."

Carnatus bowed from his saddle, and even Gad took off his hat.

"As for you, conde?" she asked. "Is what passed between us never to leave your lips?"

"I swear it with my life," said Aventis, bending his gaunt frame low. She offered him a white gloved hand, and he kissed it . . . letting go with reluctance.

Though no one there could have known, I felt a stinging rivalry—and with Catherine of Braganza, no less! I knew I had no right, no claim on Aventis's heart, but still, I could not help it.

Carnatus was the first to speak as the royal coach rolled off. His mind, as always, was occupied by one of three topics: food, gaming, or gold.

"Aventis," he said, "I saw her hand you something. Pray, what was it?"

"This." Aventis said.

As he unfolded his glove, the rest of our company gasped, for he displayed a diamond so large that it nearly blinded!

"You are holding a fortune!" cried Jeffries. "Five hundred guineas at least."

"Can your friends 'dispose' of it?" asked Carnatus.

"Oh yes," said the captain. "Let us make for London."

"At once!" Carnatus shouted, trotting off beside Jeffries like his personal guard.

I hung behind with Aventis, too flustered to speak. After a good half-league, he slowed his horse to a walk.

"I suppose," he began, "you wonder why I, a lowly highwayman, am on intimate terms with our future queen?"

"Not especially," I answered. "You are the Conde de Something and you knew her from Lisbon. I take it you are from there too?"

Aventis shook his head.

"Spain," he said. "Though my family settled here in the time of Queen Mary. Since then, England has seen great changes: all of them bad for me. Now, with the Corporation Act—"

I must have looked puzzled.

"Of course, why would *you* know? Under the Act, no man may run for office, be it even rat catcher, without first receiving the sacrament. From the *Church of England.*"

"So?" I said. Everyone *I* knew was Anglican, and besides, as an outlaw, Aventis could not run for office . . .

"You see, dear Megs . . ." Aventis leaned over his saddle and said in a comic whisper, "I am a Catholic."

"Oh."

If he had professed to be Charles, I could not have been more shocked! So *that's* why Catherine favored him—they shared the same Popish faith. I snuck a look at my friend, but, despite his facial hair, he seemed the same as most men.

Aventis gave me a grin.

"I take it you've never *met* a Catholic," he asked, "before me?"

"Well—" I thought back to those I had known, both in Middlesex and London. "Not knowingly."

He laughed, the sound filling the broad Heath.

"You need not fear," he said. "I will not force you to kiss the Pope's ring or accept the Eucharist wafer as the true body of Christ."

"But … but the *plots,*" I breathed, thinking of all the ones I had heard at the Whale.

"I know it must be difficult to hold these two thoughts in your mind, but one can be a good Catholic *and* a good Englishman."

I stared. From anyone else's lips, I would not have believed it, but there was something in his manner which had always led me to trust him.

"Is your faith—is that the reason you joined Jeffries?"

"There are few professions open to me save this," he said.

"Though I would hate to see you depart," I said, "why not return to Spain?"

He sighed.

"It is as foreign to me as to you." Then resignation turned to defiance, and he balled his fist. "No! This is *my* home, ruled by my king and future queen! I refuse to forsake them."

Especially the queen, I thought. Though it might cause me pain, I forged ahead with this subject.

"As to Catherine," I began, "it is widely believed that she has always been chaste."

"Yes," said Aventis.

"I do not believe it is known that she ever had a-a—"

"Nor should it be."

"How did you come to meet her?" I asked. Even though my blood raced, I strove to appear calm.

"As a young man," he said, "I went to Lisbon to study at seminary."

Ah ha, I knew it! Aventis had studied for the priesthood . . .

"I first spied Catherine when she was the Infanta," he said. "She had the most extraordinary ringlets, and though her stature was small, I thought her a true beauty. Alas, she had a mother who guarded her like a dragon."

I could not help but laugh.

"Mind you," he went on, "it was a no small feat to sneak past the palace and gain entrance to the convent where Catherine was held. I fear I bribed a few nuns." He made the sign of the Cross. "Well, once I got in, she took a fancy to me. It was no secret to either of us that she would be pledged to a king."

"How dreadful for her. To be forced into marriage!" I cried.

He gave me a long look.

"Our liaison could not last long," he said, "not with her sharp-clawed mama. *I* returned to England while she remained at the convent until Charles made his offer."

"Yet you are devoted to him?"

"As a subject, I am. Far better a rakish Charles than a joyless Cromwell."

"Yes," I agreed. I barely remembered the Lord Protector, but everyone around me had hated him.

"We best catch up," said Aventis, kissing to his mount.

As we both loped down the road, I asked, "Who else knows your tale?"

"Only you," he said. "I wanted to tell the others since we do not keep secrets, but . . ."

A sense of guilt overcame me. If he thought *his* secret was bad, what about my own?

As we headed toward London, we finally caught up to the others. Jeffries turned to give us both a harsh stare. *How much did he know,* I wondered, *about my feelings for Aventis?* Based on his narrowed eyes, more than Almighty God!

Yet, as I glanced at Aventis, I felt my unease diminish like a shadow at noon. At that moment, I resolved to be especially nice to Catholics . . . if I happened to meet another.

A Latter-Day Robin Hood

Our company stayed in Middlesex while Jeffries sought a broker for our glittering prize. He at last found the right "friend," and returned to where we sheltered at the home of one of his doxies. On our second afternoon there, the captain slammed through the door with a song on his lips and a fat purse in his hand.

"How now, my merry companions!" he cried, giving our landlady, Mary, a long kiss on the lips.

I felt my spirits plunge, but not from jealousy. Rather, it was seeing this woman, so soft in hair and dress, able to be openly what I could not. I looked down at my doublet and breeches. Had I become so hard—so mannish in spirit and dress—that I was no longer a woman? Was I now a sort of creature who strode between the two sexes?

Jeffries noted my sadness, clapping me on the back.

"I have something to liven you up," he said. He strode to the kitchen table as we each took a place around it. "Who wishes to see some gold?" he asked, spilling a mound from his purse. So many fat coins struck wood that the sound nearly deafened!

Jeffries turned to Carnatus.

"For you, friend, fifty guineas."

Carnatus took up a few and made a quick inspection.

"Not badly clipped," he said.

"Megs, the same."

Jeffries handed me my share.

"Thank you, captain."

I glanced down at the river of gold spilling out of my hands. I smiled, then winced as I caught the visage of Cromwell staring up from the guineas. *God's wounds,* I thought, *would we ever be free of this man?*

"Aventis, you've earned a hundred," said Jeffries. "Without your ties to Catherine, we would all be swinging from a gibbet instead of gathering here."

"Very kind," said Aventis, placing a coin between his teeth. He exhaled with satisfaction. "Real," he said.

As the sun passed through an open window, I could not help but note how handsome Aventis looked. From the top of his plumed hat down to his high boots, he looked every inch a Cavalier. It was clear from her blushes that Mary thought the same.

Carnatus turned to me.

"Why are you smiling?" he asked. "Dreaming of your own doxy?"

I laughed, somewhat nervously.

"My friend, you discern my thoughts."

The next morning, we left for London, where Jeffries had another hideout (and doxy). My God, this man had a woman not in every port but block! As we rode north toward the city, the captain did not share his plans, but when on the Great Western a sole coach rolled by, why not seize the day? Or in this case, the treasure?

Still, this coach concerned me, for it was like no other I'd seen. Two soldiers were seated at each side of the driver, and though they seemed at their ease, they still held muskets and pistols.

"Let them pass," Carnatus shrugged, as we trotted our mounts out of sight. "Such a drab conveyance with guards ready to shoot. Perhaps it is just the army moving about supplies."

"Oh, it is the army all right," said Jeffries. "But what they are moving might interest you, for *that* is the paymaster's wagon. I know it well from my years in the war."

"But, captain," I said, "Is not that money intended for soldiers? Assuredly, they are not rich. Should we as 'honest thieves' deprive them of their living?"

"God help us!" cried Carnatus, pulling up his mask. "In future, he'll ask the ladies if they be widows or orphans."

"Megs, your intent is correct," said Aventis. "We must never rob the poor or suffering."

"Do not fret," Jeffries told me. "That haul will go to soldiers. Just not the ones who expect it."

I had no time to reflect as Jeffries spurred on his horse. With a pistol in each hand and a dagger between his teeth, he looked like a landbound pirate.

"After him, lads!" cried Carnatus, and Aventis and I charged forth. We went round to the far side of the coach, where shots began to ring out. I found myself covered in powder and smoke which struck me all at once. Thankfully, a lead ball did not.

Aventis was not so fortunate. I saw him lurch back in his saddle as he clutched the top of his arm. His formerly all black sleeve was marred by a spatter of red.

"Aventis!" I cried, watching him fight to keep his seat.

"Heigh ho, lads," I heard Carnatus say to the guards on the other side of the coach. They must have been untried, for I heard steel upon pebbles as they dropped their weapons.

"Step down, if you please," drawled Jeffries. They—and the driver—complied in a crash of bodies. "Now, on your knees, in a row—with hands clasped behind your head. Just so."

"Thieving son of a whore," the old army driver cursed. "We shall raise the hue-and-cry and you will swing by morning."

"Well now," asked Jeffries, *"who* are you thinking to raise? Poor farmers with their pitchforks? Or the local watch, who make *you* look like a stripling? This road is *our* domain, and for you to pass, you must pay a toll."

"Filth!" spat the driver.

Carnatus, who I thought would be offended, merely laughed into his mask. Behind him, Gad did the same.

"Megs," Jeffries called, gesturing for me to walk round to the wagon's rear door.

I dismounted, and examined two heavy, locked doors. Not wishing to waste time with keys, I removed my pistol and blasted off that thick lock. As the doors yawned open, I was nearly blinded, for what I saw before me, piled to the roof, was a gold sea of Cromwells!

"Captain!" I shouted. "I fear this load is too heavy for us to bear away!"

"A happy dilemma," said Jeffries. "Let us then take the wagon. Carnatus? Will you and Gad oblige?"

They proceeded to march their party of five to a copse. With ease, they tied the men to the trunks of three beeches.

The captives chose not to speak except for one young soldier.

"Dogs! When you rob *us*, you rob the king!"

"Yet the king has robbed others who must now be repaid, " said Jeffries.

"Lookee—he thinks he's Robin 'ood," the old driver spat. "Where's yer bow and quiver?"

"Here," said Carnatus.

As Jeffries laughed, he crossed the road and withdrew those very items from his saddle. Returning in just a few strides, he notched an arrow and let it fly, striking the driver directly through the crown of his hat.

"Huzzah!" cried Gad. "Master's better'n Robin and Willem Tell."

Carnatus bowed.

"Hold," pled the driver, shaking. "No more darts, I beg you. You outlaws have proved your point."

"And *you* have been stuck with it!" I cried, rather pleased at my own wit.

"Enough," said Aventis weakly. He had removed his falling band and used it to staunch his wound. "Let us take the wagon and flee."

"Farewell," I bid the roped men. "Do not be uneasy. The Great Western is well traveled, and someone will come along soon."

"Hmph," the driver growled, but with an arrow clean through his hat, he decided to cut his speech short. As Gad took his place on the box, we provided a mounted escort to Jeffries's hideout on the Heath.

"Gad! Over here," Jeffries instructed, and, with little difficultly, the horses were unharnessed, and the wagon pushed by Carnatus and Jeffries into a small depression. I assisted by piling on branches until the army wagon looked like a corpulent bush!

Jeffries went round to the back. Then, he did something curious: instead of dividing the spoils, he emerged with three bulging packs. I could see the sharp glint of coins peeking out from under their cords.

"Wait for me here," he told us. "I shall not be long." He faced Aventis and for the first time noticed his wound. "My friend, you are hit! Shall I summon a doctor friendly to our cause?"

"Not needed," replied Aventis, though I could tell he was in pain. "The ball did not penetrate far."

"Thank God," Jeffries said as he tied the packs to his saddle. With a leap, he mounted and turned to me. "Megs, I leave Aventis in your care. No doubt you have skill." He gave me a hard look. Do not disappoint."

"No, sir."

I fought the urge to salute. Even if his title were honorary, Jeffries knew how to give an order. In this case, I did not mind, for I wanted, more than anything, to aid the man who had become my favorite.

As he leaned from his horse, I noticed his white parlor.

"Aventis," I said, with a hint of Jeffries's command, "let me help you dismount." With Carnatus's aid, I did so, then supported my friend as he sat. "Please, show me your arm."

He unwrapped his long falling band, while I rolled up his sleeve. Though not unaccustomed to blood, I flinched at the sight of a hole just down from his shoulder. Now that the wound was exposed, the lingering scent of powder caused my eyes to sting.

"We must remove the ball," I said. That seemed to make sense. But what to use as an instrument? Surely not bark or heath? Then my eyes fell on Carnatus, and inspiration struck.

"Carnatus, a fresh arrow, if you please. And some wine."

"Does 'e think to get the dart drunk?" Gad asked.

Carnatus swatted him on the head, then motioned toward his horse.

I was hardly a surgeon and had only "cured" scrapes and bruises incurred during fights at the Whale. What I *had* learned, though, is that most men don't die of their wounds: it's the infection that follows which leads them to Heaven or Hell.

"Carnatus," I asked, once Gad had returned, "if you had a wound on your arm, what would you do to clean it?"

He stood there and thought.

"As much as I loathe the practice, I would take a hot bath."

"Hmm." I thought for a moment. "Gad, could you fetch some fresh water?"

He seized up and jug and scampered through the trees, allowing me to return to my patient.

"You should drink this," I said, and presented Aventis with a cup spilling over with wine.

"I do not require encouragement." He easily downed the whole contents. "I believe I am presently fortified against your barbarous surgery."

Noting his pun on "barbers," who often served as doctors, I grinned.

"Good. Hold onto your humor."

"Even if it's bile?" he asked.

"Ha. Carnatus, would you mind lighting a fire?"

The giant stomped off and soon had a small blaze going. Once Gad returned, I poured water into a pot which I hung over the flames. Carnatus flinched as I broke his arrow in two and plunged in the business half. After letting this heat, I fished it out with my sword.

"Careful, lad," said Carnatus. "No harm must come to Aventis."

I nodded but my hand shook as I held the heated dart over Aventis's arm.

"Now!" I cried, more for my benefit than his.

Using the arrow's sharp tip, I probed for the hidden ball. As Aventis had surmised, it was not lodged deep in the flesh, and with a steadying arm, I drew out the round piece of lead.

"*Par excellence!*" said Carnatus.

Aventis nodded as he downed wine straight from the jug. I tried not to look as the blood coursed down his arm.

"Very well," I said. "Now . . . we must close the wound." I tried to keep my voice firm, for I could not show weakness—not in front of Carnatus.

"I have the matériel," that very man said, withdrawing from his coat pocket a needle and packet of thread! "It is to mend *my* material. One never knows when a rent in one's stocking can ruin an entire day."

"Of course," I said, thanking God that he was a fop. "Hand it here, will you?"

After threading the needle (at which I excelled, I confess), I first bathed the wound, then set about stitching it up. After a lifetime of mending, I was well up to the task.

"Superb, Megs," said Carnatus. "A London tailor could not as well."

He clapped me heartily on the back.

I coughed.

"Thank you, friend."

I, along with Aventis, now surveyed my handiwork. It was true, his arm was whole, but tinged with a thread of bright blue!

"I thank you, Megs," said my patient. "You have saved my life. Though I am not a popinjay, be assured I value your work."

His words brought tears to my eyes—always a danger before Carnatus. In an effort to distract him, I did the manliest thing I could think of: I cursed like father on a bender.

"Those bastard sons of bitches!" I yelled. "How *dare* they shoot at us! Dammee, I'll be dam'd if I don't go back and send 'em straight to Hell!"

As Carnatus threw back his head and howled, I made sure to wipe my eyes. Again, just barely, I had escaped detection.

After a week had passed, I felt a nagging worry: Captain Jeffries had not yet returned. Several scenarios—none of them pleasant—unspooled at the back of my mind. Was he running through all that gold as highwaymen frequently did? Throwing it at doxies, French wines, and gallery seats at the theatre? Or, after all these years, had he finally been apprehended, to stand trial at the Old Bailey and swing from the highest gibbet? I said nothing to the others, for Carnatus would have laughed and Aventis was still resting. In the meantime, we did not starve, for Carnatus was a great hunter with both bow and pistol. I spent *my* days doing what I liked—which meant taking care of Aventis. When he at last he grew stronger, we took a walk in the woods.

"Tell me, Megs," he inquired, as we made our way around brambles, "how came you by your fine speech? Not many innkeeper's daughters express themselves as you do."

"Ah," I said, gratified he had noticed. "I had few pleasures at the Whale, so when I went into London, I was sure to read all the newspapers and the pamphlets left by others. Books, of course, were rare, though I had my Bible and some plays by Shakespeare. The latter stolen, of course."

"So, you embarked on a life of crime even before the road?" he asked. "I don't know why, but I'm glad of it."

"You and Jeffries were not my sole corrupters," I said.

He nodded, then sighed.

"I wish that none of us had to lead the lives we do."

"Might as well wish for fairies," I said.

"Look! There's one—in a circle, behind that rock!"

He tapped me unseen on the shoulder, pretending to be one. How I wanted to answer back, but the sight of his pale face stopped me.

On the ninth day since Jeffries's departure, I knelt to examine his wound. Thankfully, it had healed cleanly, and there remained but a single detail: to remove those silly stiches.

"Pity," Aventis remarked, as I bent over him with a knife. "I felt the blue accent made me more alluring."

"You should wear brighter colors," said Carnatus. "Not the somber hues of a priest."

"Perhaps you can lend me that yellow doublet that makes you look like an overstuffed

bird—"

They quickly ceased their talk as the beat of approaching hooves sounded over the Heath.

"That must be is Jeffries," said Aventis, inclining his head as he listened.

"Or not," I answered, taking out my pistol.

"Stand down, Megs," Jeffries shouted as he galloped into view. I saw that his packs, formerly bursting with gold, were now flat as the Great Western.

"Captain," I inquired, as he dismounted, "may I ask where you have been?"

"Everywhere!" he cried. "Essex, London, Dover, even bookish Cambridge."

"Whatever for?" I asked, bracing myself for anything.

"Why, to pay the army," he said.

"Was that not the purpose of *this?*"

I pointed to the paymaster's wagon under its leafy disguise.

"Indeed, it was, to pay *present* soldiers, those who preside over peace. The men whom I've reimbursed fought long and hard in the war."

"Yet Charles did not acknowledge them?"

To me, it seemed a strange notion.

"Ah, Megs," said Jeffries, taking a welcome seat on a rock, "while *you* were playing with d—" He stopped himself. "—tin soldiers, we men of flesh were bleeding and dying for the king." He sighed. "The one who ended up without a head."

I nodded. I even knew some from London who had witnessed the event.

"Yet before that sad day," said Jeffries, "I followed Prince Rupert as we drew with Cromwell at Edgehill, then lost to him at Naseby. I was a *real* captain then—in charge of a cavalry troop. Would you like to see my medal?"

With that, he laughed bitterly.

"B-but," I stammered, "I can well understand why you took to the road under

Cromwell . . ."

"Yes, we Cavaliers were the losers—translation: traitors—and our lands were seized. Those of us with the ill luck to live were forced into hiding." He stared at me. "Or worse."

"Yet under this king?" I asked. "Can you not reclaim what was yours?"

"It would seem so," said Jeffries. "But Charles is more concerned with funding his lavish court. As for those who served his father—we are a lingering nuisance."

"But surely if you appealed—"

Jeffries looked at me kindly.

"Oh Megs, you are so young it breaks my heart! The king's character is thus: he loves what is right before him: *this* woman, or *that* advisor. Be out of his sight for a moment, and that love disappears. As for us old soldiers," he sighed, "we are a sad reminder that his majesty's side once lost."

I confess I felt the same fury as when I'd hurled that basin at father. It made me want to go out and denounce Charles in the streets.

"What of the queen?" I asked, trying not to look at Aventis. Still, he answered.

"She does not mingle in politics. That is why she will stay queen."

From his rock, Jeffries's head drooped.

"Yet we all remain loyal," he said.

"But why?" I asked. I wanted to give him a good shaking.

"Because we are military men," he said. "And who else is there to lead us? Cromwell's idiot son, Richard?"

Though I rolled my eyes, I was not yet satisfied.

"Why not repossess what is yours?" I asked. "Your lands belong to *you.*"

Carnatus seemed ready to ride, but Aventis and Jeffries just smiled.

"They lie in Somerset," said the captain, "and were granted to a Roundhead. At present, I hear, they belong to a royal favorite."

"It is so unjust," I moaned, stamping one long black boot.

"Megs," said Jeffries, "surely you more than anyone know how unjust life can be."

"How so?" asked Carnatus, curious. Gad stood close to hear.

"Once the dice are cast," said Jeffries, "the result cannot be reversed." He looked at each of us in turn. "That goes not just for Megs but us all."

Not a word passed anyone's lips until Carnatus spoke.

"Apropos of dice," he said, producing a pair from his pocket, "if I draw a ten or above, *I* hunt for dinner. If not, the rest of you form a party."

We all hunched over the ground as we watched the small cubes tumble.

"Eleven!" crowed Carnatus. "Mind you—I require six quail and a haunch of venison!"

A Double Crossing

The night of Jeffries's return, we all rode back to London to stay at the house of *another* doxy. This one was called Moll.

"Ah, Captain Jeffries," she sighed, taking his arm as if she owned it. "If only you wasn't running about the country, stirrin' up trouble and God knows what else."

"You are best ignorant of the 'what else,'" he said, allowing her to lead him upstairs. Carnatus, Aventis, and Gad were to share a small guest room, which left me alone downstairs with a couch as my bed.

The timing could not have been better, for I was stricken with my monthly "flowers," an event hard enough to manage even without sleeping rough. Now, I could attend to myself and even unbind the cloth which constricted my chest. As I let down my dark hair and combed it, I shuddered: no longer wrapped like butcher's meat, I was free to be myself.

But who *was* that, exactly? Margaret Tanner, tapstress, an object of beatings and scorn? Or feared highwayman Megs, who rode with the best of men and could even best them? If only I could bring them together: be a true "woman of the road" who need not conceal her gender. Yet, I knew this could never be: I would be despised by everyone, even other high tobys. My bones would fester by Hines's as a clear warning to my sex.

The next morning, when my friends joined me, I was fully dressed—as Megs. I would never let them know—not even Aventis—how it felt to be a pretender.

"Sleep well, Megs?" he Aventis, giving me a wink. "It must be nice to have a whole bed to yourself."

"Divan," I corrected, as we walked into the kitchen. I saw Moll preparing breakfast and stifled an urge to join her.

"Where to today, Jeffries?" Carnatus asked with a yawn. He buttered a giant oatmeal pudding.

"I am going to see some friends, get about and learn what's what. I shall not be long," said Jeffries. "Meet me at the Garden fountain at precisely noon."

We lazed about at Moll's until Aventis took out a pocket watch.

"We should go," he said. "Gad, please fetch the horses."

Once mounted, we proceeded down cobblestone streets in the center of London. Having spent so many weeks sleeping rough in Epping and Hounslow, I could hardly adjust to the crowds, not to mention their livestock, shouting, and smells! When we reached Covent Garden, I saw a throng of flower sellers who perfumed the foul air with the scent of their wares. This sparked in me an odd notion, and I tossed down a shilling to a grateful girl. She in turn handed me up a white rose, which I gave to Aventis.

"To adorn your hat," I said, blushing.

He bowed from his saddle, adding the pale bloom to his band's black feathers.

"I should get something for you, Megs," he said. "You were after all the agent of my recovery."

"Someone fetch me some hemlock!" Carnatus bellowed while holding his hands to his throat. "All this sweet civility makes me want to take leave of this world."

"That goes double for me," said Gad.

"I may accommodate your wish," I told him.

"Hold!" said Jeffries, trotting up to the fountain. "I have news from an innkeeper friend. He reports a party at the Oak large of purse and small of sense. It is only for us to enact our 'befriend and warn them' scheme."

"Not my favorite," said Carnatus. "Still, as long as there's food and treasure, I will fell the mighty Oak."

Jeffries gestured for us to follow and we left London and its smells for the clearer air of Hounslow. I wondered what this latest scheme offered, but after his Robin Hood venture, I knew I would follow Jeffries into the Whale itself!

We trotted two leagues on the Great Western before spying the Oak. It seemed a nice enough inn, though there was not an oak in view. After handing over our mounts, we were seated by the fire near a table boasting six merchants. As Jeffries's friend had avowed, their purses were indeed heavy.

"Good man," Carnatus barked at the owner, "be quick and fetch us some ale."

"Do not forget wine," said Aventis. "Preferably, from France."

"Aye, good sirs," said the man, who soon returned with refreshments. "Shall I order up a calf's head, fish fin, or humble pie?"

"Straightaway," said Carnatus. "And two to three roast fowl. I am famished!"

"Very good, sir."

Jeffries turned to a merchant at his back. This man wore simple black garb, topped by a hat so tall I wondered he'd fit through the door. Despite the fire, his lack of finery chilled me, for there was no doubt what he was, a . . . a dam'd Dissenter!

"Good day to you, sir," said Jeffries. "May I ask where your road leads?"

"To Essex," the merchant answered, "if it pleases God."

"I can't imagine why He'd object," said Jeffries.

I noticed that he and Aventis were suppressing smiles.

"What takes you to that fair county?" asked Carnatus, draining his mug.

"We have just sold our goods in London," a young man volunteered. "So, we bring our profits home."

Carnatus nodded.

"No place like home for profits."

"And did we not do well, Ted?" the merchant cried, patting his purse as if he expected it to purr.

"Indeed, father."

I narrowed my eyes. Could these men be so untutored that they offered tales of riches to strangers in an inn? Something about their frankness caused my skin to prickle.

"Surely it is God's reward," said Jeffries. "For prosperity comes to the good."

"To the *godly*," the first merchant said. "We know that we will be saved as members of the Elect."

Ugh, a Puritan, I thought. *What an annoying sect.* Too bad the king was so soft with these damn'd Dissenters. Then I glanced at Aventis and stared into my cup. I knew that Catholics too could be snared in a net of hate.

Jeffries pretended to agree with the merchant's pious sentiment.

"Too right," he said. "Mister—?"

"Winthrop."

"I am Smith. When do you set out?"

"At first light."

"Oh, happy day," said Jeffries. "We too are headed east. With your permission, we will form one merry party."

I stared at the black-clad merchants. "Merry" was hardly the word I would use to describe them. During the rest of the evening, Carnatus ate four fowl, but I could tell he was downcast for he could not bring out his dice.

At last, Winthrop and his brethren went upstairs to their rooms. We remained by the fire, quiet until I turned to Jeffries.

"Captain, these men are not to be trusted! Why in the name of their God would they be so open with us?"

"Friendly?" asked Carnatus.

"Bah! They are baiting some trap—you may count on it! Captain Jeffries, you more than any must know this."

"Megs," said Jeffries, "it may surprise you, but some men are free in their speech. They have no more distrust of strangers than a newborn babe."

Aventis nodded.

"Especially those who believe they are selected by God."

"Even so," I answered. "These Dissenters chill my blood. I have long heard how they cheered when the old king lost his head."

"We must take care not to lose ours." Aventis looked round the table. "Once we join their party, we keep our pistols at the ready. I assume they travel unarmed, trusting God to protect them."

"They'd be better off with a musket," said Carnatus.

Jeffries smiled.

"We wait here until dawn and keep our pistols loaded. If they attempt to deceive, they will lose both purse and life."

Everyone looked satisfied. In truth, I myself felt better having voiced my concerns. Lulled by wine and fire, I confess I dozed at the table, but opened my eyes when I heard boots thudding on stairs. Yawning, I looked out the windowpanes: first light was breaking, promising a fine day.

"Ready, lads," whispered Jeffries. "How meet!" he said to Winthrop, rising to greet the merchant. "We have arisen early. What say we make for the road?"

"Gladly," said Winthrop. "We have already gathered in prayer."

"As have we," Jeffries lied.

I could hear Gad snicker.

"In nomine Patris, et Filii, et Spiritus Sancti. Amen," said Aventis softly to me.

Once out in the courtyard, we found that these men had fine horses. *After we rob them,* I thought, *we must perform an exchange.* I took a quick look about me and saw that the road lay empty. By my side, Carnatus chuckled.

"Easy as robbing women," he said.

I tried not to react.

Meanwhile, Jeffries called to the merchants, "I say, gentlemen, shall I and my men ride ahead to ensure there is no danger? One cannot be too careful these days."

"Very good," said Winthrop.

"Megs, stay here," Jeffries ordered, then galloped off with the others.

They were gone for just a few minutes, but when Jeffries returned, *alone*, his face bore a look of terror.

"Bandits ahead!" he cried. "*I* managed to thwart them, but alas, they have taken my friends!"

It was then that "befriend and warn them" took on its full meaning.

"Stand and deliver!"

Two men appeared in all black, masks shrouding their faces. One raised his horse on its hind legs while the other pointed a pistol—straight *at me,* I might add.

"Our purses are not worth our lives!" Jeffries shouted, throwing his to the mounted Carnatus.

"Take mine, sir!" I told Aventis.

"But . . . this is outrageous!" Winthrop yelled, his voice full of hurt bluster. "I recognize those horses! You shall have to kill us, you tobys!"

As if on cue, there emerged from each merchants's cloak a loaded flintlock. I *knew* they were loaded, for all commenced firing!

"You are under arrest!" Winthrop barked. "By order of His Majesty, the king."

"Some merchant," Jeffries groused as he returned fire. He hit one of the "godly," who fell, clutching his chest.

"Who are you?" Carnatus asked.

"King's men," said "Winthrop." "Captain Collins at your service, sir."

Both sides paused to reload. What saved us from certain ruin were the clouds of white powder choking the morning air. When they cleared, I saw that Carnatus was hit while Aventis smacked his friend's horse to send him to safety. If one counted Gad, that left us two men down.

"Pray, halt your fire!" Jeffries told Collins, but his words fell on stone. Jeffries's horse was shot dead from under him, which left him no choice but to duck behind some scrub. "I too am a king's man," he yelled. "I served at Edgehill."

"You are an outlaw, Jeffries, and we mean to halt your career! Besides which, there are fifty guineas on your head."

Jeffries rose to full height, his expression one of disdain.

"*Only* fifty? Hmph. *That* you shall never collect."

He brought up his pistol, aimed at Collins, shot, and killed him.

Even *I* recoiled, for I had never seen so much blood. Still, I gathered myself and breech-loaded my gun, holding it steady as Jeffries had taught me. After cocking the hammer, I gently squeezed the trigger, at which point the dam'd thing blew up!

"Ahhh!" I cried. *Why did this always happen?* And more pointedly, *to me?* Could not this modern age build a decent flintlock?

As I grasped my burning hand, Jeffries ran toward me, the mounted Aventis at his heels. The captain reloaded his pistols while Aventis used his sword to cut down two more men.

"You must fly!" I gasped to Jeffries, my hand now dripping blood. "Aventis, take him and ride."

"Never!" said the two together, but they jumped at the sound of pounding hooves. Round the bend came a tightly bunched cavalry, each man in a red coat.

"Go now!" I shouted. "You must."

They exchanged a helpless look, then crouched as more shots rang out.

"We shall not desert you!" cried Jeffries, grabbing Aventis's saddle and hoisting himself behind. "Megs, do not despair."

The horse with its twin riders raced off pursued by soldiers. I heard receding hoofbeats, the sharp reports of pistols, and then, nothing at all.

A Glimpse of Hell

When I awoke on a cold stone floor, I knew *exactly* where I was. It was the bane of every highwayman who ever sat a horse. Outside my barred cell, I saw a gaoler boiling something in a large pot. Seeing my curiosity, he held up a severed head with a grin.

"This way the fowl don't get 'em when they put 'em up on the Bridge," he said.

Nice.

If this was not enough cause for revolt, my nostrils were soon assailed by the stink of unwashed bodies. London had its particular scent, but the coal dust polluting its air was like a garden compared to here. To make matters worse, I heard the sound of heavy groans echoing all around me.

I fought the desire to join this chorus. Looking down, I saw I was manacled hand and foot by thick restraints of iron. There could be no escape, and there could be no doubt: I was in London's Newgate Gaol, from which few ever returned. Few, that is, like me.

Feeling pain in my left hand, I saw that it was bound by a filthy white cloth. Though I wanted to cry out, I knew a display of weakness would be punished by jeers or worse, so I sought to distract myself by studying my new quarters.

I lay on a ragged blanket, surrounded by other prisoners much more wretched than I. I saw lice crawl over their heads, while the rags that they wore were so thin that flesh could be spotted in places. There were perhaps twenty-five of us crammed into a space no larger than a chamber. Who these men were or the nature of their crimes was as unknown to me as how I'd arrived beside them.

I turned to the inmate next to me—the one with a rasping cough. *Gaol fever*, I thought. Luck would be in his favor if he lasted the week.

"Beg pardon, sir," I addressed him. "This is Newgate, is it not?"

"Thas' right." I could barely see his grimace beneath his bristling beard. "*The wor' part:* Common Side, Felons. Hope ye enjoy bread and water. You'll get nothin' else 'ere."

I looked down at my barren belt.

"Where is my purse?" I asked.

"Emptied. By the garnish—yer price fer entrance; by payment to the cook, an' the rest to th' gaolers. They picked ye clean, my friend."

"They *charge* you to stay here?" I asked.

The man tried to laugh, but instead broke into coughs.

"Good 'un, ain't it?"

I slumped back on my blanket.

"Is the pretty young one awake?"

A man on my other side, his hair standing straight up, gave me a gap-toothed smile.

"When ye came in, ye was out," said the first prisoner. "I been sittin' watch so ol' Tom don' get a piece of ye."

"I am appreciative, sir," I said.

"Not sir," he said, "name's Sam. Samuel for long."

"I owe you a debt, Samuel."

My chains clinked as I moved them to look down at my belt again. Of course, my weapons were gone. At least they'd left me my boots.

"What have these men done?" I asked. "Incurred a debt or two?"

"Oh no," Samuel coughed, "them's 'as got their own place. Us 'ere is *thieves*: we stole more'n forty shillings, or more'n five from a shop."

"And your penalty is to rot here?"

"Oh no, sir. For that, we get death."

I should have known.

"And you, Samuel? What is *your* crime?" I asked.

He sighed, the sound more like a rattle.

"Chicken," he said.

"Beg parson?"

"Was 'ungry, so stole un."

"Good Lord," I said. By these rules, Carnatus would merit the Triple Death!

And ye?" Samuel asked.

I shifted. *How should I answer?* Since those who brought me here well knew what I was, I thought it pointless to lie.

"I am called Megs," I said, "and I am a tobyman. Member of Jeffries's crew."

Samuel whistled in admiration, then called out to the whole cell.

"'Ey gents! We got us an 'igh-class thief here! And 'e's not even in the Yard!"

Some inmates turned to stare. I could not tell what they felt, be it disgust, worship, or both. Perhaps it was sorrow, for "men" like me didn't last long.

"Do you know if they've caught Jeffries?" I asked. "Or any of his men?"

"Nah. We woulda 'eard. Guess *yere* the lucky one."

He endured a fit of coughing. Privately, I thought the best luck that could befall us would be to avoid the gaoler's pot.

I lowered my voice.

"What can I expect?" I asked.

"Oh, the regular," said Samuel. "Quick trial, sentence o' 'guilty,' then an 'anging at Tyburn. Should all 'appen pretty quick."

"I am glad."

I meant it, for I had no wish to prolong my stay. Better to swing at Tyburn than to linger at Newgate.

I was almost relieved when they came for me the next morning. Two gaolers unlocked my chains and marched me out of the cell to an old building next door.

The Old Bailey.

Once inside, I was led to the dock in a courtroom heavy with statues. Looking up, I saw that a mirrored reflector shone down on my face, joined by a sounding board so that I might be seen and heard. *Good,* I thought. I will give them a show.

I observed the unruly onlookers gathered on pew-like benches both behind and across from me. There was a shocking lack of barristers (and of guards, which I thought odd). Rather, the place was filled with merchants and others of the middling sort, while some were clearly in need: of judicial strategy or a good diversion. I turned my head to the left, where a panel of five white-wigged judges sat solemnly in their robes.

"Silence!" a heavy voice called.

"So-called 'Megs,' of the Jeffries gang," the judge closest to me began. His wig shook with indignation. "State for the court your full name."

"'So-called Megs,'" I answered. The courtroom rang with laughter.

"Order!" the voice called again.

"No matter," said the judge. "You may be called Sally Stuart for all we care."

The judge to his right shuffled some papers.

"You," he said, "stand accused of two heinous crimes: highway robbery and murder. How do you plead?"

"Murder?!" I cried. "Of whom?"

I thought back to the skirmish on the road. To my recollection, I had not even *hit* anyone!

"King's officer Captain J. Collins. Shot point-blank on the Great Western. Are you or are you not guilty?"

"Guilty!" the crowd shouted, as if they were watching a cock fight.

"What does it matter?" I asked, my voice strangely amplified. "On its own, robbery gets death. And of that I am surely guilty, as your soldiers can attest."

A cry went up round the courtroom. The judge to the far right leaned back. In the window behind him, there hung a lovely cameo of bodies swinging at Tyburn.

"Attestations are not required," he said with a wave of his hand. "*This* is a trial for murder."

I knew that to be true. No witnesses need step forth—not for my side or theirs. No barrister need bother to speak on my behalf.

The chief magistrate in the middle, backed by a throne-like panel, pounded his gavel on the bench.

"Order!" he cried, and the crowd went silent. "Well …" He looked to his four peers. "This case is simplicity itself. GUILTY! I sentence so-called 'Megs,' high tobyman of Hounslow Heath, to death by public hanging at Tyburn Tree tomorrow."

"Next please," cried a voice.

I was barely aware as my gaolers led me next door: not to the Common Side but a place far above it: the condemned men's hold. I saw that though the room was ill-lit and must be entered though a spiked hatch, at least there was a wood bed—even a window. Most blessedly, I was *alone,* free from the smells and infection which lurked somewhere beneath me. Here, I was unchained, and could tread the small space to my leisure. I determined there were worse places to spend my last night on earth.

Though I had never been devout, when the candle went out, I prayed for the morrow to come. I knew there would be no remedy: no dashing, last-minute rescue; no pardon from the king; for Newgate was a fortress and I was a stranger to Charles. What pained me chiefly was leaving behind my friends, those "honest thieves" I considered closer than brothers. As for Aventis . . . I closed my eyes tightly . . . perhaps, despite his Popish faith, there was a chance we might meet again in a next, better world …

Later in the darkness, I heard a sexton tolling his hand bell outside the gaol gate. He recited, for me and the others about to die:

> You Prisoners that are within, Who for Wickedness and Sin, after many mercies shewn you, are now appointed to dye tomorrow: give ear and understand, that tomorrow morning the greatest bell of St. Sepulchre's shall toll for you, in form and manner of a passing bell, as used to be tolled for those that are at the point of death. To the end that all godly people hearing that bell, and knowing that it is for you, going to your deaths, may be stirred up heartily to pray to God to bestow His Grace and Mercy upon you while you live: I beseech you, for Jesus Christ, his sake, to keep this night in watching and prayer for the salvation of your own souls, while there is yet time and place for mercy . . .

But who would show mercy to *me?* Our Lord might but not those on earth. It briefly entered my mind to reveal my true sex, but then I laughed bitterly. As a woman, my behavior must be *more exemplary* than a man's, and thus would result in worse treatment. *No,* I thought, I resolved to go to my death as I had lately lived: not as Margaret Jane Tanner, but as so-called Megs, the scourge of Hounslow Heath!

I knew that morning had come when I heard boots on the stairs. I tried to still the blood which coursed like a stream through my ears. My two guards chained me, then led me back past the spikes and outside, where the sexton (being paid) again tolled his bell.

As light assaulted my eyes, I was led to the Press Yard where I and six more prisoners had our fetters removed. Then a cord was wrapped round our bodies, leaving enough room to pray, while our nooses were (thoughtfully!) placed around our necks. Perhaps so we wouldn't stumble, the remainder of the long rope was loosely coiled about us. We seven were then led to three open carts, where we were provided a seat—upon our own coffin.

Things could only improve from there, for the City Marshal who led us allowed us to stop at the Bowl and then the Mason's Arms for a last glass of beer. How those draughts tasted sweet!

After that, the procession to Tyburn slowed, as if we rolled down the streets caught in a giant wave. We acquired admirers, for mobs had started to gather on every possible corner. Did not these people have trades? But of course, hanging day was a public holiday! Every sort had turned out, from the gentry in their coaches (unfortunately safe from *me*) to the indigent in their rags. The general air was as festive as dancing around the Maypole. Well, let them be joyful. Better than a somber trek.

We rolled the three miles to Tyburn where I saw, with some disappointment, that the hanging tree was not really that: rather, it was a gallows, Hines's gibbet on a grand scale.

As our carts came to a halt, our ropes were uncoiled, and I resolved to do Jeffries justice. Thus, when I stood up, I gave an expansive bow.

The sexton (damn his hide!) made a second pronouncement as tedious as the first. While he droned, I looked over the size of the crowd—perhaps some *hundred-thousand!*—with the rich seated, as always, in Mother Procter's Pews. I noted some enterprising tradesmen selling fresh pies or pamphlets—as long as there were customers, why not make a shilling?

At last, from his high platform, the hangman dropped his hands for silence. He solemnly recited the crimes of my six fellows: some had clipped the edges off coins; one had stolen cattle, and another a sheep.

Naturally, the best was saved for last. The hangman increased his indignation.

"And, so-called 'Megs,' member of the Jeffries gang, robber of coach and killer of men! His exploits know no shame, for he waved his pistol at a lady and even our very queen!"

The crowd gasped before it jeered.

"Do not delay!" they cried, "hang him!"

"Indeed," said the hangman, eyeing my length of rope which now draped over the gallows beam. "It has long been our custom to give tobymen leave to speak. Let this 'Megs' atone."

At this, the crowd cheered, and I embarked on a speech which I hoped would not disappoint.

"Londoners!" I cried as loud as I could, "atonement is not in my blood. In truth, I regret nothing."

A huge roar rang out as I stood atop my coffin.

"The loftier my quarry, the prouder I am of my deed," I cried.

"For I put to you: in what other trade may a man of my estate meet our great king's . . . lady friend, or even our gentle queen? How else could I have made three fortunes and ridden with the noblest of men, those who defended our realm against the scourge of Cromwell!"

While many applauded, some ladies before me even wept.

"Captain Jeffries is no blackguard—he bested your courts of law, for he paid back to the Cavaliers that which was rightfully theirs."

I saw some older men throw their feathered hats into the air.

"I would be negligent in my duty," I said, "if I did not mention our band's great gift to England. We have spent so much on wine, women, and dinners that if the whole were summed, it would refill the Treasury!"

This received a great cheer, for Charles had nearly emptied it.

"You should know that one of our band once bet two hundred guineas on a single game of dice."

The crowd gasped as I thought of Carnatus.

"I go to my death a ma—a *person* unafraid, with the words of Shakespeare's Caesar echoing in my ears: 'It seems to me most strange that men should fear/Seeing that death, a necessary end,/Will come when it will come.'"

I actually earned applause almost fit for a Caesar! Then, I threw off my hat and cloak, waving away the chaplain. The two thieves at my sides began to moan and tremble. A shroud was placed over their heads, but I, thinking of Jeffries, demurred. Our cart's horses were whipped forward harshly, leaving us to dangle from our ropes as the noose did its work.

I had never thought overmuch about my manner of death: on the road, I had hoped a well-placed bullet would do its work in a flash. But *this* was a terrible way to die: as the rope pressed against my windpipe, I gagged and struggled for breath.

Goodbye, Jeffries, I thought. *I tried to do you credit. . . Aventis . . .*

Then memory ceased as I thought I saw three angels—but what were they doing on horseback? Did they not have wings?

Just before I passed into darkness, I felt something shoot by my neck. It made a whooshing sound as it severed my noose from its rope. I found myself falling forward onto my own coffin!

"I have not bet above a hundred!" a booming voice cried, and, as I rose to my knees, saw it came from Carnatus. From his saddle, he nocked a second arrow and sent it spiraling toward the hangman. *That* fellow leapt off his platform like a tumbler at a fair.

There followed a pistol's close blast and as the smell struck my nostrils, Aventis, sword in one hand and gun in the other, raised his mount's front feet in an effort to frighten the guard. It worked, for they ran off in a body, deserting their post and the platform.

"Jump!" Aventis ordered, and I sprang from the cart to the back of his saddle. The first thing I did was to remove that hated noose. Though I was weak with my near-hanging and my throat ached like ten devils, I still waved to the crowds who almost went mad. Some even parted like the Red Sea so that we could flee, our horses careening past walls made not of water but flesh.

Of course, it was Jeffries who gave the final flourish.

"God save the king!" he cried, firing his pistols skyward.

I merely strove to hang on as we flew from Tyburn and onto the Great Western. Nursing my hurt hand, I was vaguely aware of the Heath and our arrival at a new hideout.

"We cannot stay here," said Jeffries, leaping out of his saddle and placing his ear to the ground. "All is quiet now, but guaranteed, they will come."

"Where should we go?" asked Carnatus.

Jeffries stood.

"Let us make for Epping by nightfall," he said. "I know it is far, but we travel light."

"Except for Megs here," said Aventis. "To my mount, he appears heavy." He gave me a backward pat.

"Tell me, Aventis," said Jeffries, "have any of us ever struggled to procure a horse?"

Aventis laughed.

"We *are* rather good," he said. "Let Megs acquire the skill."

As Jeffries remounted, I felt a strange sensation: Aventis squeezing my hand! I was filled with such joy that the pain from my burn did not sting. Now back with my friends, thoughts of Newgate and Tyburn floated off on the warm breeze: not to be forgotten, but replaced with present, happier ones. As I returned Aventis's touch, I believe I felt I more festive than even the crowds at Tyburn!

Companions Only

Now I had what I needed: A Cavalier pistol from Jeffries, and a gleaming new sword from Aventis. How well they'd prepared for my rescue! Once back on the Great Western, I managed to "persuade" a dandy to part with his dappled gray. He seemed more than a little put out.

"Do not worry yourself," I called, trotting off. "Vigorous exercise is what *this* doctor recommends."

"Damn you," he growled, but kept most of his oaths to himself.

Just as Jeffries predicted, the king's cavalry was fast behind, and after riding a brisk half-league, we heard the pounding of hooves.

"Halt!" Jeffries ordered.

We pulled on our reins and waited.

"We may outrun them here but will not be able to do so all the way to Epping," he said.

"It is likely they have fresh horses," said Carnatus.

"That is why we make our stand *here.*"

With one of his pistols, Jeffries pointed to a hill.

"Ya!" he cried to his horse, and we all strove to keep up. "We shall conduct this raid as we would any other. With *one* notable exception: we do not rob the king's men."

"Damnit," Carnatus swore.

I nodded, loading my new pistol and testing the heft of my sword. *This* time, unlike Tyburn, I could be a help to my friends.

“Ready, lads?” Jeffries asked as ten mounted soldiers loped by in a cloud of rocks and dust. He raised his own blade as if he were still at Edgehill.

“CHARGE!” he cried, and we formed a cavalry of our own.

Jeffries and Carnatus plunged to the foe’s left flank while Aventis and I closed on the right. The red-coated soldiers kept up near-constant fire, and, in the heat of the fight, I did not know at first I was hit—on my lower left arm. Still, with Tyburn fresh in my mind, I gritted my teeth and kept on.

“Separate them!” Jeffries cried, and we did, five against two on both sides of the road. Aventis whirled dual blades as the rest of us used ours to swat guns from the hands of men trying to reload. Though numbers were against us, we left two red coats in the dirt: then three, and six. The rest threw down their weapons as if they would explode.

“Is this how you defend your king?” Jeffries shouted, dismounting. He toed one man’s boot with his own. “Prince Rupert would have had you flogged for lack of effort!”

“Yes, sir,” said one downed soldier who spit out a mouthful of pebbles.

“Your captains should teach you,” said Carnatus, “how to keep your seats.”

“And not surrender like women!” cried Aventis. He shrugged as he surveyed me. “Sorry,” he whispered.

I was so rattled by my new wound that I barely heard him. Carnatus made short work of tying up the soldiers. He seemed especially tickled to use their rope for the task!

From beside Aventis, I clutched my arm, blood now marring my cloak.

"What of the wounded?" I asked between gritted teeth.

"No need to fret," said Jeffries. "Soldiers look after their own."

I nodded, then groaned. Aventis's sharp eye swept over my arm. He yanked off his falling band, deploying it as he had done for himself.

"Alas, this must wait until Epping," he said, his eyes clouding over his mask.

"No worries," I said, hoping I spoke the truth.

Jeffries stood over the fallen soldiers and threw them six handfuls of guineas.

"For when you are questioned," he said. "Now, we must say adieu." He nodded to the men. "Long live the king!" he cried.

"God save him!" came the reply.

After Jeffries and Carnatus mounted, we recommenced our ride. It was sixteen leagues to Epping—and for me, each seemed as long as a day in gaol. Though my wound had been stemmed, it pained me with every stride, and I moaned from the saddle.

"How fare you, Megs?" asked Aventis, loping up beside me.

"The fare is fine," I said dreamily, "though I loathe pickled salmon."

The concern in my friend's eyes grew.

"You must be strong," he said, trying to sound cheerful. "After Newgate and Tyburn, this must seem a trifle."

I nodded, clinging to my gray's mane as my head fell forward.

When I revived, reins still clutched in my hands, I saw we were in a deep wood. Had we reached Epping, at last?

Aventis leaped from his horse and ran to my side.

"Megs, let me untie you," he said, and proceeded to undo some knots. So *that* is how I had survived the journey!

Aventis lifted me up and placed me gently on the grass. Yet, instead of administering aid, he dashed into the forest and was soon lost in the trees. Carnatus and Jeffries looked puzzled as they gazed at my ashen face.

"Steady there, Megs," said Jeffries. "Luck has not been with you of late."

"I should never play cards," I mumbled.

"Though I hate to place odds at such a somber time," said Carnatus, "I'd bet two to five that is a serious wound."

"Thank you," I said.

Strangely, I no longer felt pain in my arm: just an encroaching numbness.

When Aventis returned, he bore a large leaf in his hands. Kneeling beside me, he applied a foul-smelling salve.

"Perhaps it does not seem so," he told me, "but you were fortunate, Megs. The ball exited your flesh, leaving only a broken arm."

Only?

"What is that potion?" I asked, pointing to the liquid inside the leaf.

"Yarrow," he said. "If one believes the wise women, it is especially good for gunshots." He tore off one of his cuffs and began to rebind my wound.

"I might suggest applying live pigeons to Megs's feet," said Carnatus. "After all, it worked for the queen."

Jeffries nodded.

"Perhaps a good bleeding with leeches."

"I thank you, friends," said Aventis, "but let us adhere to my method at present."

He rose, finding a branch to make a hardy splint. For the brace, he used the bottom of his own shirt. Poor man! With his clothes in tatters, he looked more like a beggar than a count!

After he set my arm, Aventis placed me full-length on the grass. "Now you must rest," he said. "That arm should be mended inside seven weeks."

"*Seven weeks*?" I cried. "I am young—perhaps it will heal quicker."

"Perhaps," Aventis chuckled.

Now that the numbness was gone, I felt pain at the point of the break. My grimace acted as a trigger—for Carnatus to hand me an overfilled cup.

"Nothing dulls the hurt like a pint of ale," he said. "Or a good thrashing of one's servant."

I could not speak for the latter but after I finished the brew, I could swear to the former.

'S-speaking of servants," I slurred slightly, "where the devil is Gad?"

"I dismissed him!" roared Carnatus.

"For the sixth time," Aventis whispered, "since I've known him."

"Carnatus," I asked, the ale loosening my tongue, "how . . . how came you to be a gamesman? W-were you always such?"

He sighed as he stood before me.

"Alas," he said, "I was born under a betting planet! Before the age of sixteen, I had gambled away my inheritance."

"Oh no," I said.

"And my family seat. And coaches. I once even pawned Gad to pay off a debt at the races."

"Good Lord!" Aventis breathed. "How much have you run through?"

"Hmmm, let's see . . . " Carnatus counted on his large fingers. "Perhaps . . . six-thousand."

"Guineas?!" I cried.

"They were not pence," he said.

My slightly dazed brain fought to control my mouth.

"S-so you took to the road not out of necessity—"

"It was necessary at the time," he said.

"What I mean is . . . all these years, you could have sat snug by your fire, your favorite hound at your side."

"And a drunk could stay sober if only he did not drink," said Jeffries.

Carnatus smiled wryly, then noticed I seemed forlorn.

"Do not cry for me, Megs," he said. "There is no adventure so fine as watching the dice tumble or throwing down just the right card. And let us not forget doxies or eating the best fowl in England! Truly, I would rather bask in these pleasures than sit by my fire at York."

In one way, I understood him, but in another, I could not. Though riding the road was great fun and the guineas beyond my dreams, what seemed the final consequence—a hanging at Tyburn Tree—must pale beside the gift of wealth. *Well, what did I know?* I thought, shaking my addled head. The only "valuables" bequeathed me were endless beatings and chores . . .

"Speaking of fires, let you and I go so we have reason to light one," Carnatus told Jeffries, and they both went off in the woods, intent on catching some game.

I sighed. All this talk of another's plight caused me to think of my own. Not my born station, for that was set in stone: no, seeing Aventis kneel at my side, I bemoaned the *other* me: Margaret Tanner, woman. In my sodden state, it seemed my limbs were laden with muscle, my hair coarse and wild. Alas! With Aventis so close, I felt more Hercules than Diana.

"A-aventis," I asked, hating what to my ears was the voice of a man, "do ya think of me as . . . as a woman? The same way as Mary and Moll?"

"Why do you ask, Megs?" he said with perfect complacency. "Or as we are alone, I should say, Margaret."

Hearing him speak that name made me smile despite my arm.

"Of course, you are like those women! Why would you not be?"

"But . . . d-donning a man's clothes, using his weapons, r-riding th' road—"

"It is just a charade," said Aventis, taking my good hand in his. "It no more makes you a man than if I affix a bridle and proclaim myself a horse!"

I laughed, perhaps louder than I should. Sitting up, I peered at his face.

"Thas' not it!" I yelled, getting angry without a reason. "Do you—do you think I'm pretty?"

His black eyes sparkled.

"Margaret, you will recall I saw your natural gifts." He cleared his throat. "*All* of them."

I blushed, thinking back to that day with Barbara.

"But I have seen nothing!" I protested, knowing this made little sense. "I do not think it is fair."

Aventis's shoulders shook as he laughed. *That* really inflamed me.

"Mother of God!" I cried, "if you admire me, are you still so priestly so as not to attempt a kiss? *You,* who bedded a queen!"

Through my haze, I could see him color. He sat motionless for some time, staring into the woods. Just when I thought he might fall asleep, he dropped to both knees and put his lips upon mine. I moved my arm around his back, feeling the muscle beneath his cloak. That kiss, my first real one, felt so sweet that I wished to prolong it as long as we two lived.

He was the first to pull back.

"Count," I whispered, "I-I must tell you—"

I halted as our two friends marched out of Epping, both bearing a sturdy log from which hung a freshly killed buck.

"What madness is this?!" yelled Carnatus, dropping his end of the burden as if it were made of fire. He wiped a hand across his eyes.

"No more ale!" cried Jeffries, likewise dropping the buck and stomping toward me and Aventis. He seized a near-empty jug and turned it upside down. "You have *both* had quite enough!"

"Are they drunk then?" Carnatus asked with relief.

"Ha!" said Jeffries dismissively. "So often I have seen this with soldiers—they get thoroughly raddled and think they embrace their sweetheart."

"Oh. So . . . there is nothing . . . unnatural then?" asked Carnatus. Just to be sure, he retreated behind his kill.

"Not in the least," said Jeffries. "Why don't you start gutting that buck? I could use a hearty supper."

Shrugging, Carnatus took out his dagger and applied it to the deer's hide. Jeffries, looking stern, motioned for me and Aventis to follow him into the woods. He halted by a stream, then whirled and turned to Aventis.

"Tell me, count—what good were all your studies if you cannot *think?* Carnatus would shoot the two of you as easily as skin that buck. Is that your secret desire?"

Aventis looked down at the water struggling between small rocks. I had never seen him so sad.

But I must have matched his expression as Jeffries turned on *me.*

"*Megs*!" he barked, as he had at the king's soldiers. "It was *you* who begged to join me—as a tobyman, not a doxy! I believe I made that quite clear?"

"Yes, sir," I said softly.

Now, within the hour, another real name was unfurled—this time by Jeffries.

"Conde Bernardino del Castillo," he said, "I am shocked at your behavior! Are you so depraved that you would corrupt a young girl? And what's worse, a companion of the road."

The captain turned his back in disgust.

"I beg your pardon, Charles," said Aventis. "I do not know how it happened. You have my word as a gentleman it will never do so again."

Jeffries nodded, the blood returning to his face.

"Please understand," he told both of us, "as your captain, I am duty-bound to protect you. And to keep our company whole."

"Yes, sir," I said again.

Aventis bowed, turned on his heel, and left. Jeffries gave me a searching look before heading after him. As I stood there, surrounded by trees, I knew at last what I was. Not a man—that was clear. No, I was a woman to whom love was forbidden. This seemed worse than anything I had been through—even Tyburn. But, if I were to stay with Jeffries, I must obey his rules. That meant accepting Aventis as a companion only.

1663

Accept it I did.

In truth, he made it easy, for after that day, he would scarce notice me, and when he did, spoke as he would to Carnatus. There was no heat in his glance or passion in his voice, and, hard as it was, I attempted to follow his model. Though my heart protested, the rest of me remained calm, and, to the observer, I was as Megs-like as ever.

As Aventis predicted, my arm healed inside seven weeks. It was such a relief to cast off that splint and its hated brace!

During my convalescence, we had kept on the move, which proved a successful strategy: no King's men were to be seen. Once I had recovered, Jeffries hastened us to London. It seemed the same as always, with its noxious air and bustle, though perhaps the palace at Whitehall was a bit bigger and grander.

"Has Charles really been back for three years?" I asked Jeffries. To me, my days at his side had seemed to pass in a flash.

"Yes," said the captain, "and he has, amazingly, not started a war."

"Give him time," said Carnatus.

Aventis cleared his throat.

"Not if the queen has a say."

I looked over at him on his horse as we clomped down a cobblestone street. Did he still have the ear—or hinder parts—of Her Majesty? If he did, I thought, I would surely be the last to know. Besides, Jeffries kept such a watch on us that Aventis would have to sprout wings if he wished to visit the palace. That was at least some recompense.

It was thus in 1663 that I determined to lose myself in our band's adventures. And we did have a few . . .

The first one of note passed on Salisbury plain, a popular spot for our trade due to its public coach. One fine spring day, our company hid behind tall rocks which were assembled in a circle.

"How boring," said Carnatus, looking up from his saddle. "What pitiful knave thought to pile stone atop stone? Could they not have spent their time on something more amusing?"

"Like Cribbage?" Aventis asked.

"Or Hazard?" I added.

"Shhh!" Jeffries warned, putting a finger to his lips. "Listen."

We heard our favorite melody: the groan of wheels upon dirt. Jeffries drew up his reins as a plain black coach approached.

"On it, lads!" he cried, a pistol now in each hand. We set out from behind the rocks with the fury of the Four Horsemen. The coachman, a timorous sort, instantly fell from his box and prostrated himself in the dirt.

"Brave man," said Carnatus.

"Do not hurt me, good sirs!" the man cried. "I am a poor but honest man."

"The worst sort," huffed Carnatus. He threw a rope from his saddle and casually ensnared his prey.

"Your turn, Jeffries," said Aventis.

The captain moved toward the door nearest him. It contained neither curtain nor glass.

"Out with you!" he yelled. "Only do as you're told, and I promise you'll come to no harm."

The first to emerge on the road was a frightened young woman, her raiment none too fine. She offered an arm to her companion, a man at least twice her age. He possessed strong features and wore a long fair wig. What struck me most was his gaze: distant and unfocused. It was clear that he was blind.

"Stand and deliver!" cried Aventis, though I felt somewhat bad. Who would we rob next? The lame and the infirm? Still, we both dismounted and prepared to search our victims.

"Please, sir," said the girl, her lashes tinged with moisture. "We have nothing. My
husband—"

God's legs! He looked like her father!

"—has of late been hounded for wanting a civil state."

"You mean an uncivil one!" spat Jeffries. "With another Cromwell! Hand him over to me, and I'll set *my* hounds on him."

He gestured to me and Aventis.

The woman moved closer to her spouse as she hugged his arm.

"Poor John was even arrested," she said, "and it could happen again." She looked at Jeffries, trembling. "We have no money, sir. Not ten shillings together."

"Yet you keep a coach," said Carnatus, running a hand over its roof. Far more than the rest of us, he knew what such things cost.

"Oh no, sir," said the woman, "this is lent by a friend. We must return it at Basingstoke."

Jeffries sighed and lowered his pistols.

"Megs, tell the gentleman what he must do."

I smiled, though of course this was lost on the man. *Well did I remember playing the barmaid for Jeffries!*

"As you have no money," I said, "you must practice your profession. It doesn't matter what it is. If you are a barber, then please deliver a shave."

Now it was *his* turn to smile.

"A curious custom," he said, in tones so lofty he might have been onstage. He stood in the center of the road, his sightless eyes turned to me. "I am a poet by trade."

We all laughed except for Aventis, who regarded the man with respect.

"Then pray, sir, recite us some stanzas," he said. "If they are good, we shall praise them. If not, we will take your friend's coach."

The man, rather than being offended, almost seemed to beam.

"Very well," he said. "*Someone* at least shall hear them. I have but lately produced a new work. I shall skip the introduction."

"Please God!" yelled Carnatus, and I too felt relief.

The poet tugged on a coat nearly as black as ours, thrust his wig from his face, and began:

> The infernal serpent; he it was, whose guile
> Stirred up with envy and revenge, deceived
> The mother of mankind, what time his pride
> Had cast him out from Heaven, with all his host
> Of rebel angels, by whose aid aspiring

To set himself in glory above his peers,
He trusted to have equaled the most high,
If he opposed; and with ambitious aim
Against the throne and monarchy of God
Raised impious war in Heaven and battle proud
With vain attempt. Him the Almighty Power
Hurled headlong flaming from the ethereal sky
With hideous ruin and combustion down
To bottomless perdition, there to dwell
In adamantine chains and penal fire,
Who durst defy the Omnipotent to arms.
Nine times the space that measures day and night
To mortal men, he with his horrid crew
Lay vanquished, rolling in the fiery gulf
Confounded though immortal: But his doom
Reserved him to more wrath; for now the thought
Both of lost happiness and lasting pain
Torments him; round he throws his baleful eyes
That witnessed huge affliction and dismay
Mixed with obdurate pride and steadfast hate…

"Sweet Jesus!" Aventis cried in a rare display of blasphemy. "I have not heard such lines since the Bard's."

"My 'On Shakespeare' was published in the Second Folio," *this* poet said calmly.

I heard Carnatus mumble from his place by the coachman.

"'Adamantine chains,'" he growled. "What infernal nonsense."

"I did not comprehend a word," the bound man agreed.

Jeffries turned to the poet.

"My friend Aventis," he said, "is something of a scholar, and appreciates such effusions much more than I. Yet, even I, a simple soldier, perceive that your lines have genius."

The man, much gratified, bowed.

"Sir," I said, approaching him. He turned his head toward my footsteps. "I have not heard words more glorious except in Holy Scripture. It is like . . . the song of angels."

The man smiled.

"Thank you, mistress," he said.

I resolutely held my ground.

"Oh no, sir, I am a man."

"Then I thank you, young 'man.'"

He gave me a wink.

"We shall delay you no longer," Jeffries said to the travelers as he gestured for Carnatus to free the driver. "I am certain I speak for all when I say we greatly anticipate the day that your poem is published." He paused, then whispered to the plain, "Even if you're a dam'd Dissenter!"

The poet chuckled, for his hearing was excellent. It was then that I spoke up.

"I beg you, Mr. John. Please accept these coins. They are to further your work."

From my purse (replenished by Jeffries), I pulled out some guineas and thrust them into his hand.

"Again, I express my thanks," he said. "For outlaws, you do have a certain gallantry."

Carnatus puffed out his chest as I doffed my hat. I knew the man could not see me, but somehow, it seemed fitting.

Within minutes, we watched the coach roll off. Aventis turned to me and said, "That man's work will live forever."

Still in a daze, I nodded.

"I did not realize that mere lines could so transport one."

Carnatus, as always, had a different reaction as he mounted his horse.

"I'd like to transport *him!*" he cried. "Not a penny gained. At this rate, we'll all become beggars."

Aventis smiled, but Carnatus was not done.

"First, some fool piles up stones," he said, pointing to the rocks around us. "Then we encounter another speaking of nothing but Hell. Five to three I can't endure it."

He rode down the plain in a huff.

A few months after, we had an adventure that was not even on the road!

We were well aware that the summer sun was hiding, and, in August, the air was decidedly chill. At our various hideouts, I had taken to piling up blankets and sleeping close to the fire. Even Jeffries spent nights fully clothed.

In an effort to find some warmth, we rode again into London, where Carnatus sat sighing before a cheerful coffee house.

"Come, Jeffries, why not go in?" he asked, rubbing his gloves together. "If we stay out much longer, my rear will freeze to my saddle."

"A sorry state of affairs," said the captain, "for those who have to free you. But I fear these establishments have become a hotbed of politics. Therefore, the climate within is too hot for *us.*"

"And I am not allowed," said Aventis. Seeing me start, he explained, "No Catholics."

"Nor women," I said easily. Realizing my blunder, I recovered with, "Not that that would concern us."

"Of course not," said Jeffries. "I suggest we tie up our horses and join the crowds. It may be that the heat of bodies will serve to warm our own."

I knew I would be satisfied with just *one* body present. Still, I obeyed the captain, and, along with the others, handed my reins to a lad. We had to push past carts and flocks of sheep as

we crossed London Bridge. What I noted with relief: even the famed Du Vall could walk unremarked among these throngs!

As we stepped off the Bridge, I glanced at the river Thames. I had to shake my head: was it actually *frozen* into a solid sheet? As we came closer, we saw some enterprising folks selling pies *on the river* while Londoners of all ages engaged in that new Dutch sport—skating.

Aventis, always bold, was the first to try the ice. Though I wished to follow, I could not, for I feared that veneer would crack and pull me beneath frigid water. Like so many English "lads," I did not know how to swim.

I overcame my hesitation when Jeffries offered me his elbow. With his help, I learned to perform a walk-slide which helped me keep my balance during this very odd stroll.

I confess I felt a pang when Aventis strode out of sight), but was relieved when he soon returned, his arms full of Dutch skates. For his sake, I tried to look pleased, but would rather have taunted a bear than affix those thin blades to my feet.

"You look ill, Megs," he teased, bending to fasten some thongs onto each of his boots. As he glided off without effort, I could not help but admire his grace. Yet when he started to skate round our party, forming a tight circle, this proved too much for Carnatus.

"Intolerable!" he cried. "For a Spaniard to best us at sport! Remember the Armada!"

He seized a pair of skates, lacing them around his huge boots with difficulty. When he stood, he nearly tumbled—directly on top of me!

"Carnatus!" I cried, "do not crush me like a player at Spoil Five!"

"Sorry," he said, raising himself off me. "I'll bet three to one I can outdo Aventis."

Though I knew little of odds, *these* did not sound promising. My instinct was confirmed as Carnatus waved his arms wildly, then fell onto his rear.

"Two to one?" he asked.

Neither Jeffries nor I responded.

"Hmph," said the captain at last. "Forgive me, but I will abstain. With new pursuits, I often find that the role of observer preserves both life and limb."

I could not agree more. The sight of Carnatus laid out on the ice was enough of a caution for me.

"It is easy to laugh, dear Megs," he said, as a few mischievous lads hurled snowballs in his direction. "Far harder to do."

I could not dispute him. My sense of shame deepened as small children whirled past me, yelling with delight. What's more, Aventis was close, tracing a perfect circle. If I did not act, my chance to get him alone might melt along with the ice!

Groaning like one of the Damned, I managed to tie on some skates. Jeffries propped me up until I found my feet, at which point I half walked, half stumbled toward Aventis. When I reached him, he steadied my faltering gait by putting his arm through mine.

We both laughed, carefree for once, and after some bold glides, we were free from Jeffries's gaze. What a burden lifted! I wanted to turn to Aventis, to cry, "Come, let us flee!" but then remembered the debt we both owed the captain. Without him, Aventis would starve, and I would have no home. Not to mention that Jeffries had saved me from Tyburn! No, such a thought was best left unspoken.

My next, however, warranted a full cry.

"Oh no," I said.

I had spied a familiar figure—one which I had hoped never again to set eyes on! It was *the bishop*, the one we had robbed . . . and forced to ride backwards on his ass. At this moment, he was glaring at me as if I were Milton's Fiend!

Though I wanted to skate back to Jeffries and warn him, my skill was such that I tripped and fell, gliding ten feet on my back until I lay with arms splayed at the foot of the bishop's robes.

"A new acolyte?" asked the churchman, his tone more chill than the air. "Do I not know you, boy? And that man hence? I believe the last time we met, you were both sporting masks."

"How fare you, sir?" I asked, lifting my head. "I believe when I last saw you, *you* were sporting nothing."

The bishop shook with anger. He crooked a white-gloved finger to some men standing behind him. From my low viewpoint, I saw they looked like soldiers—of the religious kind.

"Arrest them!" the bishop shouted. "They have robbed a son of the Church, along with the Church herself."

"As have you," I breathed, reaching under his robe, gripping his ankles, and using them as a prop to propel myself toward Aventis.

"Have you managed to anger a bishop?" he asked.

"Oh yes," I said, as he helped me to my feet. "We made of him an ass, and he means to make mincemeat of us!"

"Not if I can help it," said Aventis, who promptly unsheathed his sword.

Jeffries and Carnatus, both of them now skate-free, slid their way over to join us. They were greeted by the Church soldiers, all of whom pulled out their blades.

"No pistols!" cried Jeffries, meeting a soldier with steel. "There are too many children about."

"As if that would concern you," the bishop spat.

"Rest assured that it does," I said, engaging a foe with a few of Aventis's tricks. After relieving him of his sword, I saw the fellow run down the ice, then trip and sprawl, gliding out of my sight like a seal.

"The captain has more scruples than you!" I told the bishop as I took on another man. "He does not pretend to be holy while thieving from the altar."

The bishop's face went whiter than the Thames.

"Do not heed him!" he cried to his men. "This boy is no more than a footpad."

"I beg your pardon?" cried Carnatus, dispensing two soldiers with as many flicks of his wrist. "How *dare* you insult us? *We* are high tobymen—far higher than your stout self!"

The bishop sneered as Aventis came up behind him, taking on four of his men by himself. He sent them hurtling onto the ice before they rose again to continue.

"Four to one?" asked Carnatus.

"I'll take those odds!" I said, my breath forming a cloud as I challenged another soldier. I wished with all my might that I was burdened with just one blade and could break free of those on my feet!

Aventis, however, used *his* to his advantage: he spun, he whirled, he sped to each side of his foes in a near-blur of black. At the last, all four lay still on the ice.

"Well, bishop," said Jeffries, sliding toward that robed figure. "Do you wish to continue?"

Carnatus, Aventis, and I formed a barrier around the churchman.

"I am certain we may resolve this," he said, his eyes shifting to each of us, "in the way of the Church . . . that is to say, in peace."

"Very good," said Jeffries. "In the spirit of peace, I shall ask for an offering. Your purse, if you please."

The bishop looked heavenward before throwing that item at Jeffries.

"In light of the crowds," said the captain, "I had resolved not to practice our trade today. But our meeting is so fortunate it might have been, so to speak, directly ordained by God."

"You will swing, blackguard," growled the bishop. "And I will spit on your bones!"

"Perhaps one day," said Jeffries. "In the meantime, I am glad not to have to view your *flesh.*"

The skaters on the ice, held back by our flash of swordplay, now approached timidly.

"All hail the Anglican church!" cried Jeffries. "For this generous bishop has granted you one shilling each."

A cheer went up round the Thames as ruddy-cheeked children tugged at Jeffries's cloak, their woolen gloves outstretched. He responded by taking handfuls of coin and tossing them in the air.

Aventis, myself—and even Carnatus!—mimicked his gesture, our downward drop of silver sparkling against the ice. The bishop was forced to smile and bless his flock as they heartily thanked him for his liberality.

A Good Catholic

Unlike 1663, I earnestly wished that the next two years had never come to be.

They started off like any other. We did what we did best: robbing coaches on all the main roads to London. Due to our many hideouts, I saw a great deal of England from behind my black mask. Even better, I saved quite a sum, in the keeping of a London banker courtesy of Moll. In her home, we saw her often when we took shelter while Jeffries did so in her arms.

"These are nice," I told her one evening, as she returned from the dressmaker with an armful of new frocks. Jeffries was clearly good to her. She dropped her treasure on the divan which doubled as my bed.

"Really, Megs?" she asked. "You are the first of the captain's men to notice."

"Uh," I replied, searching for a lie. "I had several sisters and was raised in a feminine home."

"It has done you good," she smiled, giving my arm a pat. "You are not so loud nor vulgar as the other high tobys."

"You cannot mean Aventis," I said, a little sharp.

"Oh no, he is so holy! But that Carnatus . . ." She shook her head. "All his bellowin' hurts my head."

I laughed as she went upstairs to join Jeffries. Carnatus and Aventis were out: gone in disguise to an alehouse so the former could sample its brews.

As for myself, I stared at Moll's purchases, trying to resist, but that was never my strong point. Handling the Indian cotton, I set on a dangerous course, stripping myself of Megs and clothing myself as Margaret. Staring into a small glass, I smiled at what I saw: despite my qualms, I was no man trapped in heavy muscle. What I saw was a young woman with long dark hair, a pretty face, and a low-necked bodice which exposed a woman's figure. If I stared long enough, I could pretend there was no Megs and only this creature that lived in her place.

"Heigh ho!" yelled Carnatus, as he banged into Moll's house. He was sodden by liquid: from the rain without and ale within. "What's this? A stunning wench? Aventis, stand back!"

The latter, when he saw me, froze in place.

"Halt!" Aventis commanded. "This is but a thief come to steal our hostess's plate."

"Raise the hue and cry!" yelled Carnatus.

"Are you mad?" Aventis asked. "Think of what we are."

Carnatus drooped.

"*This time* we do not call the watch," said Aventis, taking me—roughly—by the arm. "Consider yourself lucky. I shall see you into the street."

He opened the door with his boot and dragged me into a London storm.

"What do you think you are doing?" he hissed. "Do you *wish* to be caught?"

"No," I said softly, my tears unseen in the rain. "I . . . I just . . ." I thought. What *was* it I'd hoped to accomplish? "You cannot know how it is," I said, "to be someone else every day. To put aside not just your name but your sex. I must always be vigilant. I must always pretend. After five years . . . " I looked down, "it-it wears on a body. I no longer know who I am."

Aventis's face softened as he led me under a jetty provided by the adjoining house.

"You are right, I cannot know," he said. "You are such a hardy companion I often think of you as just Megs." He removed his coat and placed it around my shoulders. "Have you tired of this life? Do you wish to leave it? You have amassed enough guineas to do whatever you want."

"As a woman?" I asked. "That frees me to either sell fish or marry."

"And do you not want that?" he asked. "Not to be a fishwife but a—"

"—real wife?" I finished. "In truth, I do not know. I confess I enjoy my freedom. I could not stand being ruled by a man, unless . . . ."

He stood there, his face taut as he waited.

"Well, what does it matter?" I asked in utter defeat. "As long as we ride with Jeffries, we are sworn to be apart. *You* do not seem troubled."

His whole body started to shake as he balled his fists.

"Though I am not a woman," he said, "I can suffer the same as one. I can feel just as deeply and hide those feelings with skill."

"Then it would seem that the sexes are not so different."

"You should know," he said, "for you have been both."

He took off his falling band and wiped my tears away.

"Dear Megs," he whispered, "it is time for me to go in. I shall open the back door and place your daily clothes there."

"Yes," I said, and watched him leave.

After that, I tried as hard as I could to pretend that nothing had changed. As Megs, I went on our adventures—stopping this coach and that—even robbing some cattle from a group of wayward farmers. My savings continued to grow, and we stayed out of Newgate—thanks to Jeffries's wiles. While others fell to the hangman, their bones dangled upon the Heath, we kept riding across it like the kings that we were.

In the summer of '65, one a great deal warmer than that which had froze the Thames, we made for Salisbury plain, where we had encountered the poet I now knew as Milton.

"Whatever became of him?" I asked Aventis.

"Alas, the lines he spoke still have not been published," he said.

"Pity," I replied. "I hope it happens one day."

"Those with talent survive," said Jeffries. "Talent and perseverance."

"Heigh ho—take a look!" cried Carnatus, pointing an indigo glove at a line of coaches in the distance.

"That is the king's!" said Aventis, as the most ornate one flew past. "And that is his brother James's."

From behind those piled stones, we watched the royals raise a dust cloud in what looked like wholesale flight. I could have sworn I saw more than *a hundred* coaches.

"I hope he brought the Master of Spaniels," I said. "And the Royal purger."

"Let us pray," said Jeffries, "that the roads have been smoothed to satisfy the Royal rear."

"Base coward!" yelled Carnatus. "Our king has the heart of a mouse! He and his courtiers do not dare remain in London."

Even Aventis looked sour as he shook his head.

"They're off to Hampton Court, I suppose."

I sighed. While we had slept rough in hideouts, rumors of plague had reached us as early as April: it must now be so widespread that the man who guarded our safety had fled to ensure his own.

"How nice to be rich," I said. "One can simply pack up and leave."

"Expect nothing from them," said Jeffries, "and you will not be disappointed."

Aventis's thoughts were elsewhere.

"I hope he included the queen in his party."

"How could he not?" asked Carnatus. "Wouldn't do to take the mistresses and leave the wife behind."

"Yet I think him capable," said Aventis.

"My friend," Jeffries told him, "do not fret about Charles. While he and his court escape, the poor putrefy back in London."

"And Moll?" I asked.

"I do not know," said Jeffries.

By the time September came, an almost visible pall blanketed our land. We heard from the Heath's townsfolk that *seven-thousand souls* expired in London *each week*. Even we, living apart, witnessed the sting of the blight when it reached the Great Western.

Travelers on foot, either singly or in groups, had been making their painful way from the city. Some lay where they fell, and though we witnessed their agony and heard their cries, we dared not help, for they were already doomed. Thus, corpses crisscrossed the road like a giant draughts board: none who passed dared bury them lest *they* fall to the contagion.

One night around our campfire, I turned to Aventis. I thought that with his knowledge of plants, he might provide an answer.

"So . . . after all these hundreds of years, there is still no relief?" I asked.

"No," he said grimly. "Though false healers offer leeches."

"One hears that a teaspoon of emeralds works wonders," said Carnatus.

"Or exposing the stricken to certain smells," said Jeffries.

Aventis sighed.

"None of these 'cures' are effective, and the sick still die."

"Terrible," Carnatus shuddered.

Thinking of Aventis's past, I broached a belief I had often heard in my youth.

"Is the plague a sign of God's wrath?" I asked.

"Who knows?" said Aventis. "But if He is a God without mercy, what distinguishes him from Satan?"

Jeffries looked troubled.

"Perhaps He punishes us for sin," he said. "The licentious court, for example."

"Then why not simply strike Whitehall and spare the rest of us?" I asked.

"It is not for us to comprehend," said Aventis, staring into the fire. "Perhaps He has a plan so lofty we mortals cannot discern it."

The rest of us answered by sighing. Such matters were so far beyond me I determined to put them aside.

As that cruel September stretched on, I saw that Aventis became restless. One afternoon in our old Heath hideout, his shoulders sagged.

"What is the matter?" I asked.

"I must go."

"Where to?" I asked. "Spain?" My voice grew eager. "Perhaps we may all join you."

"To London."

"I beg your pardon?" I asked.

"Into the midst of infection?" Carnatus stared at him, wide-eyed.

"Do you really think that is wise?" said Jeffries, his expression relaying the opposite.

"Wise or not, I must go," said Aventis, rising to harness his horse. "There is so much death and affliction that I feel I must do something."

"And what is that? " I cried, leaping up. "Can you make the false cures true?"

Aventis looked down.

"I am not a doctor," he said, "but I *am* a human being. If I can provide some comfort, my actions will not be in vain."

'But your death *will!*" I yelled, resisting a powerful urge to slap the reins from his hand.

Aventis put his foot in the stirrup.

"That may well be the result. But when misfortune strikes, then I, as a sworn Catholic, am duty-bound to act."

"Like Queen Catherine?" I balled my fist. No doubt she was still at Hampton.

"Shall we address you as 'Father'?" asked Carnatus, crossing his arms.

Aventis mounted his horse.

"No. For the present, I bid you farewell. You are my most treasured friends, and it has been an honor and privilege to know you."

He saluted Jeffries. I had never seen that look on the captain's face: stoic, yet forlorn, in a heartfelt but silent goodbye.

Carnatus's was more voluble.

"I lay *excellent* odds on you," he cried, clapping Aventis on the back. "You will return to us forthwith. But . . . do take your time, old fellow."

He stepped back, clearly thinking of infection.

Aventis laughed, then walked his mount beside me.

"Goodbye, Megs," he said, breaking with Jeffries's rule and seizing my arm. At that moment, I would not have obeyed any man, and clasped my arms round his waist.

"Dear count," I whispered up to him, "do not throw away your life! Don't you know it has a meaning to others beyond yourself?"

Jeffries cleared his throat loudly, and Aventis moved away.

"Goodbye," I said, willing the tears not to fall.

Aventis raised a hand, then trotted down toward the road. I watched as his figure become smaller, then vanished complete, as he headed southeast to London and its raging pestilence.

The Plague

"Megs?" A loud voice asked, "what is *your* opinion?"

I blinked to see Carnatus standing before me, but I was so distracted I had not heard his initial query.

"Yes," I ventured.

"So, you *are* in favor of displaying our kind on gibbets?"

"Ugh. No. Of course not."

I gave him a tight smile, then strode over to Jeffries. We were still on the Heath, and Aventis was still absent—it had been near a fortnight.

"Any word?" I asked the captain, for at least the fifth time that day.

"No." He shook his head sadly. "I have just been on the roads and questioned those able to speak. None has any report of him."

Before Jeffries, I could allow my tears to flow: he even offered me his cuff. But how many tears could come from one person? How many days and nights could I sit here wretched, thinking that Aventis might be sick or worse? The answer came to me readily—not even one more.

"Captain, I must go," I said, heading for my horse.

"I have lately heard those same words."

"Yes."

I proceeded to bridle my mount.

"You do understand, Megs, that thousands have been stricken and die within a few days—sometimes it takes just one."

"I do," I said, cinching my saddle.

"Very well, Megs." Jeffries said the last word softly. "Please give me your word: if you find Aventis afflicted, you will return. Do not cut your life short to save one who is beyond hope."

"I do not believe," I said, "that for Aventis, there is such a state."

Jeffries nodded.

One thing more."

"Yes, sir?"

"May God bless you," said the captain.

I saw his dark eyes glisten. Fighting for composure, I turned to face him and Carnatus.

"Friends," I said, "know that the time I spent with you was the best of my life. I will never forget you—not even in death."

Carnatus lowered his head.

"Dear Megs," he said. "Though I think you have gone mad, still, I wish you the best."

"Thank you. And captain—" I turned to Jeffries, "—thank *you*. For everything."

He brought his cuff up to his face.

Spurring my mount, I set out off for London, not knowing what I would find.

What struck me on my way there was the sheer number of people leaving: I was the only one heading *into* the city. When I reached the outskirts, I heard nearby and distant chiming. This must be, I thought, the ringing of church bells to acknowledge those who had died.

Though the sound chilled, I remembered why I was there. This gave me courage enough to go on, even to the heart of the city surrounded by ancient walls. It was utterly transformed: fires burned in alleys in an effort to ward off infection; and at every street I passed, guards yelled at me harshly: "Stay out!"

Old women holding white wands sought out the afflicted to herd them into their homes. There, red crosses were painted on doors, along with the prayer: "Lord have mercy on us." To ensure the sick's isolation, more guards were stationed in front.

I saw whole families, some stricken and some not, forced indoors by these methods, a sentence of death on those still free of plague. As I rode down the streets, my horse's shoes striking cobblestones was the only sound. I traveled down blocks where every door bore a cross. It was just me, the guards, and a jumble of corpses.

What had once been mothers, fathers, children were left to rot in the sun, their flesh swollen by sores. London's putrefaction: its habit of throwing garbage out windows and living closer than rats had brought the Black Death—again.

I took out my robber's mask and affixed it to my face. This was my only safeguard and it was remarkably poor. What was there to prevent me, or Aventis, from falling prey to the scourge which had felled a great city? It was likely he was dead. But hearing those heralds of death—those bells tolling near and far—inspired in me a notion.

Where was Aventis likely to be? His priestly leanings had brought him here, so what better place than a church? London had no lack of them, and I stopped at first at St. Martin's, then St. Mary's and St. Michael's. These were either deserted or were now serving as hospitals. Still, no sign of my friend.

I rode through London's old gates, and even searched the new neighborhoods from Spitalfields to Piccadilly. Here were the mansions of the newly rich: clean and neat and orderly. But none of that mattered now, for there was no stirring of life.

Aventis, I thought, clutching my reins, *where the devil are you?*

I blinked as my horse passed row houses as silent as their rich neighbors's. I had been so distracted that I did not realize I was back in the old city.

From the middle of one block, I heard the sound of bells. They were of such volume and timber that their source could be only one: St. Paul's Cathedral. Trotting to the old place, I tied my horse in front, then gingerly made my way to what was now a church of England. How Cromwell would rail! (He'd seen fit to use it as a stable). Yet, the place still seemed decrepit, its main tower on the verge of collapse.

I entered the round-topped door, fearing what I might find. Those bells surely tolled for the dead—those who had died inside.

Indeed, what I saw before me was like the suffering of Job: there were hundreds laid out, cared for by bold family members, a few doctors who still lived, and, to my shock, a handful of nuns and priests. Despite the grimness, I chuckled: how that bishop would curse to see Papists here again!

I pulled up my falling band and went forward. It was hard to look on the sick with their pulsing sores, groans . . . even vomiting of blood. As I directed my gaze over that sorrowful space, I saw a priest and a man at his side closing the eyes of a woman. To judge by her swollen tongue, she must be glad to take leave of this world. Thinking to query the priest, I stepped between bodies to reach him, my approach muffled by the nave floor.

"Pardon me, Father," I said, "I do not mean to disturb—" then, "It is you!"

The layman beside him sprang to his feet. He looked like a fellow highwayman behind his own black scarf.

"Megs!" Aventis cried. He moved to touch my shoulder, then thought better of it.

"What in God's name are you doing here?"

I had never heard him yell with such vigor.

"I-I've come to find you … and-and perhaps aid you," I said.

"And well do we need help."

He gestured at rows of bodies stretching even to the raised altar.

"But Megs, you must be aware of the danger," he said. "If Newgate is a death trap, then this hallowed ground is far worse."

"Yet *you* still live," I answered.

"Only by the grace of God. Most caretakers have died. *That* is why you must leave."

He pointed to the front door.

"No," I said calmly. "You are not my husband and I do not have to obey you. *My choice* is to stay."

"Megs, you are so very . . . headstrong," he said, clenching both gloved fists. "I know I cannot dissuade you lest I cast you out on your head—"

"—and it is unsafe to touch me."

"You must take every precaution—"

"I will," I said. "Perhaps God, sparing you, will bestow the same favor on me."

Aventis smiled sadly.

"Yet He has taken so many: the cloistered, the healers, men, women, and children. Being a Good Samaritan reaps no reward in plague times."

I sighed, bowing my head.

"What can *I* do?" I asked.

That afternoon, he showed me: I could douse patient's foreheads; hold their trembling hand in my gloved one so they knew they were not alone; and at the last offer soft words before closing their eyes. Throughout, I was struck by my friend's restraint: he never tried to preach to those of other faiths and would not read the last rites unless a patient requested it. He even approached with gladness those whom Jeffries despised: Dissenters. In this vast tapestry of suffering, sect, along with status, were equal.

Despite the hardship, what I cherished most from those first few days was the time spent with Aventis. Though he rarely paused to acknowledge me, I, Margaret Tanner, was able to serve as his partner in something other than robbery. Though we still could not touch—forbidden not by Jeffries but the plague itself—I found a calm in his presence. I could tell that his words outside Moll's had not been idly spoken; indeed, when his dark eyes caught mine, I saw a look of real feeling.

We continued to work in concert like a black-clad priest and his acolyte. So many died in that nave that I desisted from counting, while the church bells rang so often that soon I did not hear them. Aventis's efforts were constant, until—on the fourth day since I'd arrived—my secret dread came true: he developed the first signs of plague.

It began as he clutched his groin, doubling over in agony. I could only watch helplessly as his face flushed with fever. It was not long before he took his place on the floor, lying on a thin blanket, too weak even to move.

Not Aventis, I prayed, *please God, let him recover* . . .

But my prayers went unheard, for like all the others his neck began to display horrible pus-filled sores. I could only hope that in contrast to some I'd tended, his skin would not turn black.

On the third day of his malady, I told him, "Aventis, try to drink," and bent over his poor head to offer a cup of water.

He merely turned away.

"No mortal recourse," he whispered.

I refused to accept this.

"Then implore God. He is the only one who can help."

He nodded but seemed unconvinced.

The next morning, when I woke beside him, he leaned on his elbows and gazed out a rose window sparkling with stained glass. Not trusting any blanket there, I removed my own cloak and placed it over his shoulders. Soon—too soon—his sores grew to the size of eggs and his whole form shook.

"Megs." He could hardly pronounce my name. "Please. Take this."

With an unsteady hand, he reached round his neck and pulled off a silver necklace. Hanging from it was a heavy crucifix. I accepted his gift and placed it in my coat pocket.

"I shall cherish it forever," I said.

"The queen," Aventis murmured.

I put my hand to his forehead. Though I felt a cold stab at the mention of my rival, I resolved to do what was right.

"What of her?" I asked. "Do you have a message?"

He tried to nod. "Yes . . . tell her I'm gone," he gasped. "Say . . . I was always her defender."

"You have my word," I whispered, tears bathing my face. It was a sight all too familiar in that infernal nave.

"Aventis," I said, "before it is too late . . . I must tell you – if Jeffries had relented, I would have married you."

"Yes," he said with a weak smile. "And I would have accepted."

It took all my will not to reach out and touch him.

"Margaret," he said.

"Count."

I enjoyed this brief moment where we could both be ourselves.

"I always thought . . . that before passing," he said, "I would feel a sense of peace. But there is only dread."

"It is the plague," I said. "It badly infects the mind."

Despite all strictures, I took hold of his gloved hand in mine. Then, I indulged in an act made halting by disuse. As I kneeled beside him, I prayed.

"Dear God," I said aloud, "won't you please save him? You know that we are outlaws, breakers of the laws of men, but if *You* disapproved our path, then why set it before us?"

I watched as Aventis dabbed his mouth with a white cloth—one that turned shockingly red.

I re-addressed our Maker.

"The count is a good, pious man. He came here to help others. I implore you, Heavenly Father, *please* do not take him from me!"

With that, I removed the crucifix and kissed it.

It was not more than an hour before delirium struck. While Aventis writhed, he cried my name, "Margaret!" as well as that of "Charles" and someone called "Phillip." Through it all, the word "Catherine" was unspoken.

I watched over him all night, bathed in sweat lest I had to perform that last duty: closing his eyes forever. I wished I knew the last rites, but as all priests there had died, Aventis would have to forego them.

As dawn broke through the rose east window, I saw a change come over my friend: his forehead cooled, he no longer cried out, and the ghastly sores on his body took on a paler hue. By mid-afternoon, he was able to swallow some water and even a crust of bread!

"Thank you, God," I said, not realizing I spoke aloud. "I will try to be nicer to You."

"He has seen to us both," said Aventis. "There is no other explanation."

"If you say so."

Among those we had tended, a precious few would improve, but as to why, no one could say. Perhaps Aventis, made strong by his years on the road, had been able to fight his way back. Yet, though he was better, he was far from being whole: his every movement was weak, and in place of those red sores there were now raised scars. It would be some time before he was fully himself.

"Aventis," I said, my voice urgent, "neither of us know the workings of plague. You might well be re-stricken, surrounded by its victims. Please, let us fly. We must go this instant!"

"Very well," he said. As I helped him up, he said, "Dear Margaret, I do this for you. I would not have you suffer as I have—not for a thousand guineas."

"Then I'm glad you are not Carnatus."

He gave a small laugh as I led him toward the door. *Brave as ever!* I thought. Still kept a good humor despite his ordeal. At last, I helped him out and we departed St. Paul's.

The rush of outside air, unusually fresh with few left to pollute it, gave us both new life. Aventis took me round to a stable where he had secured his horse. With relief, I found my own there, and there was better news yet: some good person had fed and watered them.

While I gave my horse a pat, Aventis came as close as he dared.

"Margaret," he said, "Truly, I owe you a debt which I can never repay."

"Yet, I feel I did nothing but sit."

"No. You gave me a reason to live."

I reached out to squeeze his hand, but he would not permit more, so I turned to the horses. After harnessing both and helping him to mount, I leapt into the saddle.

Once more, I saw the great city, as quiet as it must have been during the plague of three hundred years ago.

"Will things improve here?" I asked, as we headed northwest to the Heath.

"In my experience," said Aventis, "they usually do."

The Great Fire

When we approached our hideout, we were given a hero's welcome.

"What's this?" roared Carnatus, actually tossing away a fowl. "We are treated to not one, but *two* who return from the dead!"

He strode over to Aventis and lifted him from his saddle.

"You're a bit thinner, my friend," he said, "but I always thought you could lose a stone or two."

Jeffries and I laughed.

"I am glad to see you both," he said. "With the dire news from London, we naturally feared the worst."

"Aventis is far too dashing to die," said Carnatus, laying him gently on the heath. "As for Megs, he is too young!"

I smiled, setting myself by Aventis's side. For the next five weeks, I rarely moved from that spot, except to fetch what he needed.

As he improved, so did my spirits. Though thanks to Jeffries we must remain apart, I found I did not care: the only thing that mattered was that Aventis lived!

When he could tolerate wine, I asked, "The Lafite or the Latour?" like the barmaid I'd been.

"To a man recalled to life, even sludge will do," he smiled.

When I returned with a full cup, he put a hand to his cheek, where most of his scars had now faded.

"Tell me, Megs," he asked, "has the plague made me more tragic? Do I now bear the outer scars which reflect those within?"

I laughed, then swatted him.

"Aventis, you are no Milton," I said. "Best that you stick to your sword!"

By the sixth week, he was fully recovered. Though we wanted to be off, travel was not an option while the plague held sway. Incredibly, it lasted until *the next winter*. We lay low on the Heath until Charles decided it was safe to return to Whitehall. This was a great news for us, for in his train came courtiers, their coaches laden with treasure. We acquired so many French chairs we might have furnished Moll's house!

Of course, there were also guineas—enough to please Carnatus.

"I say, Aventis," he said, one morning after a raid. "Might you spare me some wine? I'm not entirely satisfied with this purloined ale."

"Of course," said Aventis. He filled a gold chalice to the brim.

"Very fine," Carnatus pronounced. "I declare myself happy you did not die last September."

"Thank you," said Aventis.

"Your luck was prodigious," said Jeffries. "They say that one in four has perished in London. I am grateful that Moll has survived."

"As am I," I said. "I hope the city can revive."

"As for me," said Carnatus. "I must revive *myself*. I confess myself weary even of this good Heath. A soft bed and a good meal would be welcome as a doxy."

I tried not to blush as Jeffries nodded.

"We must wait until all infection is cleared," he said. "We do not have a fortress-like palace."

"More's the pity," said Aventis, rising from his seat. "Think I'll gather wood for a fire."

"May I help?" I asked eagerly.

"Let Carnatus go," said Jeffries. "Perhaps he'll work off that partridge."

Carnatus laughed as he stomped off with Aventis. I looked down at the grass and sighed. Now that a month and a half had passed, I longed for a moment to be alone with Aventis.

Once London had been declared safe—*in June*—Jeffries wanted to visit Moll. In truth, I rather liked her, for she was friendly to me and glowed around the captain. However, I gave *myself* a stern warning: Stay away from her wardrobe!

As Carnatus had said, a soft place to sleep did wonders. To me, it was just short of heaven, though it was but Moll's divan. At night, I had my privacy, and would throw off that hated chest cloth. Once, when all were abed, I took up Moll's glass and a candle, just to assure myself that I could still pass as Margaret. There was no doubt that I could . . .

During this stay at Moll's, our company kept to itself. As Aventis had foretold, Carnatus called back Gad, whom he would send to a nearby cookhouse to retrieve groaning plates of meat. After our luck with Charles's train, we could stay off the road for a bit.

"I say, Gad, hand me round that capon," said Carnatus.

"Yes sir."

We were lounging about Moll's sitting room, enjoying another repast.

"Megs, did you sample the oysters?" Carnatus asked.

"I did. Fat and delicious."

"Like me," he pronounced. "What of the anchovies?"

"Not quite to my taste," I said.

"Gad," Carnatus ordered, "run back to the cookhouse and obtain a less fishy fish!"

So it went for a month as Jeffries cooed with Moll and the rest of us ate and drank. It was starting to get a bit dull, but we could not venture out among the much-reduced populace: the risk was far too great, and as a "man" who had cheated Tyburn, I resolved to lay low so the noose did not string me high.

The others seemed content: Aventis read his Bible while Carnatus played Gad at cards, and I attempted to mimic their calm. Still, I was restless: until my wish for action was granted on 2 September 1666.

From a deep sleep, I awoke to sounds in the street and the smell of burning wood. As an innkeeper's daughter, I lived in dread of his event.

"FIRE!" I yelled, causing Gad to run downstairs.

"Wake the whole household!" I cried, then pulled my mask over my face. I threw on what clothes I could, stumbling toward the front door. As I threw it open, what I saw was a catastrophe: a great fire was raging, flames rising in every direction, over the spires of buildings and the jetties of two-storey houses.

I ran back through the open door.

"We must depart!" I shouted, and saw my fellows and Moll running towards me while still getting dressed.

"We must get to the pipes!" cried Moll. "They are under the street."

Our company used swords and anything else we could carry—broken-off panes and broomsticks—to try to puncture the cobblestones and free the liquid below.

Our neighbors, none of them calm, joined us in their night-shirts. Within minutes, we had broken through the pipes and were handing round buckets.

"Form a line!" Jeffries ordered, raising his sword.

We complied, some thirty strong, but our efforts were laughable: we were like so many ants trying to put out the sun. After a half-hour of this, black smoke overcame us, and we fled choking from the street.

"Stay together!" Jeffries cried, as we fought for breath.

"It is the devil's work!" a woman in her bedclothes screamed.

"No, it is the baker's. Thomas Faryner of Puddin' Lane." A man pointed to where the flames were fiercest. "Left 'is oven unwatched, damn 'im!"

So, I thought, *this is all it takes to destroy England's capital?*

It clearly was. As we ran past wooden houses, many half-destroyed, London looked like a paper town besieged by a match-throwing giant!

"It may yet put itself out," said Carnatus.

"No, the wind!" Aventis cried, nearly losing his hat.

I could feel it blow strong from the east, but it did nothing to quench the fire: in a cruel twist, it merely fueled the flames. As we ran, I confess I felt fear: I could face swords, bullets, and anger; but this new threat could not be cowed by anything in my power!

"Head to the river!" said Jeffries, and we were glad to obey. Yet once we reached the wharves, we recoiled from a ghastly sight: a towering wall of fire which seemed to threaten the Thames!

"What is *in* those buildings?" I coughed, shielding my eyes from the smoke coming from smoldering warehouses.

"Only oil, tar, and pitch," said Jeffries. "And brandy."

"Mother of God!" I shouted. "Could it *be* more combustible?"

"Quick now!" Jeffries told us. "We must get across."

"How?" asked Gad. "There's not a boat that ain't full."

Carnatus, undeterred, waded out up to his ankles.

I turned from him as a monster roar shook the shacks on the bank. The air itself became heated as the smell of burning tar crept under my mask. I reeled, fearing that I might faint.

"Steady, Megs," said Aventis, grabbing my arm.

This quickly revived me.

"Ho, boatman!" Carnatus hailed a small craft. "Take us across, if you please."

"One guinea each," the man said.

"That is *outrageous!*" cried Carnatus, putting his hands on his hips. He looked like the Colossus of Rhodes.

"Sorry, gent," said the boatman. "If ya don't wanta pay, I kin find a body 'oo will."

"Very well," Jeffries spat, and handed over some coins.

We all stepped in gingerly. When Carnatus came aboard, the wood creaked in complaint. As we headed toward London Bridge, I saw that the huge waterwheels beneath it—which I knew supplied the streets—were themselves engulfed in flame.

I nudged Aventis and pointed.

"That does not bode well," he said. "If the east wind holds, I fear that London is lost."

"All because of a baker?" I asked.

"Stranger things have passed," said Aventis. "Malory tells us that a knight who raised his sword intending to kill an adder led to the fall of Camelot."

I looked around us, actually seeing *water burn.*

"But this is real," I told him.

Though our journey was short, it seemed to last an age. When we reached the farther bank, we had to cover our faces, for the air here was filled with debris. If that was not bad enough, it was near impossible to know if dawn had broken: when I looked up, I saw not the sun I knew but an orb the shade of charcoal.

"See there," said Carnatus.

As we tumbled out, he pointed back across the Thames.

We all watched as flames devoured the city's tall spires, each wreathed with black smoke as if in a last cry for help.

"There goes everything," I said. Though I was not a Londoner, I could still feel pain.

"I never thought I'd see such a sight," said Jeffries. At that moment, he realized our party was minus one. "Has anyone seen Moll?" he cried.

We all looked around.

"Not since we crossed," I said. "We must have lost her before the river."

Jeffries clenched his jaw.

"I must return for her."

"No, no!" came the shouts, from me as well as the others.

"No doubt she has found safety," said Aventis.

"I am sure of it," I said, "for she is a clever woman."

Jeffries looked torn, closed his eyes, and balled his fists. Still, he knew our advice was sound.

"Very well," he said. "Let us leave here before we choke."

Though we walked north for an hour, the landscape was much the same: buildings and shops on fire—or about to ignite. Once we came to Lombard Street and the Royal Exchange, we were privy to a sight that would otherwise be comic: a long line of bankers, cloaks blowing, rushed from its square, their arms full of bulging sacks. *While the lives of hundreds of thousands were imperiled*, I thought, *they* chose to save gold! I glanced at Jeffries, curious if he would strike, but he just looked disgusted.

"The Exchange is threatened!" one banker cried, as if mourning the death of a loved one.

"Still," said Jeffries, "it looks like you've taken most of it."

The bankers ran on, a panicked mob at their heels.

"Tell me," asked Aventis, looking around. "In all this, where is the *government*?"

"Saving their own skins, of course," said Carnatus. "Based on Charles last year, they're probably in York by now."

"This is a disgrace," said Jeffries. "Order burns along with our buildings. Where is the mayor? Or for that matter, the king?"

Finally, on what I assume was Monday, we saw a Trained Band of soldiers marching down the street. Their task must be to quell the mobs who had gathered amidst the smoke. Of course, they traded conspiracy theories: *this fire was a plot set in motion by French agents! Or worse, the agents were Papists . . .*

The soldiers first harassed the rioters, then those they sought to accuse. I had never seen such mayhem!

Frightened, I turned to Aventis. Calm as always, he gave me a wink.

"As long as I don't shout 'Long live the Pope,'" he said, "I think I'll be perfectly safe."

I tried to smile and nod. But was it not amidst chaos when people turned on each other?

I kept my worries to myself as Jeffries continued to lead us in search of a flame-free block. We ran in a pack, pursued by fire crowned with black smoke. Finally, we stopped at an unburnt house where my greatest fears came true: a mob was assailing a foreigner.

"What's this?" Jeffries cried, shouldering his way forward.

"'Ang 'em!" one imposing dyer was yelling. "Ain't 'e a Frenchie?"

"And a Papist! What's *'e* doin' 'ere?"

An enraged woman tore a crucifix from the Frenchman's throat.

"Some one fetch a noose!"

This made me clutch my own throat as I remembered Tyburn. I vowed I would not see another undergo that agony. Tensing every muscle, I prepared for a fight.

The mob acted in concert as they snaked a rope over a half-charred beam. At the other end, they knotted that hated lasso.

"Kill 'im!" they yelled. "Didn't the bloody pope bade 'im set this Jeremiah?"

The poor victim was dragged toward the noose, his expression one of terror. I prepared to leap forward.

"No."

Aventis's single word brought everyone to a halt. Withdrawing his sword, he stood before the Frenchman.

"Your talk of plots is nonsense," he said. "Neither Papists, nor French, nor Spaniards, lit this mighty blaze. Instead, it was a baker unmindful of his oven."

The dyer, his arms stained crimson, narrowed his deep-set eyes.

"Why should we heed ya?" he snarled. "Look a' 'is beard—if *e's* an Englishman, then I'm the bloody queen!"

The mob laughed, but it was not a happy sound, for it contained a violent edge.

"I stand with this man," said Jeffries, taking his place by Aventis. "As I stood with the king at Edgehill."

Faced with an actual soldier, the crowd grew quiet.

Carnatus, with a great clatter, stepped up to join his friends.

"I am a nobleman," he told the mob, "skilled in the arts of hunting and shooting." He raised his sword. "Also, this."

My turn at last, I took my place with the other three.

"Anyone who touches these men will answer to me," I said. "I may be unarmed, but that has not stopped me before."

"He near-killed a man with a basin!" Jeffries cried.

The crowd eyed us for a moment. Could we hold back so many? Or would we be swarmed, with three more nooses tied?

The dyer was the first to speak.

"Beg pardon, cap'n," he said to Jeffries. "Didn't mean no disrespect. If that gentleman—" he pointed to Aventis, "—is a friend of yorn, we won't 'arm a 'air on 'is 'ead."

The mob murmured its assent, their heat cooling as quickly as that above us increased.

"Get to safety!" Jeffries ordered, and, like good troops, they obeyed, going off in different directions.

"Merci, Monsieurs," said the Frenchman, his knees visibly trembling.

"I suggest you make your way north," Jeffries said. "Lose yourself in a crowd, do *not* utter a word, and in the name of God, hide *that.*"

He pointed to the crucifix which still lay in the dust. The Frenchman bent to seize it and stuffed it under his cloak.

"I shall commend you to good King Louis," he said with a bow, then vanished into the smoke.

"Just what I've always wanted!" Carnatus cried to his back.

"Never mind that," said Aventis, as the beam of the would-be gallows ignited into a fireball.

We all leapt back. The flames were engulfing the block, each house now falling outward with a sound like a death rattle.

"Come," said Jeffries, coughing. "We must follow Monsieur and head to the open fields."

We trekked back to the burning Thames, its waters choked with barges piled high with furniture. This would not be a way out. Instead, we trailed a crowd walking back toward Newgate, but we could scarcely make progress, for the wall that enclosed the old city now served as its own gaol. To my great joy, I saw the prison consumed with bursts of orange. Let the cursed place burn! I could only hope and pray that its inmates had fled . . .

In the press of flesh that surrounded us, there was such a pushing and shoving that we likewise pushed our way out. Another escape route closed.

"Let us try to outrun the flames," said Jeffries. Though it seemed a daft notion, that night we stayed on the move.

"I'm ready to drop," said Gad, after trudging for what seemed days.

In one bold move, Carnatus swept him up and placed him on his shoulders. As Gad fell forward, the rest of us bore witness to London's near destruction: no fancy shops, food markets, or taverns stood in our way; there were only flames, heading out to the rich neighborhoods.

"This is vexing," said Carnatus. "God's wounds, look where we are! We have come full circle to Newgate!"

I sighed. Though it was hard to see through the smoke whipped up by that cruel east wind, I recognized the gate's outlines.

"Let us make for St. Paul's," I coughed. *Why not?* It had served as a refuge before—perhaps it could be one now. As we stumbled past the row houses next to the Cathedral, I saw this was not to be.

St. Paul's was actually *melting*. This church, which had stood for hundreds of years, came to a crackling end as lead from its roof poured into the streets. We were forced to run for our lives as stones from walls gave way, chasing us like cannonballs. There was no tolling of bells to mourn the death of St. Paul's for no one was there to ring them; besides, the bells surely formed a silver river flowing at our feet . . .

"Make for Cripplegate!" Jeffries gasped, the air now so heated as to be unbreathable. It was then that I saw things best reserved for delirium: pools of fountains *boiled,* while the stones beneath my boots glowed with an unearthly red.

Using sound rather than sight, we arrived at last by the gate—this one too thronged by crowds. Jeffries turned to a tanner who held his meager belongings.

"What is the word?" asked the captain.

"Nothin' good," said the tanner. "King wants houses pulled down, but his high an' mighty Mayor ain't doin' a thing. King an' his brother finally rode out—tryin' to set up firebreaks. Mos' everythin' gone. Mos' everyone I know don't have a house no more."

"I am sorry," said Jeffries.

The tanner sighed, looking up at bilious black smoke.

"What has God got agin' us?" he asked. "Firs' the plague and now this."

"It has been a hellish two years," said Jeffries.

"Have faith," Aventis told them. "We cannot know God's plan."

"Wish He would tell us," shrugged the tanner. "No offense to ye, Lord."

It took some time to make our way through Cripplegate with its jumble of crowds and carts. As we finally broke free and walked north, we were joined by so many others we were like a marching army. The farther we moved from old London, the clearer the air became, until my throat ceased burning.

When we arrived at a field in Islington, Carnatus set down the sleeping Gad and rushed off to find food. The rest of us simply slumped by a grazier's wagon.

That night, thanks in part to borrowed blankets, we were able to eat, drink, and sleep. Of course, back in the city, we could still see the fire raging—which in turn sparked the exiles here to speak darkly of plots. A rumor swept through the camp that not only had the French and Dutch *set* the fire but were on their way to invade! I had to laugh at the powerful pull of deception—who, after all, would know it better than I?

As we lay by the wagon's wheels, I turned to Aventis with concern.

"You must have a care," I said. "These people are under a spell. Do what we told that Frenchman: hide your face, and do not speak! You may want to shave your face."

Aventis laughed.

"Do not fret, Megs," he said, from beneath his blanket. "My Spanish accent went along with my ancestors."

"It is nothing to mock," I said. "This crowd seeks someone to blame, and it will *not* be an Englishman."

For two more long days, we camped by our friend the grazier. Carnatus, growing weary, turned to us with hands on hips.

"This press reminds me of Tyburn," he said.

"*Those* crowds sought amusement in death," said Aventis. "These merely desire a refuge."

"Bah! Do not mistake me. I do enjoy great throngs—so long as they are held to no more than three."

We all smiled, then looked, as everyone did, toward London.

"Will this damn'd wind ever give way?" asked Jeffries. He gave Aventis a wink. "Perhaps it was sent by Spain."

"Though I do not believe that," said Aventis, "I observe that it must end."

As usual, he was right.

Fully five days after they'd started, word reached our camp that firemen in the city had quenched the last of the flames.

"About time!" roared Carnatus. He put a hand on Jeffries's arms. "May we *finally* resume our trade? I warrant that in London, there is bounty still to be had."

"From those who have lost all?" asked Aventis. "I thought we were better than that."

"As did I," I added, standing by his side.

"Bah!" said Carnatus. "There is nothing worse than thieves with scruples! As for myself, I require a good breakfast. Come, Gad."

The two of them tramped off.

"I must continue my search for Moll," Jeffries said to Aventis and me. "She must be *somewhere* in this throng."

"You'll find her," Aventis told him as we watched him push his way through the crowds.

I turned to my last remaining friend.

"I am glad," I said, "that you were not hanged, skewered, or trampled in the midst of all this madness."

"As am I," he smiled. "None of them sound attractive."

"You have survived fire and plague," I said. "Your resilience is near-biblical."

He threw back his head and laughed.

"As is yours," he said. "*I* never endured Newgate, the Old Bailey, or Tyburn."

"We are both survivors," I said, staring into his face. "The only things we cannot conquer are Jeffries and his dam'd rules."

Aventis looked down at me for a moment. We had both been through so much which made Jeffries look very small.

"Yet he is not here," said Aventis.

Taking me by the arm, he led me to a spot behind the wagon where we could be well-hidden. For only the second time in five years, he threw off my hat and unbanded my hair. Bringing his face close to mine, he kissed me full on the lips. If possible, it was even sweeter than the first time.

"Count," I whispered, holding him. "Is there no way Jeffries can be swayed?"

"Fair Margaret," he said with a sigh. "This courtship is more perilous than Catherine at the convent."

"Alas, no sign of Moll," a voice called at my back. "I hope she got to—"

I whirled guiltily to face Jeffries, whose eyes flared black.

"WHAT AILS YOU TOO?" he yelled. "CAN I NOT LEAVE YOU ALONE FOR A MOMENT?!"

Damn our luck, for he'd not been the sole witness of our brief embrace. Carnatus and Gad strode up, the first so red in the face that he matched the hue of his cloak.

"What is this?" Carnatus shouted. "Such unnatural acts cannot be borne!"

Though Jeffries tried to deter him, the giant pushed him away. I could feel his hands seize my collar, lift me up from the ground, and place me none-to-gently on the dirt before him. Teeth clenched, he searched my face, my loose hair, then ripped off my cloak and stretched my long shirt thin. Though a cloth still bound my chest, in this pose there could be no doubt.

"You . . . are . . . A WOMAN!" Carnatus raged.

At his side, Gad gaped like a trout.

"Did I not advise you?" Jeffries hissed to me. His eyes sparked like the Fire.

"You *knew?"* Carnatus asked, taking a step back.

"Yes," said Jeffries. "I warned them. I warned them over and over, for I know your feelings on the matter."

"*Feelings?"* Carnatus bellowed. *"Matter?!* For a full five years, I have been riding with, eating with, *sleeping* with . . . a tobyman who is *not* a man! My honor shall never recover from this stain."

He balled his huge fists in an effort not to strike me.

"Such deception!" he cried. "Such arts! And-and we risked our lives at Tyburn . . . for what? To rescue a *her!"*

This, I fear, exceeded my tolerance, and I faced him head on.

"Is my life then to be forfeit on the basis of sex?"

"YES!" he yelled. "To which you are a disgrace! You should be at home, waiting on husband and children, not riding the roads like a man! While pretending to *be* one?" He slapped his forehead. "Sweet Jesus! I-I've actually shared a bed with her."

"Sure wish I 'ad," said Gad.

"Carnatus, Lord Phillip, whoever you are," I said, "I see that your mind is closed. No locksmith may undo it."

"This is hardly the time for metaphors!" he roared. "I ought to cut you in two! Put a lead ball straight through your heart!"

Aventis reached for his sword, which seemed to have an effect. Carnatus's gloved hand moved away from his pistol.

"I can no longer trust you, *doxy,*" he spat at me, then looked with contempt at the others. "Nor you two. Gad, let us take ourselves off to find more honest thieves."

The three of us who remained watched him drag Gad by the wrist until they disappeared.

Jeffries, with great sadness, turned to me and Aventis.

"You know full well this is the end of us," he said. "Count, I expected better. Margaret, I am grieved I took you on. Farewell."

He did not bow or incline his hat as he turned on his heel and left. Aventis, groaning, dropped his head to his breast.

"God forgive me," he whispered. "I have destroyed friendships ten years in the making. And it is my fault, mine."

"Aventis—" I said.

"No. For what I have done, I must atone. Farewell, Megs."

He did not pause to look back as he walked into the crowd.

What has just happened? I thought, my knees buckling beneath me. As I kneeled on the dirt, it struck me: I was completely alone.

Home

I did not know how long I remained there. I did not rise, even when the grazier yelled, "Ho, there! You all right?"

In fact, I was not. When feeling returned to my limbs, I was sure to bind my hair and retrieve my hat. Things were bad enough without presenting this creature—part man, part woman—to a world which would show more contempt than Carnatus.

Where to now?

I almost laughed at the query.

Moll's had undoubtedly burned and besides, I wouldn't be welcome: not there, or at any of Jeffries's haunts. *Where then did that leave me?*

Along with the crowd around me, I turned my eyes to London. It was a smoking wreck; still, I joined scores of others in a slow march south. As we entered the city proper, remnants of ash crept into my nostrils, causing me to cough. That was a good sign, I thought. It meant I was still alive.

With effort, I took in the landscape. So many houses gone—and most official buildings. *How,* I asked myself, picking my way through debris, *was this to be reconstructed?* Yet, as I continued my trek, I sought hope in the landmarks still standing: The Tower; the Navy Office; even London Bridge, though it lay silent and crushed.

The fire had not consumed everything.

It was then that I realized I had a place to go. Setting my steps toward Hounslow, I sighed for my horse. When I reached the Heath, I tried not to think too much, for it seemed that every breeze whispered the names of my friends.

Head bowed, I was so distracted I hardly realized I'd arrived. Yet there it was—the old signpost. Across from it, precious little. After what I'd seen in London, the state of the Whale did not shock, though it did fill me with sorrow. The entire inn had burned to the ground, its only remnant three charred brick chimneys. Out of habit more than anything, I entered through what was once the main door, and saw in my mind: the tap room, crammed tight with barrels; the stairway which Jeffries had climbed; the chamber which we two had shared. All, all gone, cleansed by fire and gone from the earth.

I closed my eyes. When I opened them, I saw a woman of forty wheeling her things on a small wood cart.

"Hullo, mistress," I said, touching my hat.

She grunted, perhaps too heartsick to speak.

"It seems this part of Middlesex is as wretched as London," I said.

She narrowed her eyes—perhaps she was wary of city folk. But wait! Of course, it was my attire. I thought it best to get to the point.

"Do y'know," I asked, "what became of the folks at the Whale?"

She shook her graying head sadly, at last moved to reply.

"Thank the merciful Lord, most escaped except the ostler. He was so sodden with drink they could not carry him out."

"So, Claude is dead," I said. I could not have been calmer.

The woman cocked her head, no doubt puzzled by my local knowledge.

"And," I asked, "the proprietor?"

"Ah." The woman sighed. "He was raddled as well but did not weigh as much as Claude. They managed to drag him out, though I hear he's in a bad way."

"Hmm." I could not say I felt distress. "Do y'know where he might he be found?"

"Two streets over, at Sally Marpole's."

"Thank you, mistress," I said, turning on my heel before she could ask *me* questions. "You have been most helpful."

I knew well where Sally's house lay. Had we not served together as barmaids for nigh on seven years? I was relieved to find the house whole: humble, but whole. When Sally responded to my knock, I could barely contain a smile.

"Hullo, mistress," I said, with another pull of my hat.

She did not answer; just stood there holding the door.

"Uh, I beg your pardon, but I have been told that Dick Tanner lies within."

"Yes."

She regarded me with suspicion. What could a highwayman want with *her?*

"I-I am here on behalf of his daughter—" I said.

"Margaret!" Sally cried, her still youthful face beaming. "Lord, these many years, I thought her dead."

"No, she is in London," I lied.

"Unhurt?"

"Oh yes, she came through the fire."

"Thank the Lord!" said Sally, her blue eyes growing moist. "We was always the best of friends."

I nodded, trying not to recall those years of hoisting ale and getting pinched. I fixed my eyes past her shoulder and into the darkened sitting room.

"Oh, forgive me," she said. "Please, do come in. Would you care for tea?"

"No thank you," I replied, though I hadn't had the brew in years.

I looked over her place as I would the inside of a coach: there, in a corner, between the modest furniture, lay a familiar form. He was resting on a small divan, his body swaddled in blankets. Though his face was blackened and his eyelids drooped, that face was seared in my memory.

"Fa—" I said, moving toward him. "Master Tanner. Your daughter Margaret has bade me to come."

"Meg," he gasped, sounding as if even his lungs were scorched.

I nodded, expecting some message, and he did not disappoint.

"Goddamn that filthy little whore to hell!"

Unlike the old days, I did not retreat.

"I shall relay your kind greeting," I said.

"Ah."

He closed his eyes with difficulty. I tried to envision the body beneath those blankets, then shrugged in the manner of Megs.

"Well," I said carelessly, "do not despair overmuch. I lately knew a fellow who came through the very plague."

Father attempted to nod, but the effort was too much. He shakily brought up a hand pocked with bright red blisters.

"Meg requests—" I began, wondering what to say. "That I am . . . to look after you. You may call me Highwayman."

Father stared up at me, but unlike those on the road, did not display alarm. Indeed, we shared a tie: not so much of blood but trade.

"Very well," he said.

Over the next few days, I fulfilled "Margaret's" wishes, fetching him warm mugs of tea and wiping his blistered brow. To Sally, I was cordial, but no more than was required. The less I said, I thought, the less chance of being discovered. Finally, on day three, I saw that father grew weak and would not last the night.

"Leave me," he said. "I wish to meet the devil in peace."

Damn his black soul, I thought. *Why was I even here? What could I possibly want of him, now, before he expired?*

Did I desire forgiveness? Bah! Forgiveness for *what?* For being used as a servant the whole of my young life? Or did I, in some Aventis-like way, wish to forgive *him? Ha!* I thought. Such saintliness was beyond me. What then did I want? As I stood over his motionless form, the answer came to me whole. I bent down.

"Father," I whispered.

"What?" he rasped.

"I am not Highwayman. It is me, your daughter, Meg."

In one motion, I let down my hair so that it fell about my face. He could only gape.

"Yes, it is me," I said, "the one who broke your noggin and hoped that you were dead. But know before that day, there were so many beatings, slaps, and curses that I barely lived as a human. Until I left your 'care.'"

Anger inflamed my blood as much as it had when I'd first left him.

"What do you want?" father gasped. "Get it over with, damn you!"

"It is simplicity itself," I said. "I wish for an apology. I wish, at the last, for you to show remorse."

He stared up at me with defiance.

"Or do you remain a bastard," I asked, "until I close your eyes?"

He let loose a long sigh, then motioned for me to come closer.

"Very well," he forced out. "I admit I treated you ill. You have every reason to hate me."

"I do," I said, placing my hand on his. "Words cannot undo the past. Still, it is good to hear them."

He nodded, then fell into a state from which he would not awake.

"Farewell, father," I said.

As I stooped to close his eyes, I felt we were both at peace.

The Rebuilding

I laid father to rest next to mother in our village cemetery. It was not a popular event: just the gravedigger, Sally, and me. The local priest had fled—to a less fiery locale—while I made excuses for "Margaret."

"She must see to rebuilding," I said. "Of course, she would come if she could."

"Of course," said Sally, "she were always a good-hearted soul."

I attempted to nod gravely. Lord, if she only knew!

"Well," Sally sighed, as we faced the newly dug plot, "Master Tanner might not have been honest, but he were always good to me."

In response, I grunted.

"Shame about the missus, though," she went on. "Weren't in this world long."

"Ah."

Staring at her grave, I thought about the mother I had never known. *How different my life would have been,* I thought, *had I a loving protector!*

"I s'pose ye're back to London, Mr. Highwayman?" Sally asked.

"Oh. Oh yes. That is exactly right."

I doffed my hat in farewell, ignoring her looks of interest. I had things to do if I were going to revive the Whale! With a firm stride, I made my way to High Street: some shops had been burned, but the fire had skipped others, and I was happy to see that the dressmaker's still lived.

"How'd ya do?" I said, flinging open the door. My eyes met those of a woman framed by bolts of bright cloth. "Me and . . . and my wife have been burnt out, and I'm looking for something to replace her charred rags. Can you help me?"

"Certainly, sir," said the woman, withdrawing to the back and then returning with an armload of garments. "These I have recently sewn for myself, but I can do so easily again, and to think of your poor wife—please sir, I bid you, take them."

"You are very kind," I said. When was the last time I had said that to a stranger? "My wife is roughly your size, so these will do very well."

I gave her a smile, handed over guinea, and headed out.

"God bless you," I said. Aventis would have been proud!

There was now the matter of changing, and I, child of the Heath, knew exactly where to go. I headed for a lone tree which I had long used as a landmark. There, I shed the garb of Megs and transformed into Margaret: who sported a skirt and bodice; with a light skirt beneath that; and a soft cotton shirt with lace tucked at the neck! The only discordant note was my thigh-high boots—but, hidden as they were, they could easily pass for shoes. Once my hat was thrown down and my hair allowed to fall free, I felt a weight fall from me: the heavy one of disguise. Taking care to bury my highwayman's costume (but keeping hold of my pistol), I headed back to the Whale, practicing on the way: that is to say, how to walk like a woman.

Word of my return spread quickly, and, that afternoon, I was joined before the inn by a circle of friends.

"It is so good to see you, Margaret!" Sally cried, with an embrace. "Where have ye been all these years?"

"Oh, running some shop or t'other," I said, feeling strange as her arms went round me. I suppose I could do such things now, and no man might object!

"Lord knows, we missed ye," said John, a jovial sort who had served in the tap room for years.

"As I missed you," I lied. I could hardly say that on the road, there was no time to think of home! "I have a proposition," I told them.

They all looked at me with hope.

"In my absence, I have done well . . . that is, my shops have paid off. What say you to raising the Whale and having her swim once again?"

"Huzzah!" came the cheers.

"We will help!" John cried. "I'll start with the bar."

I wrote to the London bank where Moll had placed my guineas. Happily, gold didn't burn, and the bankers remained. It was thus a mere week before construction began and I, lodging at Sally's, felt hope rise along with a new stone wall.

Slowly, the Whale's belly took shape until there was a kitchen, six chambers upstairs, a fireplace and John's bar. When, after three months, panes were placed in the windows, I knew it was time to decide upon a new sign. I had never fancied the old one, with its whale trapped in words: no, *my* beast would be free, leaping above the waves!

Shortly after, I was able to move from Sally's to one of those new chambers—*the biggest.* No more bed of straw for me. After I saw to the finishing touches, we reopened at last on 1 January 1667, and before the arrival of March, I was turning patrons away!

I soon settled into my role as proprietress, serving beer, ale, and wine: all of it excellent, for I had sampled the best. I oversaw the new cook, so something like sanitation prevailed in the kitchen. In the main room, I strove to be friendly, but not overmuch: always, I must deflect questions about my past.

Of course, it did not prove easy to shift from Megs to Margaret. Even as I filled cups, my mind would flash back to those adventures with Jeffries: stopping Lady Castlemaine, the Duke of Monmouth, even the queen herself! As for our broken company, I yearned for them every day.

Ah, Jeffries, I would think, *though you played by the rules, how I admired you!* As for you, Carnatus: despite your pigheadedness, I would gladly give twenty guineas just to hear you place odds! And Aventis, dear Aventis . . . would I ever see you again? Or would I be forever haunted by that tall thin figure with a pistol in one hand and a sword in another, risking himself for others, or pressing his lips to mine?

Ned

Some say that time is a balm which can cool the heated past.

Though I resisted, I found with the passing of years that Megs gradually faded. I was now wholly Margaret, the woman who owned the Whale, and, at twenty-seven, was close to being a spinster! The very thought made me laugh: me, a woman whose blood ran so hot she was nearly hanged at Tyburn, talked to like old woman! Still, I did all in my power to encourage this view of myself.

"'Night, Sally," I called, as her shift ended and she headed for home. We had been a going enterprise for nigh on two years now, all vestiges of the Great Fire receding like a dream: not only here, but in London.

I must have made a good appearance for I had no lack of suitors: some were bakers and some were butchers; some travelers from other parts; but how could any compare to Aventis, my first and only love? To my mind, they were too stout, too bald, too crude, but in the main, they mostly *bored* me. Who could rival my warrior-priest? Certainly, none in Middlesex.

Now, there *was* one patron: his name was Ned Huntington, and each evening he liked to stop in for a bottle of beer or two. Ned was a farmer possessed of a few acres not far from the Whale. He was a good man—at least, I had never heard ill of him.

"Laid in four fields of taters today," he told me one night as I set about closing up.

"Mmm," I said.

"If the weather holds, should be a banner crop."

I looked at him with a smile, a cleaning cloth in one hand. His speech pleased me, for he was a gentleman, or as close as one could be. He was not unhandsome: in fact, his sandy hair, green eyes, and form made hard by labor were *not* unpleasant to the eye. He was older than I—perhaps thirty—and though the girls sighed as he walked through town, he seemed not to notice. Perhaps, like me, he could not set an old love aside, or simply had not found the right woman to marry.

"So." He took a swallow of beer. "I'm sure I must bore you silly, with all my talk of farming."

"No, no," I said, though he sometimes did. "You can see that my life is hardly pamphlet-worthy."

God, if he only knew!

"You work very hard," he remarked, watching me wash down the bar. "That is something I like."

"Indeed." *How many of my victims had commended me for effort?*

"Oh yes. It cheers me to see a woman who makes an honest living and is not beholden to any."

I paused to think this through. Despite the "honest," it seemed a true depiction.

"Thank you," I said.

"What I like best is the way you employ your time. Not a moment wasted."

"Yes, I-I suppose that it so," I answered. I did not want to tell him: *I maintain this state of industry so I do not have to think.*

"Well, best be getting home," he said, rising with reluctance. "There is . . . don't know if you've heard, but there's a dance on Friday. Held at my barn, in fact! I would be much obliged if-if you could favor me with your presence."

I shrugged.

"Why not?" I said.

It had been so long since I had done anything pleasant.

Oddly, all that week, I looked forward to Friday. At least it would break the monotony of washing, serving, and smiling. On the day, I dressed with extra care, even leaving my pistol at home.

When I arrived at Ned's barn with its thatched roof and smell of cattle, I saw some couples already dancing as a lone fiddler played.

"Ah, Mistress Margaret!" Ned cried, rushing over to bow.

"Good evening," I said.

From the way he looked at me, I could tell he admired my finery.

"May I have the honor?" he asked, gesturing toward the dancers.

"I beg your parson," I said, "but I do not know how to dance."

"Oh, that is all right," he said, motioning me to a bench. "I daresay that at court, I would be called a bumpkin."

"I do not know. I have never been," I said, thinking of Catherine.

"Well, you have used your time more wisely." Ned gave me a smile. "Instead of frivolity, you have devoted yourself to industry."

"Of various kinds," I muttered. I attempted to change the subject. "Tell me, how are the crops coming?"

He laughed.

"I am sure my potatoes don't interest you."

I gave a feeble smile.

"But you," he said, "when you were away in London, you must have encountered all sorts. You must have some amusing tales."

I gulped.

"I would prefer not to speak of that time," I said. "I am sure you understand—estrangement from home and all that."

"Of course," he said, and allowed the matter to drop. One thing I could credit him with: he *did* have perfect manners.

"This seems a prosperous farm," I said, glancing over the pastures and the happy cows within them. "You must do quite well here."

"Yes, but . . . must we always talk of business?" he asked.

"What else is there?" I replied. "You are a farmer and I am an innkeeper. What more do our lives consist of?"

"That is wise," he said, smiling as if I'd spoken a great truth. "Most dream of being more than we are, but you are content with your lot."

I answered by sighing heavily.

He gave me his arm and we rose, strolling past the boisterous dancers. I waved to Sally and her most recent conquest.

"Tell me, Ms Margaret," said Ned, as we passed those contented cows. "Forgive me if I am too bold, but . . .why is it that that you are not wed?" He slapped his forehead. "I am sorry! I intrude where I should not."

"No, no," I said, "I have no secrets." *Ha!* "There-there *was* someone in London, but I fear it did not end well."

"Ah," Ned said, "that is too bad," and, from the look on his face, I could tell he was sincere. "That must be terribly difficult. I confess . . . I have not yet found . . . that is—"

"Let us not speak of it now," I said, turning back to the party.

A Bold Call

Poor good-hearted Ned! How could he know that whenever he brought up That Subject, he only brought to my mind new thoughts of Aventis. I must have breathed so many sighs around him that had he been a small boat, he would have been blown from the Whale! Every night, as he sat by the fire, nursing his bottle of beer, he could not discern that he was causing me torment. Should I respond to his overtures, or continue to sit and molder, as I was doing now? It had been three full years since I'd set eyes on Aventis.

Ned pursued his suit well into winter. As rain battered at the Whale's windows, I found my defenses weakening. What was I waiting for, really? A miracle from Above? By the time spring arrived with its renewal of crops and life, I decided to put into motion a plan I had long been forming.

"Sally," I said one night, after Ned had departed, "Tomorrow, you must take my place. I have some errands in town."

"Of course, mistress!" she said. "It would be my pleasure."

"You are a good girl," I told her with affection.

I actually rode *sidesaddle* to London on one of the Whale's nags! How Megs would have

railed . . .

Once I arrived in the city, though it was mostly rebuilt, I found what I sought at once. Dismounting and smoothing my skirts, I looked to the house next door, under whose old jetty . . .

"Yes?"

A still pretty woman answered my knock, her attire much finer than when her old house h stood.

"I-I am here to see Captain Jeffries," I said. I noticed that my hands shook. "If-if he indeed be here."

"And who shall I say is calling?" Moll asked with a hint of frost.

"Please tell him it's Margaret Tanner."

"Very well."

As her tone became more chill, one thing was apparent: she was not at all pleased to see me.

"Charles," she called, "some *woman* is here for you."

She led me into the sitting room where I had passed many nights.

"How may I be of assis—?" a deep voice asked, until its owner caught a glimpse of my face.

"Margaret!" he cried, running forward to catch me in his arms. "I cannot tell you how *good* it is to see you."

"Captain Jeffries," I whispered, "does this mean I am forgiven?"

"Indeed," he said softly. "Over the past three years, I have had much time to reflect. I feel I was wrong to blame you, for you were very young. Rather, it is *Aventis* who was in the wrong."

Though I thought this unfair to the count, I mouthed a heartfelt "Thank you" as I closed my eyes and returned Jeffries's embrace.

"Hmmp," said Moll, folding her arms over her skirt. "Charles, is there something you wish to tell me?"

Jeffries opened his mouth to speak, but I intervened.

"Moll, the last time we met, you knew me as Megs, the highwayman."

She stared at me, uncomprehending.

"I know it is difficult to grasp," I said. "In any case, rest assured I have *no* designs on the captain."

"That is well," she replied, "for we are man and wife."

"Many good wishes!" I cried, stepping forward to squeeze her arm. "I always hoped for this outcome."

"Thank you," she said, now blushing. "But where are my manners? Please, sit down. I will fetch us some tea."

Jeffries and I remained standing in the center of the room. He had to wipe his eyes, for he had not seen me like this since we had first met.

"You look quite fetching," he finally said, motioning me to a chair. "Though I confess I rather miss Megs."

"As do I," I said, tucking in my skirts as I sat. "Being Margaret has its good points, but it tends to be somewhat dull."

"Yes," Jeffries whispered, glancing about the room. "Naturally, I love Moll, but when I think of my days on the road . . . "

"Galloping over the Heath," I said, "in search of some easy pickings—"

"—never knowing who you'll meet," he smiled, "the Duke of Monmouth or a poet!"

"Along with the friends you love best in the world."

We both sat there in silence. At last, Jeffries spoke.

"But that is the past," he sighed. "At present, I would not trade Moll for a hundred guineas."

"Only that?" I asked.

"Very well—two-hundred."

We both laughed.

"You sound like Carnatus," I said.

The ghosts of our lost two friends seemed to linger in every corner. Now I must find the courage to ask the question I'd come for.

"Captain Jeffries," I said, "do you know what became of the others? Have you seen them?"

He shook his head with sadness.

"Alas, no," he said.

I looked to the room with that table where we had divided our guineas. I was thrilled to see Jeffries, of course, but without the rest of our company, we lacked our brain and heart. Still, I owed it to him not to show disappointment.

"Since you are no longer on the road," I asked, "how do you spend your time?"

"I attend the races at Newmarket," he said, "but otherwise, try to refrain from being seen."

"That is wise," I said, for I would never forget the tug of Tyburn's noose.

"And yourself?" Jeffries asked.

"Well, suffice it to say that the Whale swims again."

"Huzzah!" cried Jeffries.

"Did you not know where I was?" I asked. My hurt tone must have stung him.

"I did," he confessed. "After Islington, I was not sure if I was welcome."

"Captain, how can you say that?" I cried. "For you and Mrs. Jeffries, food, drink, and lodging are *always* on the house."

Moll smiled as she returned with tea things.

"Moll, my love," said the captain, "surely you know you *cannot* serve tea to a tapster!"

He rose and from a cabinet, retrieved a private bottle of wine and poured three generous glasses.

"To Megs!" he toasted.

We lifted our glasses high.

"To Captain Jeffries!" I said. "May he ride again."

Though Moll gave me a curious look, I could not have meant it more.

Plotters

The events that preceded my last great adventure were of course unknown to me. But, with a new understanding of the character of my foe, I imagine they proceeded something like this:

Versailles, 1669

One could easily say that Versailles was a mirror image of Whitehall.

To me, Richard Cromwell, son of the sainted Oliver, they were both plunged in debauchery and the worst kind of vice. Both kings keeping mistresses openly! Bestowing *titles* upon such women and their bastard progeny! As for that reprobate Phillipe, the Duke of Orleans: he was guilty of a crime decried in our holy scriptures, one so truly terrible I cannot speak its name! I find both courts wholly devoid of religion, for they are entirely given over to the things of this world: expensive manicured gardens, great palaces wrought of marble, and enough gold decoration to forge a second idolatrous Calf!

Dear Jesus, I pray: let *me* not be ensnared by the grave sinners who surround me; let *me* not be tempted by whores displaying their bounteous flesh!

Yet, after my long years of exile, Louis XIV can hardly shock me. Was it not the Prince of Conti who once remarked while we dined (myself in disguise):

"Well, that Oliver, tho' he was a traitor and a villain, was a brave man, had great parts, great courage, and was worthy to command; but that

Richard, that coxcomb and poltroon, was surely the basest fellow alive; what is become of that fool?"

To be sure, back in England, they mock me as "Tumbledown Dick," for my tenure as Protector lasted but nine short months. But it is *they* who should quiver in fear, for though Charles sits snug on the throne, so once did his father, who, with fire from Heaven, my own father brought low. Oh, for those blessed days when the "Saints" ruled Parliament and my father laid down God's law like a second Moses! If I have any abilities—any quickness of mind, courage, and sinless men to support me, then in due time—God willing!—another Cromwell shall rule.

I attempted to calm myself as two former ministers, William Smith and Joseph Hyde, entered my infidel's chamber. Oh, the decadence! What with its gross works of "art," pure walnut table, and canopied bed which had no doubt hosted illicit trysts!

"Gentlemen," I said, "come in. Welcome to the den of the beast."

"God preserve us," said Hyde, looking around in fright. "We are at the very center of Papacy!"

"That would be Rome," Smith corrected.

Like me, they were both discretely dressed not in costumes fit for a harlot but in somber black.

"I trust you arrived without incident?" I asked.

"Though the canal crossing was rough, God saw fit to see us through."

"I motioned for both to join me at table.

"And your intelligence," I asked. "Has it proved correct?"

"Yes, sir," said Hyde. "I have it on faith from my man in Whitehall. Who would have thought that *this* Charles wishes to lose his head?"

We all laughed merrily. As Puritans, we were not joyless: not when it came to crushing our foes.

"If your man speaks true," said Smith, "the Protectorate will rise again."

"Yes," I smiled. "I swear I will make them regret digging up my father and exhibiting his head on the Bridge."

We all leaned over the table.

"This 'king' and all his court deserve to be cleansed by fire," Smith said.

"Bah! Let's leave that to the Catholics," said Hyde.

Smith looked uneasy.

"Talk of revenge is fine," he said, "but how to *enact* our plan? Anti-Papists are two a penny back home, but no one will give us credence unless we can provide *proof*."

I smiled, for I knew how. After forty-three years of life—nine of them in exile—I had at last learned patience.

"We must not act," I said, "until the thing is signed. The key is Charles's sister, married to that hateful Phillipe. My spies relay she has played the role of ambassador—from her brother to Louis."

"What qualifies her?" asked Hyde. He must have been thinking of his own career. "A mere frivolous woman, and a mistress of Louis's to boot!""

"She is distasteful," I said, "but cannot be avoided. We must follow her every movement, and, when the time is right, seize from her that which will alter the world."

"Excellent," said Smith.

Hyde nodded.

Having obtained unanimity, I reached for a gold jug of wine and poured three hardy glasses.

"To us!" I toasted. "We shall reclaim England! A Cromwell will once again rule!"

Two Proposals

Ned persisted in being so good that my opinion of him improve. After learning that Aventis had left us as if he'd died of the plague, my feelings for his rival softened.

"I see a change in you, Ms Margaret," Ned told me one night. "You don't appear so melancholy and you smile more often."

"If I do," I said, passing a cloth over his table, "it is in no small part thanks to you."

"Ahh," he said, putting down his bottle. "Am I then led to believe you have let go of your London suitor?"

He might as well have asked if I had let go of my soul. Yet, contemplating a lifetime alone, I stared down at his head: he was decent, he was upright, and would not make me his servant. I could continue running the Whale while he worked his farm.

"Miss Margaret," said Ned, looking around to ensure no one was lurking. "I have known you these past four years. I have treasured your temperament and your devotion to work. I have not yet asked outright, but now I feel I must: Would you become my wife?"

I sighed—perhaps too loudly. Yet, I was sorely inclined to accept.

"Please give me one day," I said. "This is a solemn decision affecting the rest of our lives and should *not* be made in haste."

"Of course," he said, trying to sound cheerful. "I shall stop in tomorrow night at my regular time."

"Thank you," I said, as he pressed my hand. Unlike Aventis's touch, it did not send sparks through me. Still, Aventis was gone, and Ned . . . well, he was not.

"Goodnight," he bade me, as he headed for the door. He turned to me one last time. "I shall be waiting," he said.

I waved.

What have I done? I groaned. Ned was a nice enough man: in truth, too nice for me. If he discovered my trade before he'd met me—even my true temper—he would have run over the Heath, not stopping until there leagues between us.

Did I deserve him? I thought. What's more, did he deserve *me?* An outlaw, a woman who dressed as a man, every penny sunk into the Whale earned from highway robbery! Would I be selfish in accepting him, or more so in refusing? In truth, my head spun, and it took me awhile merely to ascend the stairs.

Despite the events of the evening, I adhered to my nightly ritual: letting down my hair and combing it; dashing water on my face and neck. Yet, my agitation was such that when I peeled off my clothes, I did not reach for my nightshirt, instead remaining in my shift. After snuffing out a candle, I drew my bedclothes around me, for though it was May the air bore a hint of chill.

Let me sleep, I thought. *Relieve me from this turmoil.* Instead, when I closed my eyes, I dreamed, as always, of Aventis.

He came to me alone, his long black hair and cloak waving in the wind. He outstretched a gloved hand toward me.

"Margaret!" he called, "I am here; do not forget me!"

"No!" I cried, and I might have said it aloud.

He strode over a dream landscape that oddly had no ground, bundling me into his arms and taking my head in his hands.

"Aventis," I whispered.

As he bent me back, his lips touched mine.

"I shall never leave you!" I called.

"Good. Those are the words I seek."

"Aventis?" I mumbled sleepily.

"Close, but not quite."

My eyes sprang open, and I saw a man bending over me. At first, I reached for my pistol on the table beside me, but then, as my eyes adjusted, I saw who it was.

"Captain Jeffries?" I asked.

"Shhh," he cautioned, putting a gloved hand to his lips. Lowering it, he crossed his arms, gazing down at me fondly. "I still can't believe you once passed as a man."

"Captain," I said, "may I ask how you got in? Did you fly through the window?"

"Climbed," he said, pointing to an open pane. "Who do you think taught Carnatus how to swing a rope?"

I chuckled.

"Captain, though I know you like to be bold, why not simply knock on the door? Why sneak into my bedroom like a . . . " I thought. "Like a thief in the night?"

"Margaret, your mind is not dull," he said. "Can you not conjecture?"

I blinked the sleep from my eyes.

"You do not wish to be detected?"

"Brava!" he said. "Now it is your turn to ask *why.*"

"Very well," I shrugged. After my rude awakening, I was in no mood to quarrel. "What then brings you here in stealth?"

He knelt at the side of my bed.

"Adventure," he said. "Excitement. Remember how we both spoke of riding the Heath once more?"

My blood, which I felt over the years had thickened, now flamed as if by a tinder.

"Will it be a great robbery?" I asked.

"Yes," said Jeffries. "But not of gold."

"The Crown Jewels?" I asked, my eyes shining.

He let out a low laugh.

"One might say that what we seek holds a far greater value."

"Do not tease me, captain!"

He motioned for me to quiet.

"It is a difficult task," he said, "and for it, we must reform our company." I smiled from ear to ear. "Not to go on the road. To retrieve something so perilous that its mere existence might threaten the life of the king."

"Good God!" I whispered.

"Know that spies are everywhere," said Jeffries. "I even have one of my own. He's a crusty old Cavalier who still retains the king's favor. He was privy to a discussion—or at least the rumors of one. Knowing what trade I'd practiced, he came to me at once. What he relayed was so fantastic I hardly believed it myself."

"Tell me at once," I said. "Who wishes to kill King Charles?"

He strode to the open pane, closed it, then leaned over me.

"Margaret, what we attempt will be our most risky adventure. Guineas may come and go, but what *we* seek affects two kings and a duke."

I leapt up from my bed, then began to gather my clothes.

"I am ready to leave now, sir."

"First," said Jeffries, "you must comprehend the danger—"

"Do you think for a moment," I asked, "that I would stand by? I have many capable workers. They will not miss me as we … save two realms, I s'pose."

The captain nodded, smiling in the near dark.

"For this mission," he said, "I do not require Margaret. What I need is Megs, armed and ready for action."

"Huzzah!" I yelled, raising my arms. Then I put them down. *Damn!* What about Ned? His timing could not be worse.

Jeffries must have sensed the change in me.

"If you have a prior obligation," he said, "something to hold you here . . ."

I pictured Ned in my mind: sturdy; reliable—he would never put a foot wrong. Then the image shifted to Aventis: black-clad; an outlaw; yet still willing to do what was right . What a choice was before me!

"Well, sir," I said, pausing before my dresser. "You see . . ."

"Yes?"

I saw that his jaw was set for disappointment.

"It's just that . . . uh . . . my old clothes are under a tree."

Jeffries flashed a smile as he led the way: as always, I followed, clutching my pistol and powder.

Amongst Vacancy

"I would recognize that tree anywhere," I told him as we rode across the Heath.

Jeffries—being Jeffries—had thought to bring a spare horse and now, after all the long years, we trotted together again.

"There is only one trouble," I sighed. "I cannot see in the dark."

Jeffries laughed.

"Let us wait for the moon."

We could see her, a vague sphere crossed by tendrils of clouds, but she took her time to unveil like a modest woman. When she did, I cried out.

"I see where we are!"

With a gesture, I bid Jeffries follow until we sat before my lone birch.

"Captain, may I borrow your sword?" I asked.

He handed it over and I commenced digging. As soil flew all around me, I spied the corner of a black cloak and the sheen of a green doublet! There followed breeches, stockings, hat, mask: even *my* old sword. Though they had the fresh smell of dirt, they had *not* been savaged by worms!

Jeffries turned his horse away as I shed the skin of Margaret and assumed that of Megs.

"You may look, sir," I said, clambering into my saddle.

"Great God!" Jeffries exclaimed. "My old companion is back."

I smiled, reveling in the freedom of sitting my mount astride, of being unconstrained by tight bodice and stomacher.

"This is better," I proclaimed, stretching out my arms. "I am just as I once was."

"Let us hope our friends are too."

"Yes," I agreed. "But where *are* they?"

"That is what we must discover," said Jeffries. "I suggest we start with Carnatus. He, at least, is likely to be in the country."

Carnatus.

In my excitement, I had not thought on the way we'd parted at Islington. Did he still want to skewer and shoot me?

"Do you think he will . . . accept me?" I asked.

Jeffries nodded.

"It is a risk," he said, "but we need his strength. We must take our chances."

"Where do you think he could be?"

"His range is vast," said Jeffries. "He might be in York, or London."

"But London itself is vast!"

"True. We should start with his usual haunts: taverns and cookhouses."

"Did he have a particular favorite?" I asked.

"Yes," said Jeffries. "All."

If he was cowed at the prospect of finding our friend, Jeffries did not show it. Once we rode into town, we visited various taverns—all of them rebuilt—and every cookhouse in sight. After a day of this hard duty, we put up at Jeffries's house.

"Oh, Mr. Megs!" Moll cried, as we entered, "I beg your pardon, Mistress Margaret. That

is—"

"At present, please call me Megs," I said.

I withdrew a handful of guineas and placed them in her palm.

"Please accept this small token as a wedding gift for you both."

"Thank you, Mr. Megs," she said.

"Just Megs, if you please. We are practically family now."

As she rushed off to dispense with the coins, I elbowed Jeffries in the ribs.

"Since you are an old married man," I said, "are you sure you're fit for our endeavor? Perhaps you have grown soft."

He gave me a swat on the head.

"May I remind you, Megs," he said, "that this 'old man' can still hit a twig from fifty paces. And swing a sword almost as well as Aventis."

"I do not doubt you, sir."

Alas, his skill with a weapon could not aid our present mission. Over the next few days, we tramped and rode over London, until I thought we'd seen every block. We visited so many taverns that by week's end the smell of beer nearly turned my stomach.

On the seventh day of our search, a young boy in rags appeared on Moll's doorstep.

"Have you heard something, Jack?" Jeffries asked.

I assumed that the lad must be one of his "spies."

"A bit," Jack said. "'eard Phil's man was 'angin' about the Garden. Lookin' shifty as ever."

"Excellent!" Jeffries cried, handing the boy a shilling before turning to me. "Megs, we're off! Perhaps Gad can be collared."

"Yes sir," I said with a sigh. After all our walking about, I confess I was weary. Still, I slapped on my hat and followed the captain out.

How different the Garden appeared, compared to my last visit! Flower sellers shared space with folk hawking produce from a line of booths. Though the colorful fruit looked inviting, Jeffries's mind was elsewhere.

"Megs, head west and north," he said. "Meet me by the fountain at ten."

I nodded, keeping my eye on the crowd as I moved among their numbers: there were housewives bargaining mightily, dandies posing like peacocks, and scores of children getting underfoot. How changed was London! One could never imagine that only five years prior, it had been a burned-out hulk . . .

I made my way through the mob, members of which gave way to my not-so-gentle entreaties. Where *was* that devil Gad? If I knew him, and I did, then he was up to no good. After a fruitless search, I waited for bells to strike ten before striding back to the fountain. Approaching me was Jeffries, holding a reluctant captive by the ear: *Gad!*

"Nabbed the blackguard before he could run," said the captain.

"Well now, what's this?" I asked Gad. "Do you dare flee from your master's master?"

"I have been instructed," Gad said, drawing himself up, "to say that Mr. Carnatus does not wish to witness you." He nodded up at Jeffries. "An' that goes double fer *'er.*"

Jeffries practically shoved him into fountain's pool.

"Shhh!" the captain hissed. "Have you no brains in your head?"

As Gad considered the question, Jeffries put a hand on his sword.

"Take us to Carnatus," he ordered. "Or I will skewer you like an eel."

Gad placed both hands on his stomach.

"Please don't, sir!" he pleaded. "You kin let go a' me now."

It did not take long to march him back to Moll's so we could retrieve our horses. Gad, still gripping his stomach, leapt behind Jeffries on his saddle.

He led us down several blocks, crisscrossing back and forth, until we reached one of empty plots where I knew that houses once stood.

"This better not be a ruse," I growled. "Why would Carnatus choose to be amongst vacancy?"

My answer arrived in the form of a merry sight: on one dusty plot sat the portly frame of a man, ensconced on a French chair and waving a turkey leg!

Jeffries jumped off his mount.

"Carnatus!" he cried. "My old friend."

"Jeffries!" Carnatus roared.

Despite his strictures to Gad, Carnatus seemed overjoyed. He leaped from his chair, upending it, and nearly smothered poor Jeffries like an affectionate hound.

"What the devil are you doing here?" Jeffries gasped.

"Had a bit of a contretemps—at a cookhouse," said Carnatus. "I thought it might be safer to enjoy my repast alone."

He gave Jeffries a wink, but when his glance fell on *me*, his good humor turned to menace.

"It is *him*. Her," he spat. "That unnatural creature! Did I not make it clear at Islington that the sight of it disgusts me?"

"You were clarity itself," said Jeffries. "However, there is a matter at present which requires our full number."

Carnatus narrowed his eyes.

"What would you say," asked Jeffries, "to learn that the king's survival depends wholly on *us?*"

"Preposterous!" roared Carnatus. "How can *we* be of such consequence?"

Even though the plot was otherwise deserted, Jeffries lowered his voice.

"There are great webs woven at court," he said. "Charles seeks to ally with France to fight against the Dutch."

"Bah!" said Carnatus, waving a hand. "We just waged two wars with Holland. Of what import is a third?"

Jeffries moved closer.

"There have been . . . secret dealings with Louis," he said. "Charles is to receive millions if he favors France."

"Pfft." Carnatus shrugged. "What care I for these millions if they are not *mine?*"

"There is something else." As he had at the Whale, Jeffries sounded grim. "Something so peculiar—dare I say, *doltish,* that Charles risks his own crown."

"Will he permit the French to invade us?" Carnatus asked.

"My friend, I regret to say that the truth is a thousand times worse."

Carnatus adjusted his sky-blue cloak.

"Is he being wrought up then?"

"Well . . ." Jeffries thought. "In a sense. But this scheme, I fear, is mainly of his own doing."

"The fool!" Carnatus cried. "Gad, you were right. 'Stupid lies the head that wears a crown.'"

After giving me a rancorous look, he bid Gad to fetch his horse.

"I will join you," he said, "but I have terms: under *no circumstance* will I be forced to speak to, nay! even *acknowledge*, that person known as Megs."

He leaped into his saddle as Gad clambered behind.

"You have my word," said Jeffries.

What about mine? I thought. Was I to be thus despised, lower than Gad as far as our company's order? It would seem so, for as Jeffries rode north, Carnatus kept to his side, with myself firmly behind.

A False Robbery

Despite my misgivings, I gave a wide smile when we stopped at a particular road: none other than the Great Western! I took a moment to marvel at the dusty expanse which to me was like a chapel.

Yet why stop here? I wondered. Was it the captain's desire, in order to finance our mission, to rob a coach or two? If that were indeed the case, I confess I *could not wait!* All thoughts of respectability—mingled with those of Ned—left my head and did not return.

"Shall we make for our usual hill?" asked Carnatus.

"Yes," said Jeffries, "but we wait on a given coach. I learned at the Garden it is due to pass this way soon. One of us should keep watch while the others remain out of sight. I shall take the first shift."

I sighed, since that left *me* with Carnatus. He rode up the hill and wheeled his horse, deliberately, so that its backside faced me. I knew I should feel slighted, but instead, stifled a laugh.

"Carnatus," I cried, addressing his horse's tail, "Cannot we settle this feud? Regardless of my sex, was I not a true companion during our years on the road?"

My words were greeted with silence. Still, I made a second attempt.

"Did I not heal Aventis?" I asked. "Allow myself to be taken to spare Jeffries from the king's men? Endure the horrors of Newgate while not breathing a word of *you*?"

The only effect of my queries was that Gad's back grew stiffer.

"Very well," I said. "Wish me out of existence. But when the moment comes and you need him, Megs will be at your side."

Three *very long* hours later, Jeffries called for me to relieve him. From behind a copse of beeches, I observed the passing of coaches, yet not the one we sought. In an attempt to stay alert, I dismounted and practiced my swordplay, glad that Aventis was not present to see me defeated by a tree . . .

That night at our old hideout was one I never wish to repeat. Carnatus, once so generous with his ale, refused to pass me a mug. When it came time to distribute our supper, he made Jeffries hand me my plate. Though the captain was kind, I felt the sting of rejection when half our party decamped to sleep away from me. Well, if they did not wish to share the fire, that was their misfortune!

"Our coach should appear today," Jeffries said the next morning. "Let us all ride to await it."

As I affixed my mask, I smiled widely beneath it. To be a high tobyman, even in this broken company, sent a chill through me which I had not felt in years. I made sure my pistol was loaded as I sat my horse with the others and calmly awaited our prey.

This was not long in coming, and when it did, there could be no doubt: not with that gilt finish or distinct coat-of-arms. This time, the coach was accompanied by four others.

"To it, lads!" Jeffries cried, and I set off with Carnatus, all thoughts of discord between us ground like dust beneath our horses's hooves.

More than anything, I wanted to give the cry.

"Stand and deliver!" I shouted, blocking the road with Jeffries. Six magnificent horses came to an ungainly halt. "Well," I said to the coachman, "I believe you know what comes next."

Carnatus and Gad held him, and though he was armed with a pistol, he wisely decided to throw it down when faced with four of ours.

I watched Jeffries dismount, then approach the gilt coach's nearest door.

"Bom Dia," he said, removing his hat and bowing. Slowly, silk draperies parted, and, as if the past were replaying, I saw Queen Catherine's head.

"Do I not know you?" she asked, staring at Jeffries's mask.

"Yes, Your Majesty. We met when our band contained a man we call Aventis."

Her expression did not change.

"That is to say," said Jeffries, "Count Bernardino of Spain."

"Ah," said the queen, tossing her head which caused her pendants to swing. Idly, I wondered: *how much would they fetch in London?*

"I beg your pardon," said Jeffries, "but we desperately seek our friend. We need him to foil a plot against your husband."

"What is this 'plot'?" she asked haughtily in her accented English.

"Queen Catherine," said Jeffries, "the king's wishes with regard to France are known to me."

She arched her dark eyebrows.

"So?" she asked. "We must oppose the Dutch merchants."

"*That* is not the danger," said Jeffries. "It comes from others who have reason to hate your husband and wish to see him dead."

The queen looked unalarmed.

"All monarchs have enemies," she said. "It has been so since the days of Rome."

"And before," Carnatus muttered.

Catherine looked us over if we were inmates at Newgate.

"Tell me," she asked, "why should I give credence to criminals?"

Carnatus's face turned crimson. With his hot head, would he dare chastise *the queen?* Thankfully, Jeffries stepped in.

"Your Majesty," he said, "we rode with the Count of Castillo and he is as spotless as—" he gulped, "—the Pope. Surely you trust *him?*"

She stared at Jeffries through her large dark eyes. Though I had seen more comely women, her air lent her a dignity that beauty could not bestow.

"Bernardino," she whispered. "Yes, I would trust him with my life."

"Then I *beg* you to help us find him," said Jeffries. "Is it possible he corresponds with Your Majesty?"

Catherine looked down and sighed.

"Very well," she said. "He is at the Abbey of Saint-Germain-des-Prés."

Though Jeffries and Carnatus nodded, I had no notion of where this place could be. Perhaps the Holy Roman Empire? After all, Aventis had said that the Romans once called it Germania.

"Thank you, Your Majesty," Jeffries said, his voice infused with deep feeling. "You will *not* regret this confidence."

She surveyed us again.

"See that I do not."

The queen offered her gloved hand, and, like Aventis before him, Jeffries kissed it with reverence. She tapped the roof of her coach, causing her train to depart with the clank of iron on dirt.

Now that she was gone, the realization struck me.

"She could have hanged us all!" I cried. "And strung us up next to Hind!"

"Happily, she did not," said Jeffries. "Now, we ride south."

The Abbey

We traveled near twenty-four leagues in a day and a half, at last stopping at an inn. Though Gad was permitted to sleep in the bed beside his master, *I* took his place on the floor.

Very well, Carnatus, I thought. *I shall not gripe out of respect for Jeffries.* The next morning, despite my stiff neck, I gave him and Gad a nod.

As we sat down to a quick breakfast, I addressed Jeffries beside me.

"Excuse me, captain," I asked, "but how do we get to Germania by riding the English countryside?"

"What nonsense does it spout?" Carnatus asked in amazement.

"His name is Megs," said Jeffries. He turned to me. "Saint-Germain lies in France. Which means we make for Dover."

"Ah."

Why must I appear the fool before Carnatus? I agonized. Gripping my beer bottle tightly, I determined to keep silent.

We continued our southward trek and finally arrived in Dover, its dock teeming with ships. Jeffries sold our horses for far less than they were worth, but due to our mission's gravity, even Carnatus shrugged. That day, we bided our time in a tavern until the sun finally set behind Dover's white cliffs.

Carnatus, Gad, and I rose (a bit reluctantly, perhaps), and proceeded to follow Jeffries as he led us down to the docks.

"I have some old friends here," said the captain as he scanned a tangle of masts.

I could just imagine who these "friends" were: smugglers not far removed from the pirates of Barbary. Still, they looked friendly enough as they indulged in their banned trade.

"Hullo! George, is that you?" Jeffries called down to one such fellow.

This George was young, with shoulder-length hair constrained by a woolen cap. His boots, cracked and waterlogged, must have seen their fair share of weather.

"Captain Jeffries!" George cried. "Been a long time, ain't it? Las' time I seen ye, you was with the king."

"These days," said Jeffries, "I don't keep such grand company. But I do have a request. Can you ferry my friends and me? Price is really no object and circumstances demand that we depart with haste."

"Like, for instance, *now,*" Carnatus growled.

"Sure thing, cap," said George. "Everyone climb aboard. She ain't much too look at but she's made the trip least an 'undred times."

He pointed with pride to his boat . . . dingy . . . *rowboat*, and I found my heart sink even faster than this craft would!

I approached it with trepidation.

"You are . . . quite sure," I asked, "that this bark can make it to Calais?"

"My 'friend' here is cautious," Carnatus said. "Delicate constitution."

Behind him, Gad sneered.

"Shall we?" I asked, jumping into the boat with more assurance than I felt.

Jeffries followed my lead, as did Carnatus. Surveying the cramped space, he yelled to the dock, "Gad, stay here!"

I could see Gad grin. Of course, so would I, if I could remain on dry land!

When Captain George swung aboard, I feared his craft would swamp. As I looked over rotting wood, patched here and there with tar, I tried to maintain my calm. In fact, I was terrified, but would drown than be mocked by Carnatus.

"Need ta wait for high tide," George said.

"How long will that be?" I asked, as I tried to settle in despite the moored boat's rocking.

"Not ta much longer."

When his boat rose on the waves, George blew out his lantern, leaving the moon as our guide. Hearing his oars move against water only increased my unease, for God knows I was no sailor! This was made more than apparent as I leaned over the side. Though our voyage on the canal consisted of but twenty miles, I silently cursed each one.

"Steady, Megs," Jeffries whispered. "Remember our ultimate aim."

I nodded weakly. *What was it again?* We bobbed in blackness in the world's smallest sailboat to . . . to rescue the king! What must we do beforehand? *Of course!* We must rescue, uh, find Aventis.

When morning finally broke over the grey-green sea, I saw a hint of land in the distance. Having never been out of England, I assumed that this was France. I watched George take down his sail and row slowly to shore. I nearly ran as I splashed my way to the sand, where I promptly collapsed. My inner demons rejoiced, for Carnatus was in even worse shape, splaying on the beach like a seal.

"Damn Aventis!" he spat. "Couldn't he have gone to Spain so we could sail like gentlemen?"

As Jeffries laughed, I turned to surveil Calais. What I saw was an English-style seawall, and, if I strained my eyes, the Cliffs of Dover behind me. But Jeffries had not made this journey merely to lead a Grand Tour. He ushered Carnatus and me into a seaside tavern, where he ordered (perfectly, based on the waiter's reaction) in French. Carnatus added some flowery phrases, which made me sink into my chair. It was clear I was alone in not comprehending a word!

After a simple breakfast of fresh bread and butter, washed down of course with French wine, Jeffries hurried us from the quay and made for a stable. It was the matter of a few moments for us to secure borrowed mounts, which Jeffries led south down a road which seemed familiar to him.

"How long until Saint-Germain?" I asked, as my new horse loped at his side.

"Sixty leagues," he said, as if it were round the corner.

I sighed. That meant more stays at inns, and, despite Gad's absence, more backbreaking nights on the floor. After two such sojourns, I had the urge to approach Carnatus and shove him into a vineyard. There, he might be pressed into a more pleasant vintage.

Still, as we rode through the countryside, I was not unhappy, with my view of sloped-roofed farmhouses and cows contentedly chewing. It was shocking to note that the French raised the same livestock as us and toiled in similar fields. They had been so maligned at home that I half-expected the Pope to swoop down in his robes, hands extended like talons. But what I saw from the road could not have been more peaceful.

The small villages we passed looked just as bucolic, each with their small stone church. But there was no time to remark them for Jeffries did not waste a moment. Changing horses frequently, we rode like a thunderclap all the way to Paris.

The great city at last! Yet, I had to confess, it seemed not so great as London, despite the majesty of Notre-Dame. How I wished to see the sights! Alas, Jeffries rushed us through so that every avenue blurred. If we had not been pursuing Aventis, I might have made an outcry to visit at least one cathedral!

I soon had my wish, for Saint-Germain was just beyond and we dismounted before the Abbey. I confess I had envisioned a small, quaint refuge housing perhaps ten monks: in fact, the grounds were monumental!

Still shaky from our epic ride, I trailed Jeffries through a tall iron gate, where we beheld what seemed an adjunct of Paris. Any vows of poverty must have been set aside, for the Abbey had *three* huge towers flanked by squares of lawn each housing a single tree. The weathered stones of the walls looked ancient—older even than St. Paul's . . .

"Where might we find Aventis?" I asked Jeffries, taking in the walled enclave of buildings.

"We must inquire," said Carnatus, striding into a wide basilica framed with stained glass windows. "Hullo there!" he cried, "anyone home?"

"Yes." A voice echoed from within. As its owner came forward, I saw a youngish monk in his robes. "Who enters the house of Benedict?" he asked.

"Friends," said Jeffries, in an attempt to sound convincing. Carnatus and I knew how he hated Catholics—except, of course, for Aventis.

"You are English," said the monk, in perfect English, "and no friend to our order." He noted our dusty attire. "You have ridden far to get here. Perhaps impelled by a desire to convert?"

"Well—" I began.

"Not today," said Carnatus.

"We wish to find a man who resides here," said Jeffries. "Or so we've been told. He is a Spaniard and goes by the name of Aventis."

"How do I know you will not harm him?" asked the monk, shifting in his robes.

"God's wounds!" cried Carnatus, his words echoing to the roof. "Jeffries, allow me to shoot this infidel."

"Calm yourself," said the captain, then turned back to the monk. "Uh . . . brother . . . Aventis is our friend. Give him my name, Charles Jeffries, and gauge his joyful response."

The monk stared at Jeffries as if to divine the truth.

"Very well," said the brother. "He is in the Bibliotheca. Look for the long building next to this one."

Of course, I had no idea what a "Bibliotheca" was, but my companions seemed to. They led me outside to a narrow structure heavy with domed windows. As we strode toward the main door, I found I could barely breathe. The prospect of seeing Aventis—after *five whole years*—made me as queasy as if I were still at sea. As I attempted to calm myself, Jeffries shot me a glance, and I well knew its meaning: *Behave.*

As I followed my friends, I found myself in a stone hallway marked by round-topped doors. They seemed to go on forever! *Where* in this ancient labyrinth could we find Aventis? We entered each room in succession, so strange to me since they were bursting with books! This Abbey must have been—and still was—a great center for learning, for clusters of monks worked tirelessly with pen, ink, and parchment. As they maintained a silence, we did not wish to disturb them. After walking for what seemed ages, we finally reached the penultimate door. Inside was a figure leaning over a scroll. Even from the back, I well knew who it was! After so many dreams, there was no mistaking his form, long hair, or sword which hung from his belt. I let out a breath as I noted his lack of priestly garments, for he was dressed the same as when we two last parted.

"Aventis!" Carnatus shouted, striding up to his friend and clapping him on the back.

"Carnatus!" Aventis coughed, rising from his chair.

"Count!" Jeffries strode to the center of the room.

"It is good to see you, Charles."

They exchanged a warm handshake.

"Hullo," I said shyly. I had not moved from the doorway.

"Megs!" Aventis called. He came over to where I stood and grasped my hand in his. Unlike my dreams, the heat of his touch was real. I managed a weak grin.

"Carnatus?" he asked me softly, thrusting his chin toward the giant.

As I shook my head sadly, he patted my shoulder, then moved back to the others.

"To what do I owe this distinction?" he asked. "May I offer you some wine? It is made in Saint-Germaine."

"Shall we refuse?" Carnatus asked the stone walls.

Aventis left to retrieve some glasses, then returned and played barman, filling them to the brim.

"To Aventis!" Carnatus toasted, throwing back his head.

"To the count!" said Jeffries, following suit.

"To the end of his penance," I said softly.

"Dam'd right!" said Jeffries. "Let me tell you what we face."

As he told the tale of Charles, Aventis's face went pale.

"Well," he said, "I had planned to retire here, to aid the monks in their work." He laughed. *"And* do penance for my sins."

"But, Aventis," I said, recalling my Bible, "would not the greatest sin be to stand by idly? Does not the Proverb say: 'Whoever is slack in his work is a brother to him who destroys.'?" I paused. "Or something like that."

Aventis sighed.

"I'm afraid you have me there, Megs."

"Then you will join us?" asked Carnatus.

"Hmph. I will."

I could not recall such happiness since the last time he'd kissed me!

"Yet," Aventis said, as I struggled to listen, "I fear that to have an effect, we must infiltrate the French court. And I am as much a stranger there as I am to Whitehall."

We all stood silent. How then to gain access?

Aventis stroked his chin.

"You are convinced," he asked Jeffries, "that Charles's sister Henrietta plays a part in this intrigue?"

"The main role," said Jeffries. "My Cavalier spy had no reason to say otherwise. I saved his life at Naseby."

"Hmmm." Aventis thought for a moment. "I know her to be the unhappy wife of the Duc d'Orleans. Who indulges, they say, in an unpleasant custom."

"I have heard," said Jeffries. "The Italian vice."

I stood there uncomprehending.

"If I may," said Aventis, "I suggest one of us visits Versailles. I modestly put forth myself, for a Papist scholar will be unremarked."

"Excellent," said Jeffries, though I felt downcast. I would not only miss Aventis, but a chance to view Versailles!

"Now, Megs," said Jeffries, noting my posture, "there may be more chances to view that ever-expanding palace."

"Damned French," Carnatus muttered, "always trying to be bigger."

Since Versailles was not far off, we agreed to meet Aventis in a *taverne* by the Abbey at three after he'd made his visit.

When he left on my horse, the rest of us traipsed to le Coq Royal where we were led to a table. I looked around at the other patrons, glad to see that unlike the Puritans, they shared a bottle or two!

Carnatus ordered in French, a recital which went on so long I feared we would never eat. However, our server soon emerged bearing a rump of beef with cabbage, Sweetbreads *en papillot*, capon fried eggs and breadcrumbs, and another dish called *Caux fowl* with *consommé. I* contented myself with a cheese. Despite Carnatus's jab, the French were indeed capable of outdoing us at table. As I raised my fourth glass of wine, I felt as buoyant as the light which struck it . . .

By the time the massive bells of the Abbey chimed three, I was thoroughly sated. On time, Aventis swung through the door, a hood masking his face. We bade him sit, then offered him food and drink.

"Friends," he said in a whisper. "I did indeed visit Versailles, saw the king from a great distance, and obtained a report of great value. From a gardener!"

We all leaned closer.

"It appears that Louis himself will escort Henrietta to Dunkirk," he said. "So that she in turn may be landed … at *Dover.*"

"What the devil?" cried Carnatus.

"Shhh!" said Jeffries.

Aventis threw off his hood.

"My friend with the clippers informed me that Henrietta . . . " he looked around, ". . . has not set foot in England these past nine years."

"Why go now?" asked Carnatus.

"Alas," said Jeffries, "I fear I know the reason."

We all stared at him, waiting.

"I will divulge it," said the captain, "when I feel it is safe. In the meantime, we must fly."

"Where to?" I asked.

"Dover."

He rose from his chair with a scrape.

"But we have just left there!" I cried.

"And have achieved our goal in France. For now."

Slumping, I took a last gulp of wine and placed some cheese in my pocket. Thoughts of George and his rickety boat almost cleared my head!

Aventis noted my expression: one of sheer terror, no doubt.

"Do not be troubled, Megs," he said. "I foretell a grand adventure!"

Dover 1670

Aventis borrowed a horse from the Abbey, while Jeffries led us all north, this time not to Calais but Dunkirk. There, as the sun set on 24 May, I witnessed my first royal spectacle.

Princess Henrietta must have been there for the train which accompanied her numbered into *the hundreds*. King Louis must truly esteem her to approve such an escort! As we tied up our horses and strode down to the docks, we caught sight of a ship flying sails enough for all France. I heard one fellow shout to another (in French), which Jeffries translated:

"Those festivities in Lille! I have not seen such in my life."

"The fireworks were especially good," said his friend.

"Why does *the king* not escort her?" I asked, searching in vain for Louis.

"It is not a good sign," said Carnatus.

"Think," Aventis ordered. "How would it look for the King of France to land upon our shores?"

"Like an invasion?" I offered.

"No, an alliance," said Jeffries. "With the hated Papists."

Though Aventis *was* one, he nodded. I determined it best to stay silent and leave matters of state to him.

"How shall we get to Dover?" asked Carnatus, taking note of the French court's raiment. "Would you look at those heels!" he cried. "Higher than any woman's."

Jeffries was unconcerned about finery.

"By the same method we arrived," he said.

"No," I groaned.

The captain hailed another small boat, *its* captain loading in some "duty-free" wine. Within minutes, Jeffries had paid for our passage, and I must say with great reluctance, I walked with my friends down to this crumbling craft.

"Lord save me," I moaned as we set off, the sight of Henrietta's fleet not enough to cheer me.

"It will be fine, Megs," Aventis said. "The first time I embarked from England, I never left my cabin."

Miserable, I nodded.

Carnatus, sensing blood like a shark, haughtily turned to Jeffries.

"How like a woman," he said. "The slightest hardship and she is 'ill' or 'down with headache.' What a frail, useless sex."

I actually stood to face him.

"Without us, you would not be in this world," I said.

"Pity," said Aventis, looking straight at his friend.

"Enough," Jeffries ordered, as Henrietta's flagship set sail. We kept a good distance behind as we trailed her to Dover. I was not too aware of our progress, since I spent most of the voyage hanging over the side.

"Look, Megs!" Aventis called at about five the next morning. Ahead shone the white cliffs of Dover, but this natural wonder paled beside the spectacle below! Being rowed at full speed from the shore were *four* richly clad nobles, whom Jeffries identified as: King Charles II; his brother James, Duke of York; the Duke of Monmouth (now a young man!); and Prince Rupert of the Rhine. It was as if the sea had opened and delivered up four gods!

"I am beside myself," cried Carnatus. "Would you look at those jewels!"

Even our captain/smuggler instinctively doffed his hat. A young woman in sumptuous dress was helped to the side of the king, and I saw her smile and weep as the two of them embraced.

"Princess Henrietta Anne," said Aventis.

I felt like an unwanted spy as I watched the touching scene. Our craft remained offshore until the royal party landed. Then, our captain rowed us to the beach, and our boots again touched earth! Though I was tempted to bend and kiss it, Carnatus never took his eyes from the royals.

"Where are they headed?" he asked.

"Dover Castle," said Jeffries, pointing to an old keep which overlooked the sea. "It is the only place here truly fit for a king."

"But not for us," I said. "Surely *we* cannot enter."

"True," said Jeffries, "they will not invite us to their talks."

"How do you know such talks will take place?" I asked.

"See that man?" Jeffries pointed to one who wore an embroidered cloak. "He is the French ambassador, Colbert de Croissey. And I can guarantee he is not here to take the air."

"Two to one," said Carnatus, "he's on hand to advise the princess."

"I'll take those odds," said Aventis.

Jeffries looked around.

"Let us talk in a less public place," he said.

"Don't tell me," I said. "That tavern at seaside."

"Just so."

He led us inside, where we found a familiar figure hanging about the bar. Of course, it was Gad.

"Thank heaven you've come!" he cried. "I just run outta shillings and they cut me off."

Carnatus relieved his plight by ordering ale and wine.

"What have you seen, lad?" he asked. "Anything we should know?"

"Nah," said Gad with ill humor. "Dover is boring as oats. Saw a fight 'tween two sailors but they pulled 'em apart."

"Very well," said Jeffries, taking a corner table. "Let us keep our eyes and ears sharp."

We sat there till afternoon and enjoyed a bit of their fare. Just as I became restless, a party of three entered. *Bah!* Puritans! Ever since "they" had shot me, I could not abide their presence.

"Listen well," Jeffries whispered. He pretended to oil his pistol.

One of the three, who seemed the leader, led them to a center table. This man, whose fair hair fell to his shoulders in defiance of the "Roundhead" tradition, leaned forward to speak.

"So, it has come to pass," he said. "Smith, your informer at V. was first-rate."

I inclined my head to hear better.

"Hyde, you were well-advised: that coxcomb Buckingham is ignorant as a babe, and it is likely he and the others do not know 'the great secret.'" He snickered. "That's what the fool king calls it."

"If we could secure the kings's letters," said the man called Hyde. "*That* would be proof enough."

"It would be," said the leader, "but such letters are usually hidden inside those addressed to others. If they *do* exist, they are likely written in cipher. Louis *loves* cipher."

"Where does that leave us?" asked Smith.

The leader, who might have been forty, smiled.

"In the perfect locale," he said, "to seize the final papers."

The three fell silent before ordering wine.

At our table, the four of us turned to the captain.

"God's wounds," hissed Carnatus. "Jeffries, you must enlighten us. That *whole exchange* was a cipher."

"Patience," said Jeffries. "The fewer who know the details, the less there are to tell."

Gad scrunched up his face, trying to understand.

"I will tell you this," said, Jeffries, lowering his voice so we had to bend forward to hear him. "A treaty will be signed. The one presented to the public will declare we ally ourselves with France."

"What of it?" I growled, ignoring my vow of silence when it came to politics. "Everyone hates the Dutch. It will be good to see them crumble."

Even Aventis nodded.

"Far better for trade."

"Oh, for God's sake!" Jeffries hissed. "Did I not say that those terms are *strictly for the public? I* do not care if we battle Spain, Holland, and France along with the Holy Roman Empire."

The rest of us fell silent.

"There is a secret provision," he said, "which concerns every man in England."

I cleared my throat.

"And woman," he added.

"As to our mission?" I asked. For once, *I* was the one who remembered!

"Two copies of the secret treaty will be drawn," Jeffries said softly. "One will be given to Louis—the other will stay with Charles."

The captain balled his gloved fist.

"We *must* seize both and destroy them," he said. "Never let them fall into enemy hands." He jerked his head slightly toward the Puritans's table. "Do you know who that man is?" he asked, pointing his chin at the leader.

"Cromwell's ghost?" guessed Carnatus.

"You are close. *That* is Richard Cromwell."

"God's legs!" Carnatus cried, rising with a crash and putting a hand on his sword.

"Silence!" Jeffries hissed. *"Sit down."*

Carnatus did so reluctantly.

"Ha, what a fine joke!" Aventis shouted. This shocked me, for it was so unlike him. "Pray, tell us another!"

The Puritans turned their gaze elsewhere.

"Carnatus," Jeffries said, "in order for us to succeed, you must master your temper."

Carnatus nodded sheepishly, taking a mouthful of ale.

"That applies to us all," said Jeffries, looking around the table. "We must display the discipline and rigid self-command of . . . of Louis XIV himself!"

Unexpected Friends

Over the next few days, we laid low, taking care to avoid Cromwell and his black-garbed men. On the first of June, proceedings at the castle ceased, for Charles and Henrietta took a brief sojourn. Upon their return, the princess and her train made haste to depart from Dover.

"Please, captain," I said to Jeffries, as we stood together on the beach, observing Charles embrace his sister.

"What is it, Megs?" he asked.

"Tell me," I pleaded, "that it is not back to France for us."

Jeffries chuckled.

"Happily for you, no. We *must* get Charles's copy before he returns to London."

I nearly collapsed with relief. All this to-and-fro-ing by boat had caused me to lose a stone!

That afternoon, I contrived to slip away from the tavern, alone. Since Jeffries and Aventis were trying to work up a plan, I felt my presence superfluous. Whistling a sailor's tune, I went back to the beach to view those shining cliffs. Indeed, they were pristine—white as the frost on the Thames—and as I looked them over, I enjoyed the fresh sea air. How fine the ocean could be when you were not upon it!

"Good morning," said a voice behind me. "Lovely day, is it not?"

I turned, expecting to find more tourists like myself. Indeed, they were this and more, for I faced Cromwell and his two men: all with pistols drawn. I thought of the last time I'd been ambushed—when Aventis had done so at Epping—but *these* men would not prove to be my friends.

"Your weapons?" Hyde asked.

Defeated, I threw them to the rocky sand where they were retrieved by Smith.

"Out on a stroll?" Cromwell asked. In a menacing tone he added, "We well know who you are and why you are in Dover."

"Likewise," I spat. "You must wish to end up like your father: remains put in chains, and head placed on a pike."

The son began shaking with rage.

"You should not have left the three dunces," he said.

"The only dunces *I* note are those standing before me."

"Do you not note this?" Hyde smiled as he brought his pistol closer. "Richard, a wit."

And that was the last I recall until I awoke in a cold stone cell.

I clutched my head in pain, surmising that Mr. Hyde must have struck it with his barrel. I saw that as at Newgate, I was chained hand and foot, but unlike my ghastly first cell there, I was this one's sole inmate.

Now what? I thought. Would the Puritans attempt to use me in some effort against Jeffries? I smiled. If so, they did not know fierce highwayman Megs.

The throbbing in the back of my skull forked down to my eye. While I clenched my fists, I tried to think through the pain: where exactly *was* I?

Groaning, I saw that the stones of the walls were aged, though not as much as the Abbey's. There was only one place in Dover whose walls matched these exactly: its castle.

There was no time for more reflection as Cromwell and his two men clanged through a barred door to join me.

"Well, Megs," said Cromwell. "That is your name, is it not?"

Of course, I would never tell. The best I could offer was an ill-remembered verse from "The Whiskey in the Jar":

> And 't was early in the morning, just before I rose to travel
> Up comes a band of footmen and likewise captain Farrell
> I first produced me pistol for he stole away me rapier
> I couldn't shoot the water, so a prisoner I was taken.

"That does not even rhyme!" cried Smith.

I tried to revive my tobyman's swagger.

"Do you think a crack on the head can loosen the tongue of one such as I? For I have been shot and near-hanged!"

"Impressive," said Cromwell, "though Jeffries likely provided you aid. He will have a hard job of it, though, finding you down here."

"Still," I said, "he has the will of your father and the gold of a king. Besides, why would he come for me? I am but a lowly apprentice."

"But not despised," said Cromwell. "I could tell by the looks he bestowed on you."

"Say what you will," I yawned, pretending indifference. "My friends will be off shortly, having obtained the treaty."

"Perhaps not," said Cromwell, "for at this very moment, they are reading my note."

I looked down, hoping that Jeffries and Aventis would prize their mission over their fondness for *me*.

We all waited a silent few minutes while Hyde cleaned his dam'd gun. Then, just as the throbbing behind my eye gave way to a lesser stab, a lad ran breathlessly in, holding forth a small folded paper.

"Give it here," said Cromwell.

The boy was only too glad, and as Crowell read the note, his pale complexion turned red.

"They shall burn in sulfurous fire!" he cried.

I tried to hide my smile.

"How did Jeffries respond?" I asked.

"'Go to Hell.' That is the entirety. I cannot fathom a highwayman turning down five-hundred livre. He need only abandon his quest and we would give him the money and you."

"He has gold enough," I said, wondering what Jeffries was up to. "Besides, I am not worth five shillings. Why not permit me to go?"

Cromwell motioned the boy out the door.

"Ha! We can use you," he said. "You are cunning, and you are a thief."

"Did you mean to rob some coach?" I asked.

His icy blue eyes surveyed me.

"If you do not aid us," he said, "I will see that your favorite, Aventis, is exposed as the queen's former lover."

I started, rattling my chains.

"One learns so much at Versailles," he smiled.

I sensed from knowing his past that Cromwell's resolve had been forged by failure. This man would not stop until Charles was dead.

"Very well," I said calmly. "Where do we begin?"

A Theft but Not of Gold

Hyde bent to unchain me, taking care to show me his pistol. I rubbed my wrists to ease them as he and the others marched me into the sunlight. I was able to view at close range the expanse of Dover Castle: indeed, its several rock towers could have withstood an invasion.

"This survives due to my father," said Cromwell, gesturing toward the fortress. "He seized it during the war without having to fire a shot."

"It has been restored to the king," I said. "That is, its rightful owner."

Hyde answered by to prodding me with his gun.

"Easy," I cautioned. "I cannot help your master if I am full of holes."

"I wish, "he growled.

I joined this "godly" crew as they led me toward three waiting horses, subjecting *me*, *Megs,* to having my hands roped before me and being plopped like a sack behind Cromwell on his saddle. *God's blood, did they think me Gad?* Still, I held my tongue as we reached the Dover Road. Where would Cromwell go now? How did he mean to steal the treaty? If I could act as a helper, perhaps it would be to my good.

"We should make for Shooter's Hill," I suggested.

Cromwell grunted, then applied the whip to his mount. He rode twenty-five leagues without stopping, nearly killing our horses. I likewise suffered, for the constrained pose of my arms soon caused me to groan. To Cromwell, none of this mattered: he would gladly see us all dead in the pursuit of his prize.

At last, after dawn the next day, we arrived at Shooter's Hill. This had long been fabled—since the time of the Henrys—as the province of highwaymen, more so than even the Heath. Now, Cromwell bade me dismount, untied my hands, and shoved me back in his saddle.

"Recall," he hissed up at me, "if you do not take the treaty, then Aventis is good as dead."

"That is . . . not . . . something . . . one . . . forgets," I groaned, as the blood returned to my hands. I looked at Smith calmly. "My weapons, if you please."

He reluctantly gave me my pistol as he and his two friends aimed *theirs* squarely at me.

"My sword," I requested. I would not let these dogs have the pleasure of besting me!

Smith slammed the hilt in my hand. Now that pain now longer consumed me, my mind was able to work.

"What makes you think," I asked Cromwell, "you've outpaced the king and his party from Dover? They *do* travel by coach."

"They will have stopped," he said. "Charles will brook no discomfort on a journey of such length. No doubt he has taken his leisure at some Royalist country keep."

This man is no fool, I thought. *I must keep my wits about me.*

In my wilder, younger days, I might have fought him, and his two men besides, but now three against one were odds I preferred not to take. What I needed was that gamester, Carnatus, along with my two other friends! But who could say where they were now? In Dover, in London, or any parts in between . . .

"There they are!" Cromwell cried, gesturing toward the gilt coaches which must contain the king, his brother, and likely those who had parlayed at Dover. It was a considerable train, the largest I had yet viewed,

with so many men on horseback it looked like a charging cavalry. Seeing so many opponents, I considered feeling, but then thought of Aventis. If his affair with the queen became known, it would mean his head. Shaking my own, I waited for the royals to pass, and then, mask affixed, galloped toward the gentry. *Their* coaches, with all their ornaments, seemed dreary compared to the king's.

"Stand and deliver!" I yelled, wheeling my horse into their path. I wanted to follow with, "Your money or your life!" but, oddly, money was not what I sought.

"All coachmen, dismount!" I cried, "or I shoot *this one* between the ears."

I aimed at the first coach's box.

The two drivers behind him must have been friends, for they hastily clattered down.

"What's this?" A bass voice thundered from inside the first coach.

"All will be well, sir," I said, recalling my training. "In the meantime, if you care to enjoy the view . . ."

"Damn your dam'd effrontery!" I heard, as a door slammed open, revealing a richly dressed lord.

"I'll thank you to stop your progress sir," I said, "or, like those in the Press Yard, your next steps will be your last."

"Impudent!" roared the lord, but he halted where he stood.

"Coachmen, face down in the dirt," I ordered, "with hands behind your backs. That's it, gentlemen."

How I missed Carnatus and his skill with a rope!

"Very good," I said to the lord. "Let us enjoy the morning while I search your person and coach."

I raised my hat: how was I to know then that he was Henry, 3rd Baron of Arundell?

I could almost hear Jeffries's instructions as I searched his clothing . . . including the waistband of his breeches.

"Outrageous!" Arundell fumed, "I have just returned with the king."

"I know," I said with sympathy, then noticed the large gold crucifix hanging over his surcoat. On a whim, I withdrew my own. "God bless the True Church, sir."

"What's this?" Arundell cried. "A *Catholic* robbing another? Has the whole of the world gone mad?"

"It has, sir," I said, using my sword to sweep his coach's rich lining. Besides a thick Roman Bible, I found no other books or papers.

"Sorry to disturb," I said. "Now, if you'll just follow me."

And so I continued. Though I was unaware of their titles, I held up in succession: Secretary of State Lord Arlington; Sir Thomas Clifford of parliament; and one Sir Richard Bellings. The first two had nothing I wanted (besides their fat purses, which I *did* consider taking). However, the last least-ranking gentleman proved to be the best, for, inside his waistcoat, I found a folded document. Though it was all in French, I could discern English signatures, along with that of Ambassador de Croissey! If *this* was not what Cromwell sought, then I best hang up my spurs!

While straightening Bellings's coat, I found my hand brush *another* Crucifix! For a sect with so few numbers, they certainly had their nobles!

"Best of health, sir," I said to Bellings. "And to the Pope as well. What's his name again?"

"Clement. Clement X!" Sir Richard replied in a huff.

"Of course. Well, I thank you for your time," I told the three gentry who all huddled by the last coach. "For now, you may keep your coin, but we may well meet again."

"Impudent dog!" said Arundell.

I gave them a merry wink as I vaulted onto my horse.

"God save the king!" I shouted, riding past their train and back up Shooter's Hill. By the time I stopped before Cromwell, he was shaking with impatience. Snatching the papers from me, he began to read. I could see his smile grow as he perused each page.

"Glorious!" he cried. "Charles has, with his own hand, consigned himself to the headsman! There is not a moment to lose. We must seek the queen directly."

"The queen?" I asked. Was she expected to wield the ax?

"Quiet!" Hyde ordered. "Hand down your weapons." As he and Smith wielded pistols, I thought it best to comply. Hyde turned to his master. "May I kill him?" he asked.

Cromwell shrugged, then thought a bit.

"No," he said. "We may require an extra hand when it comes to breeching Whitehall."

Dear Lord, I thought. *Has he come completely undone?* After robbing three prominent gentry—two of them lords—he was actually proposing we break into the royal palace! For a fleeting moment, I longed for my life before Dover: one devoid of nobles, kings, and even the errant knight!

Her Majesty

It did not take long to arrive in the heart of London. As always, there were crowds about, and I considered crying out to alert them to my plight. But who there would believe that a Puritan—Richard Cromwell, no less!—had taken a highwayman hostage? People would think me a madman, and Bethlam, where such were kept, made Newgate look like a spa. Far better for me to determine how Cromwell intended to enter the palace . . .

Before I could think on it more, we halted before the Banqueting House, where old Charles had lost his head. I prayed that despite my company, the new one would hold onto his!

"You are a Catholic," said Cromwell, as he and his men dismounted. Hyde reluctantly slashed my ropes with a glinting dagger.

"Actually—" I began.

"For the purpose of this visit," said Cromwell, "you are a Papist come to plead for your people in the north."

"And who are *you?*" I asked, my voice laced with contempt. "Dissenter friends I've had to supper?"

"I represent a similar sect. Just like Her Majesty's."

"This plan is so wild," I said, "it surpasses even Jeffries."

"Enough," Cromwell hissed, pushing me toward the Hall. He must have been a gifted player, for his whole air altered as he addressed four guards.

"Begging your pardon, good sirs," he said, the model of servitude, "we are poor Dissenters seeking an audience with our queen." He pushed me forward. "This young man is a Papist and bears a shocking report of how

Her Majesty's brethren are treated up in the north. It is quite shameful and even affects great peers."

"Hmph," said one of the soldiers, placing both hands on his pike. "Think you to merely appear and be granted a royal audience? Such simpletons I have never—"

We did not hear the end, for Hyde lunged quickly, stabbing the man through the heart. Cromwell and Smith dispatched the others with daggers. As their bodies fell to the pavement, we dragged them to a side alley, covering them with the refuse that littered all of London.

With a knife at my own back, I entered the Banqueting Hall. My eyes were drawn to the ceiling painted with creatures awaiting their doom. Cromwell, noting my interest, spat with contempt, "Rubens."

I followed the once Lord Protector as his minions followed *me*. Cromwell marched through the halls with such confidence it was clear he had been a resident. To his fortune and my detriment, we encountered no more guards: Charles's recent arrival must have required their presence. Hesitating just slightly, Cromwell entered a suite of chambers which would not have been out of place during the reign of the Tudors.

This was plainly the realm of women: both the painted and earthly kind. The latter, I knew, were considered the beauties of the age, clad in such silken finery and sporting such ornate hairstyles that I openly gaped. There was one surrounded by others who earned much applause and laughter, for she wore the costume of Charles, including his wig and "moustache"!

Cromwell only *looked* disgusted, but I felt the sensation down to the pit of my soul. *This woman,* I thought, *wears a disguise to amuse, while* I *adopt mine in order to be free.* When I looked at her, what I saw was not an ally, but a mere pretender.

"Boy!"

Cromwell, noting my distraction, shot me a warning look which caused me to recover by bowing and clutching my crucifix. He repeated to the women his false tale of persecution, inspiring in them soft sighs and even tears. They were only too happy to take us deeper into the suite, where I saw the queen—Catherine of Braganza herself!—dining, attended by even more ladies. Luckily for me, a newly made "Catholic," there were several priests around her. The chamber itself was hung with so much velvet that one knew in an instant it had been fashioned for royalty.

Catherine nodded as one of her ladies whispered to her.

"Very well, you may come forward," she said, and the four of us did, kneeling before her table which stood on a great dais. I noted that Cromwell and his men did so with great reluctance.

"You come with tales of our people," Catherine said.

I looked around, then realized she spoke to *me.*

"Yes, Your Majesty," I mumbled.

"The times are dire indeed," she said with a shake of her curls. "Lord Clarendon's Codes are oppressive, and my husband hates them, but in light of current feeling, what is he to do?"

Looking truly distressed, she saw my blank face, and said, "It may not have reached you, but the Codes mandate that Catholics cannot travel more than five miles from their homes. We are forbidden to worship lest we be transported. We cannot attend school, and we may not serve in government, or even as doctors. The fine for marrying a Catholic is one hundred pounds."

I closed my eyes, feeling sorry for Aventis and anyone of his faith.

"It is beyond disgusting," I said.

It was then that Cromwell rose.

"Madam," he said, "these laws oppress more than Catholics. They are for Dissenters as well."

"Yes."

Catherine waved a hand.

"On the subject of Catholics," said Cromwell, flashing a smile, "I happen to have on my person a document of interest."

With a flair, he produced the papers I had stolen from poor Sir Richard. He handed them up to a priest, who in turn gave them to Her Majesty.

She sighed, then unfolded the papers and read. As she did so, her face became pale and her hands started to shake.

"Querido Deus!" she cried, rising so quickly that her ladies-in-waiting scattered. "From where did you obtain this?"

"That is moot," said Cromwell smoothly. "As you see, it is a treaty. Not the false one pursued by Buckingham. The *secret* one, signed by your husband."

"Has Charles gone mad?" the queen cried. "Who could have convinced him to agree to such terms?"

"One he loves and esteems," said Cromwell, "perhaps more than Your Majesty."

He bowed.

'Minette," Catherine said, steadying herself on the dias.

"Just so," he replied, "the king's beloved sister. In truth, she surpasses our finest diplomat."

"Oh não," Catherine groaned, and I felt pained to see her in such distress. "This treaty," she said, "it must be destroyed."

"Unfortunately," said Cromwell, "there is another copy. No matter." He smiled. "Since Charles's relations have such sway over him, we depend on you, dear Catherine, to counsel his abdication."

"And your elevation!" I cried.

"Just so—" he started to say, but halted when we all heard a scuffle in the outer chamber. This was succeeded by the sight of a massive body tumbling headfirst into the room. Based on size and garish dress, there could be no doubt who it was: Carnatus!

Despite his loathing of me, I was never so glad to see anyone in my life!

"Huzzah," I yelled, as Jeffries and Aventis burst in, trailed by twenty soldiers. It would seem that unlike Cromwell, they were *not* familiar with Whitehall, and had stumbled into a nest of Life Guards!

At the welcome sight of my friends, a new boldness seized me, and I in turn seized my weapons while kicking Hyde to the floor. I ran full-tilt toward three guards, engaging them in swordplay which I trusted would please Aventis! I thought to use my pistol, but it seemed vulgar before the queen, so I persevered with my blade: thrusting it through one guard's doublet, the second's coat, and, I hesitate to report, the third's red breeches. The guards fell in succession, but a fourth—a captain by the looks of him—engaged me with his own blade which he used to free my lace cuffs from the constraints of their sleeves. *The blackguard!*

He did not desist as he lunged for me, and I feared I would lose my shirt if not my life until Aventis whirled and gave him a thrust of steel. I saw Jeffries and Carnatus deal such punishing blows that the queen looked on in amazement while Cromwell cringed at her feet.

"Halt! Halt!" came the cry, as a crush of more Life Guards swept in. Though the four of us faced them together, they outnumbered us ten-to-one, and so we put down our swords.

"Hold them!" cried an officer, and we were divested of weapons in seconds. *This* captain seemed indignant. "How dare you engage my men before her Royal Majesty?"

I exchanged a look with Jeffries. Was there an appropriate answer? Unfortunately, Carnatus opened his mouth . . .

"Querida Catarina. Um momento."

The giant closed it again as Aventis stepped forward. *Of course!* How could I forget his long past the queen?

"Bernardino," she said, smoothing her skirts. I saw a handful of guards scramble up to surround her.

"Your Majesty," said Aventis, kneeling, "surely you know in your heart I would never oppose you."

"*Sim,*" said the queen, nodding. "Rise."

He did, removing his hat.

"That treaty—" Aventis motioned to the papers she still held in her hand. "It has the power to destroy. If its contents become known, your husband will be killed."

At my side, Cromwell and his men smiled. I fought the desire to strike them with my bare hands.

"Please," said Aventis, lifting his hands in supplication. "Turn it over to me and I will see it destroyed. Along with its twin in France."

From her dias, Catherine looked down at his face. She seemed to regard him as a dear, beloved friend.

"Very well," she said. "Ensure that they are both burned."

Aventis bowed low.

"Consider it done."

She folded the papers and handed them down to him.

"Thank God," Carnatus muttered. "This damnable business is done."

At the captain's signal, the guards stepped back.

"Uh . . ." I began awkwardly.

"What is it, Megs?" asked Jeffries.

I inclined my head toward Cromwell and his two henchmen.

"Of course." Now Jeffries addressed the queen. "Your Majesty, I fear it is me again."

"I can see that," she said tartly.

"I must inform you," said Jeffries, "that this man is no common Roundhead. In fact, he is Richard Cromwell, son of the late Oliver."

The queen shook with anger.

"Such treachery," she muttered. "Will it ever end from this family?"

"I would lay odds—" said Carnatus, but Cromwell interrupted.

"My father was a great man!" he cried. "He desired rule by parliament and an end to the tainted Church. I am glad he did not live to witness your husband's lechery!"

"Charles has his faults," said Catherine, "but still, he is King of England. *Your* father was a usuper who brought us war, not to mention misery."

"It was for your own good!" Cromwell yelled. "To stem the Papist scourge, which even now strangles this palace." He cast an accusing finger at the priests on the dias.

"It is true," Catherine said evenly, "that we follow two different faiths. Yet, as both are oppressed, I should think you would stand by us."

"Never!" cried Cromwell. "Only *we* are especially chosen by Him!"

"I fear it is useless," said Jeffries, shaking his head. "He must be put to death."

"Shall I summon the headsman?"

Carnatus gave Catherine a wink. The queen thought for a moment.

"Death?" she asked. "Like my husband's father? And all those who died in the war?" She straightened. "Richard Cromwell?"

"Yes," he said unwillingly.

"It is my desire that you be granted a pardon. These fine guards will escort you out of our realm. You are not to return, upon pain of death."

From Cromwell's wide smile, one might have thought that he'd just been given her hand!

"Thank you, majesty, thank you!" he cried. "You are truly gracious."

"But—" Jeffries began.

"Suficiente," said the queen. "The events of this day have wearied me." She brought a silk cloth to her face, then looked down at Aventis. "Do not fail me, count."

The Duke

I begged, I pleaded, I actually thought of employing tears (though, as I regarded Carnatus, I quickly abandoned this thought).

"Please, Captain Jeffries, I said, before the Banqueting Hall, "can we not secure a berth more refined than a dinghy? After all, we have just seen the queen."

Jeffries tried not to laugh, though Carnatus, despite himself, chuckled.

"Megs, you shall get your wish," said Jeffries. "On this voyage, we sail in style."

I exhaled in relief, then thought of our rival travelers.

"The queen will provide Cromwell with similar fittings," I said. "When, by rights, he should be chained to an oar."

I looked at company, each member astride an elegant mount. Each, that is, except me.

"Megs, climb aboard," said Jeffries. "You will ride with me until you procure your own."

Not *another* dual ride as if I were a servant! That reminded me.

"Where is Gad?" I asked.

"At home," said Carnatus, forgetting his vow not to speak to me. "I am punishing him for overspending at Dover."

"Speaking of which," said Jeffries, "we must make for the Dover Road."

He set off at a brisk pace, and, once we'd arrived, we spotted a fine gentleman who had the courage—or stupidity—to venture alone.

"On him, Megs," said Aventis with a wink. "You know how it is done."

Indeed I did.

As Jeffries leapt off his mount, I took his place in the saddle and approached this coxcomb.

"Hullo!" I cried, trying not to laugh at his hat's profusion of feathers.

"What do you want?" he asked coldly, staring at my drawn pistol.

"Not a great deal," I said. "I'm afraid I must borrow your horse."

"*What?*" he huffed. "You mean steal."

"Call it what you will," I said, "but I am in a great hurry. Your horse, if you please."

His feathers ruffling, he reluctantly left his saddle.

"You're nothing but a common diver!" he cried.

"Oh no, sir, I am a highwayman. And since you are so rude, I must ask for your purse."

With great indignation, he threw it at my head.

"You could learn a great deal from us," I said as I changed mounts. "I am sure you'll have ample time to think during your walk."

I rode back to the others, where I returned Jeffries's horse.

"Well done!" Carnatus cried, forgetting his rule *again*. "How *dare* he call us divers? You should have whipped him where he stood."

I smiled as we began our ride south in earnest. Now that I knew the way, I found I could relax. As we pounded down the road, passing travelers without a thought of robbery, I spurred my new mount to ride alongside Aventis.

"Megs," he said with a smile, "I cannot tell you how glad I am that we found you safe. We were all quite troubled." He pointed at Carnatus. "Even him."

"How did you know I had been taken?" I asked.

"The lad who delivered the note. It is amazing what a shilling can purchase."

I nodded.

"Still, I must apologize for wandering off on my own."

"No matter," said Aventis. "We have secured the treaty."

He felt in his coat pocket, withdrew those cursed papers, then took out a match.

"Aventis," I said, "before you destroy it, can you tell me what it says? I do not read French."

"Of course," he said. "But I must warn you—keep a firm grip on your reins!

He proceeded to read, translating for me into English:

> The king of England being convinced of the truth of the Roman Catholic religion is resolved to declare it, and to reconcile himself with the Church of Rome as soon as the state of his country's affairs permit . . . . But as there are unquiet spirits who mask their designs under the guise of religion, the king of England for the peace of his kingdom, will avail himself of the assistance of the king of France, who, as he is quite anxious to contribute to a design glorious not only for the king of England, but for the whole of Catholic Christendom, promises to pay to the king of England the sum of two million tournois, the first half payable three months after the ratification of the treaty, the other half three months later. In addition, the king of France undertakes to provide, at his own expense, 6,000 troops for the execution of this design, if they should be required. The time for the

> declaration of Catholicism is left entirely to the discretion of the king of England.

"God's wounds!" I shouted, "I'll be damned if this is not dam'd stupidity!"

Aventis shook his head.

"It is not the smartest thing that Charles ever did."

"'Unquiet spirits'?" I asked. "*Is he mad?* To restore ENGLAND to the Catholic faith with Bloody Mary still fresh! And . . . and those Clarendon laws, the people detecting plots in their very soup! Aventis, I must ask you: is this man fit to rule?"

Aventis sighed as he fired his match, transforming paper into a clump of ash.

"Understand, Megs," he said, "that Charles has been, so to speak, heavily wrought upon."

"His *sister* has that much influence?" I asked.

"And his old Catholic mother, who left this world last year."

I had a thought which chilled me.

"Is Charles himself," I asked, "an actual Catholic?"

I regretted these words after they left my lips. *Such absurdity!* The head of the Church of England?

"In his heart, I believe he is," said Aventis. "If it were up to him, he would convert."

"A disaster," I muttered. "I cannot imagine anything worse."

Aventis waited for my sighs to subside.

"Now," he said, "I am going to tell you something which, in regard to the future, is in fact far worse."

"Dear God," I moaned.

"James, the king's brother and heir to the throne, has secretly become a convert."

I could not speak for several moments. Finally, I cried, "*Are* all *the Stuarts lunatics*?!"

"One could say," said Aventis, "that they are mainly Catholics."

Jeffries slowed his horse to fall back and join us.

"I could not help but overhear," he said. "Charles may be wanton but be is not a fool."

"How can you say that?" I asked. All the evidence pointed otherwise.

"He is a politic gent," said Jeffries. "That is why he maintains the throne. There is a very real chance that the 'secret' clause of the treaty will never be known."

"In the meantime," said Aventis, "he collects his *tournois*."

"And Louis's love," said Jeffries.

"Very well," I said, "but what if Cromwell gets his hands on the treaty in France?"

"That is why we ride," said Jeffries.

After a breakneck journey, we arrived *for the third time* in Dover. I confess I was feeling bone-tired, but after what I had learned, I was anxious to get to France.

"Do not forget your pledge," I told Jeffries, and he laughed as we boarded a ship fit for Henrietta. Now *this* was the way to travel: instead of a leaky rowboat, we strode on a deck of good wood surrounded by billowing sails.

"Ah," I said, leaning over the side, and for the first time at sea, my insides did not heave. "On such a vessel, I would not mind going to Spain, or even the Americas."

Both Jeffries and Aventis laughed.

On *this* voyage, I was aware of my surroundings: the spray of the grey-green water; the whip of the summer wind. In just a matter of hours, we crossed the canal and disembarked at Calais. I saw that our journey from there would likewise be one of comfort, for, once off the boat, Jeffries hired a coach-and-four.

"Captain," said Carnatus, "this is how we should *always* travel."

We joined him within. It was a tight space for four "men," but we lightened discomfort with discourse.

"Would you have us rob coaches to secure one of our own?" asked Aventis.

"Why not?" shrugged Carnatus. "After the theft, we might join our victims for supper."

"He fancies himself a Du Val," I mumbled.

What I quickly realized by being inside a coach and not outside with a gun was the sheer hell of this kind of travel. The roads in France were equal to England's: in other words, strewn with potholes the size of my head. How I longed for a horse which at least had a spring in its step!

Since we changed our own so often, it took but five days to arrive in Paris—which involved me, naturally, sleeping on inn floors or in truckle beds. I could not say the French versions were less hard than the English, though the excellent food cheered me.

When we finally arrived at the capital, I could hardly contain my excitement. *At last,* I would see Versaille and all her fabled beauty! Yet my joy gave way to despair as our coach did not venture east.

"I do not understand," I said. "Does not Henrietta live in Louis's palace?"

Aventis shook his head.

"You will recall," he said, "that she is wife to Louis's brother, the Duc d'Orleans. Phillippe has two estates: the Palais-Royal in Paris, grand enough on its own; and the Château de Saint-Cloud, which is said to rival Versailles."

"Dam'd French," said Carnatus, "always trying to one-up each other! But I'd bet that he's in the city. Who wants to lay down a louis?"

Since none of us spoke, he sighed, then picked at a cheese he'd brought.

"Forgive me, Carnatus," said Aventis, "but I must disagree. Phillipe is said to despise Versailles, and Saint-Cloud is his passion. Upon his wife's return, he would surely take her *there.*"

"Our decision is crucial," said Jeffries. "We cannot, as Carnatus would say, place all our bets on one hand. Therefore, we shall split our party: with Carnatus and I in Paris; and Aventis and Megs to Saint-Cloud."

I could not have been more astounded. Why would Jeffries divide us thus? Did he think to dispense his best minds—his own, and Aventis's—to each destination? I snuck a glance at Aventis, but he did not look my way.

Once we reached the Palais, Jeffries bade the coachman halt and stepped out with Carnatus. Before I could speak to Aventis, the captain appeared at the window.

"I am putting my faith in you both," he said. "Do not forget the gravity of our task. If Cromwell beats us to Henrietta, he will become Lord Protector."

"Yes, sir," I said, feeling both the tug of duty and that which pulled at my heart.

"We understand," said Aventis.

We watched our two friends stride down a crowded boulevard.

"Well," I said to Aventis, trying to fill the silence, "how would you propose we get to the chateau?"

"By boat," he said, and I put my head in my hands.

"Do not bestir yourself, Megs—it is but a short trip. A dawdle down the Seine and—*voila!*—we arrive at the back of Phillipe's. When I was at the Abbey, I used to study his plans of the gardens."

"Very well," I said, trying not to sound petulant. "You and Jeffries know best."

It took no time at all for our coach to reach the Seine. Stepping out, I saw that it teemed with traffic like its English cousin the Thames. Aventis approached the owner of some small craft and spoke to him in French. After handing over some coins, he motioned for me to join him. Once again, we were off, with Aventis taking the oars and a westerly route. *I* lay back on a bench, noting how the calm water picked up flecks of sunlight. *If only we could float away,* I thought, *going on an uncharted voyage where there were no rules, no Cromwell, no foolish kings to be saved . . .*

"Megs!" called Aventis, shattering my reverie. "Look! It is the Grande Cascade."

I sat up with reluctance, but this soon fell away, for I saw a pool adjoining the Seine whose backdrop was a waterfall, its own deep waters lined with postlike fountains. The visitors before it, their clothes colorful as Carnatus's, and the manicured trees behind made me give a cry: "How beautiful!"

"There is nothing like it in England," said Aventis.

He steered over to the pool, then tied up the boat. Leading the way, he climbed onto a walkway filled with sauntering French, then headed for the trees before shoving me through them.

"Is the entrance through an arbor?" I asked, wiping leaves from my mouth.

He gave a low laugh.

"Did you think we could knock at the door and simply ask for Monsieur?"

I shrugged, recognizing his wisdom. After a time in this planted forest, we stood at its perimeter, both of us staring at the gardens of Saint-Cloud's. At that moment, I lost all regret about not seeing Versailles, for *these grounds* were like Paradise. Perfect plots of grass bordered by cheerful fountains stood off the bank of the Seine. When I gazed opposite, I sighted a stone chateau that frankly put Whitehall to shame.

"Megs," Aventis said sharply. "Stay with me. We must find the back entrance."

I nodded, feeling more dwarfed by Saint-Cloud the closer we came to it.

"If anyone asks," said Aventis, "I am a priest and you are my parishener."

"Not again," I groaned, trying not to gape at a perfect tree-lined walk. "Why must I *always* be Catholic?"

"Shhh," said Aventis, sidling his way toward a promising door. With a push, it opened: onto another world. As we tiptoed inside, I saw delicate white marble statues; ceilings painted with scenes that overwhelmed in their vibrancy. From every corner hung tapestries, overlooked by chandeliers secured by velvet ropes. *If this is not Heaven,* I thought, *then I do not want to go there . . .*

Of course, we were apprehended by the time we reached the hallway. An unhappy maid stood before us, wielding her duster with menace. Aventis engaged her with French and a smile, until she too smiled, followed up with curtsy. Leading us through silver-and-gold-plated doors, we found ourselves in what must have been one of the chateau's wings. Stopping before a wide door, the maid knocked softly, then motioned us into a chamber which made Catherine's look like a milkmaid's!

The decorations were lavish yet tasteful. Directing my eyes to the maid, I saw her curtsy before a young woman who was no stranger to me. Though I had only seen her from a distance, there could be no doubt: she was Princess Henrietta of England, the Duchess of Orleans. After conversing with her servant, she turned to Aventis. I felt only frustration as French swarmed all around me.

"What are you saying?" I asked, tugging Aventis's cloak.

"Just some pleasantries about the health of Monsieur and Louis," he said. "The king, it appears, has recovered from a bad cold."

"Can't you tell her," I asked, "that we are in a great hurry?"

"Why is that?" Henrietta asked. Of course, she spoke perfect English. "Must you return to England? I have but lately been there myself."

"We know," I said.

With a clear desire to exclude me, Aventis switched back to French.

"What are you saying now?" I asked when he paused for breath.

"I am relating," he said, "the great danger that treaty presents to her brother. She does not understand." He smiled at the princess. "She has been gone for so long that she is no longer sensible of how the English hate us."

By "us" I knew he meant "Catholics."

As their discourse went on, I began to question my presence. Was I there merely to admire the paintings? Just when I thought to leave, the princess's tones grew heated, then became amenable as she gave Aventis her hand.

"She has agreed to give us the treaty," Aventis said with relief. "Though it is not in her hands, she'll have de Croissey deliver it here."

"Thank God!" I breathed, then bowed and smiled at the princess. "You have saved England," I told her.

"That is my hope," she answered.

Her maid cordially led us to the back door where we'd entered.

"Avoir," said Aventis, then turned to me. "That could not have gone better."

"No," I said, as we hiked back through the trees. "But what of Cromwell?"

"He has not seen her," said Aventis. "He must have gone to the Palais."

"Wouldn't it be rich if he ran into Jeffries?" I asked.

We both snorted with laughter.

Retracing our steps on the walkway, we set off in our boat down the Seine. Looking back at the Grande Cascade, I truly felt grieved to leave such beauty behind. Would I ever see it again, or the chateau for that matter? Despite the warm July sun, I felt beset by gloom.

Once back in Paris, we hurried to a *taverne* which Aventis had set as a meeting place. As he made his report, Carnatus raised a fist in triumph.

"Superb!" he cried. "*Magnifique!* Don't you think so, Jeffries?"

"Indeed," said the captain, but he still looked anxious. "Still, I would like to know: where the devil is Cromwell?"

"He can go to him for all I care," said Carnatus. "What concerns me now is French fare—a great deal of it." He called to our serving girl, *"Du vin tout autour! Et vos plus beaux vittles!"*

His plea was answered shortly as food and wine arrived at our table. When Carnatus had eaten his fill, he turned to Aventis and said, "Our mission is near complete! Who knew it would be this simple?"

"Do not tempt fate," said Jeffries. "Until that treaty is in our hands, *I* will not rest easy."

Yet rest is what we did that evening, in *two* beds this time at an inn. The captain, true to his word, remained restless at my side, while *I* thought chiefly of Aventis, who dozed just just a few feet away.

I gave a long sigh.

"Do not fret, Megs," Jeffries whispered, "for there is an end to all things."

What did he mean? I thought. An end to our company, or merely that cursed treaty? Too afraid to ask, I remained awake until morning.

After the others dressed, I followed them down to our *taverne.* When I walked in, I could feel something amiss, as if a deep sense of grief lay over the place like a pall. The serving girl from yesterday worked in a kind of daze, while others, both patrons and waiters, were openly shedding tears.

"What has happened?" I asked Jeffries, who had gone to speak with the girl before returning to us.

"Madame se meurt," he said, sinking into a chair.

I looked to Aventis.

"Madame is dead," said Aventis.

"I am sorry—which madame?" I asked. "Do you mean the French queen?"

"No," said Jeffries, holding his head. "Princess Henrietta, the Duchess of Orleans."

"How could that be?" I cried. "When we saw her yesterday, she seemed perfectly well."

"I noted that her skin was pale," said Aventus. "And her eye dull."

"Great God! Was she poisoned?" Carnatus asked.

I turned in my chair.

"Who would do such a thing? Monsieur?"

Aventis shook his head.

"Phillipe may have his oddities, but he would not kill his wife. For her, he reserved a great tenderness."

"But . . . the treaty!" I cried. "How is it to be obtained?"

"If de Croissey has come," said Aventis, "as he would in light of this news, I should think that all Madame's papers are now held by Monsieur."

"Thirty July," Jeffries muttered, raising his ashen face. "This is the worst day for England since Oliver Cromwell won."

"Cromwell!" we all said as one, then ran into the street to hail a public hack (or whatever they called them here). It was a short ride to Saint-Cloud, where we clambered out amidst a tangle of coaches. Many were ornate, but none could rival one boasting a gold face wrought into the sun. *My God,* I thought, *King Louis himself is here!*

It was no trouble for us to go down that tree-lined walk and enter Saint-Cloud from the front. Even from outside, we could hear a great melee, and once we entered, we saw servants openly sobbing. In the main room, conclaves of richly dressed nobles stood talking in whispers. As we passed one, I heard the word "poison" (pronounced as a haughty "pwa-zone"). *Could Carnatus have been right?*

As former visitors, Aventis and I showed the others the way through marble and velvet. We found the princess's chambers by following solemn mourners who lined up before it. Staring at the silks and frills of the men, more foppish than even in England, my eye was naturally drawn to three in plain black dress.

"Jeffries!" I hissed, *"there."*

I pointed out the Puritans, some thirty bodies ahead of us.

When Carnantus spied them, he put a hand on his sword.

"No," said Jeffries softly, "we cannot make a scene. Not when Monsieur has just lost his wife."

Aventis nodded.

"It must be left to him," he said, "to dispense the treaty as he will."

I wondered at that moment who was more disgusted: Carnatus, or myself. For once, I doubted our two wise men. What if Monsieur hated

Charles? What if Cromwell intended to offer him dazzling bribes? Had it been left to me, I would have stormed the chamber with my pistol, stolen the treaty, and run. With their three-inch high heels, these nobles could never catch me!

"Megs," Aventis whispered, "you're shaking. How may I help calm you?"

"Tell me about Phillipe," I said. "What sort of man is he?"

Over the next half hour, I strained my eyes from the sheer effort of widening them. What stories I heard! Such contradictions! By the time Aventis had finished, I was using the wall as a prop.

It was then that Jeffries acted.

He stepped forward in line, beckoning us to join him. *He* in turn joined Cromwell, Smith, and Hyde.

"Richard!" cried Jeffries with a smile, "*so* happily met! Whatever brings you here?"

"Away with you," growled Cromwell, fumbling for his pistol. Carnatus cut the act short by digging his own into the Puritan's back. Smith and Hyde did not look pleased.

"Let us make this a merry party!" cried Carnatus. "We shall enter the chamber *together.*"

After some minutes passed, we heard a stir from within. When the door opened, I saw at least twenty nobles in extravagant dress. But they were merely planets revolving around the sun, for at their center was Louis XIV, the finery of his costume at great odds with his countenance. How he'd loved his sister-in-law! It was spread across his face for all of France to see. As he stepped down the hall, all gave way and bowed deeply. I turned for one last glimpse: though his dark wig caught the sun, his stride was slow and mournful.

At last, it was *our* turn to pay respects. We jostled with the three Puritans in our effort to reach Monsieur first. I saw that on the bed lay poor Henrietta, her face as pale as her sheets. I prayed that she had died naturally and not at some poisoner's hand.

I looked up at Philippe, who stood in the center of the rooom. What struck me at first was just how *handsome* he was: he was comelier than his brother, his features perfect beneath his wig.

Both Jeffries and Cromwell took turns offering sympathy. Monsieur nodded, though he seemed in a daze, and who could blame him? One moment, he had a young, vibrant wife; the next, a colorless corpse with hands folded demurely. If I were him and the body on the bed was Aventis, I would have gone mad with grief: but, being a royal, he could not threaten God or weep.

I could see the time had come to bring up the matter of the treaty. *How*, I wondered, *did Jeffries intend to do it?* Of course he was beaten by Cromwell, who ran up to Monsieur, practically grabbing him by the collar. What I heard next from them both was a babbling stream of French.

When there was silence, my three friends looked disgusted.

"What did he say?" I asked.

"What one would expect," said Jeffries. "He has offered Monsieur sixty-five-thousand pounds—once *he* becomes Lord Protector."

"Bah," I said. "What does a duke need with money?"

"There is more," added Aventis. "he gave a promise of land: no less than the port of Dover."

"It is not his to give!" I roared, and, pre-empting even Carnatus, unsheathed my sword.

"That's the way, Megs!" he yelled, swinging his pistol around to aim it again at Cromwell.

Hyde tried to defend his master by firing his own. Happily, he missed, causing Carnatus to do so as well.

"Dammee!" cried my former friend.

Outside in the hallway, we heard the French nobles scrambling. But that was as nothing compared to the rage of Phillipe.

"Qu'est-ce que c'est?" he cried. *"Comment oses-tu me parler d'un traité avec la duchesse, pas même froid ?"*

"What did he say?" I yelled to Jeffries.

"Well," the captain replied, embroiled in a duel with Smith, who had grabbed a sword from the wall, "he wants to know why we talk of a treaty when his wife is hardly cold."

"And well he might," I said, hooking the tip of my blade to the lining of Smith's coat and hurling him to the floor.

"You can't win, Jeffries!" cried Cromwell, picking up Smith's stolen sword as he ducked through Carnatus's legs. "You have nothing to offer! Nothing but fealty to a king who cast you onto the road."

"That may be true," said Jeffries, feinting like Aventis. "But loyalty *has* no price. And either, I think, does the duke."

This sparked something in me. As I hurtled toward Hyde, who was wrestling a sword from the wall, I yelled to Aventis, "Please translate for me!"

"Duke," I said to Phillipe, as my blade now clashed with Hyde's, "your late wife loved her brother. Who, this man, Richard *Cromwell*, wishes to dethrone."

There followed some French from Aventis, then the duke.

"He says," said the former, just escaping Smith's upturned blade, "that he does not care who sits on the throne in England. His only concern is for France."

"Then please tell him," I asked, as my blade ripped a tapestry in two, "that a king deposed in England could mean trouble for France."

Phillipe stroked his chin. In disgust, he seized back his sword from Hyde, then used it like a master to stab him through the shoulder. Hyde collapsed with a groan.

"Thank you, Monsieur!" I cried. "I have heard you were a great general. But your brother will not let you fight due to your . . . uh, proclivities."

"That is true," said Phillipe in halting English. Beside him, Jeffries and Cromwell toppled a priceless chest. "Also, he is jealous. None may outshine the sun."

Giving Hyde a push with my boot, I nodded.

"Monsieur," I said, "all these years, you've been despised for what you are: a man who loves both men and women."

"Yes," said Phillipe, watching Carnatus stab Smith and dangle him off the floor.

"I too am despised," I said. Lowering my sword, I swept off my hat, letting my long hair fall. "*I* have dressed as a man so that I may be free. And *you* have dressed as a woman for much the same."

He nodded as Cromwell went flying across the room.

"We two have more in common than you do with him," I said, pointing to the bloodied Puritan. "You and I have been scorned for vice, but in our hearts, we believe in king and country."

"That is all we can offer," said Jeffries, a bit breathless from his skirmish. "Not money or land. Merely loyalty to our king."

"I see," said Phillipe. He turned to Smith, who was creeping up behind him, sword back in his hand. "Put down your arms, you Puritan pig!" Smith quickly complied. "Well," said the duke, "I think the choice is clear. For Charles and my brother, and—" he turned to me, "—and comrades-in-arms, I grant you this."

He turned to the chest of drawers now in pieces on the rug. Removing a handful of papers, he displayed them to Jeffries.

The captain nodded.

Monsieur then seized a lit candle from a now-bent table lamp. As he drew the wick toward the treaty, Cromwell shouted, *"No!"*

"You're getting blood on my Persian rug," said Phillipe.

All of us watched as this last copy of the treaty took on an orange hue, then blackened around the edges. When darkness had finally engulfed it, Phillipe flung it to the floor, grinding the embers down with his heel.

The duke extended his hand to Jeffries.

"C'est fait," he said. "It is done."

He gave me a wink.

Honored Guests

After the strains of our adventure, we were relieved to sail home, then procure horses (legally!), and ride to London. On the streets, there was still talk of Papist plots and the king's involvement, but now at least—*praise God!*—there was nothing damning in writing.

"My dear friends," I told the company, as we picked our way over cobblestones, "why not celebrate tonight at an inn I know in Middlesex? Since I am the owner, food and drink are on the house."

"A wonderful plan!" cried Carnatus, who was speaking to me again. "After that fancy French fare, I could do with a simple fowl—or four!"

"Sounds heavenly," said Aventis. He gave me a smile. "Much like Saint-Germain."

"Not as grand as all that," I said, "but at least *my* walls are new."

"Let us ride," said Jeffries, and we followed him to the Heath.

Once there, I bid the company pause before a lonely birch. After some digging, I hid behind the trunk and transformed: this time, back to Margaret. How cumbersome were these skirts! And the side saddle posture! Still, I was anxious to see how Sally had gotten on. Handing my horse to young, pleasant ostler, I motioned for the others to follow me through the main door.

I was pleased by what I witnessed. The tables were overflowing with patrons, served by staff so obliging I needn't have bothered to return!

Seeing me there, Sally ran toward me.

"Ms Margaret!" she cried, grasping both of my hands. "We been eatin' ourselves up wonderin' where you been."

"As long as customers are eating," I said, "there is no cause for concern. I have been . . . abroad," I told her, pointing to my companions. "You remember Captain Jeffries? Well, these are his friends, and are to be treated like earls."

"Why not a prince?" asked Carnatus, sliding onto a chair. "I shall have two of everything. Including two tankards of ale."

"Yes, sir," said Sally, then drew me aside. "Ms Margaret, Mr. Ned's been beside himself since you up an' went. He stops in every night, hopin' you've come back. And, I must say, he drinks more'an his fill."

"Oh no," I groaned, my stomacher digging into me. God help me, but Ned had not crossed my mind—not for these many months. And he had been waiting on my answer. What was I, as Margaret, to do?

As the shadows lengthened outside, I tried with all my wiles to usher my friends upstairs.

"You will each have your own room," I said, "with feather beds soft as a babe's bottom. Food and drink will be brought to you the whole night if you wish."

"Let us go!" said Carnatus, rising.

Of course, Ned chose that moment to swing into the Whale. He *did* look careworn, his usual cheer having given way to gloom. And, as luck would have it, once he entered the room, he faced none but Aventis!

"Ned—" I began, wondering what to say.

"Margaret!" he cried, with a beaming smile. In his joy, he ran toward me and *took me in his arms.*

"Heigh ho," said Carnatus. "What's this?"

From being my staunchest foe, he now fancied himself my guard!

"Who is he?" asked both Jeffries and Aventis. They each bore a look which was usually accompanied by gunfire.

"I am Margaret's fiancé!" cried Ned, as he removed a *gold ring* from his coat.

"WHAT?" cried my three friends.

"Ned," I whispered between clenched teeth, "I never gave you an answer. Do you not think—?"

It was then that he fully noticed my company: three men, dressed in all-black, bristling with weapons, and wearing on their faces scowls fit for the road.

"Margaret," asked Ned, "who are they?" He took a step back. "Have your spent your time in their company?"

"Well . . ." How to explain?

"And what if she has?" growled Carnatus. "Do you think us not up to riding with the fabled Megs?"

Now *this* was a turn of events!

"I do not know a 'Megs,'" said Ned. "I see only Margaret."

"It is a nickname," I told him.

"And you are 'fabled'?" he asked, "and ride with these blackguards? Why, they are cutthroats and outlaws! The high tobys who plague our roads!"

"You should not have said that," I told him, as Carnatus withdrew his pistol and pointed it straight at Ned's heart.

"Stand down," Jeffries ordered. He sighed, looking at me. "If this is Margaret's betrothed, we must respect her choice."

For the first time, Aventis spoke.

"Must we?" he asked, stroking his chin.

We all turned to stare at him.

"You, sir," he said to Ned. "May we infer from your speech you do not like our profession?"

"Indeed!" cried Ned. "I cannot think of anything lower."

"Then logic would require," said Aventis, "that Margaret, by having such friends, is tainted by association."

"Dam'd right!" Ned cried. "If I hadn't seen it directly, I could not have believed it. Mistress Margaret: so decent, such a hard worker, in the company of men like you!"

"You do not know her," said Aventis.

"And I do not wish to!"

Ned quickly snatched back his ring, then backed toward the door.

"I am sorry," he said to me. "I must withdraw my proposal. Your companions are not to my taste."

With that, he swept out the door.

"Ah, Megs," said Aventis blithely, shaking his head in mock sorrow. "God forbid we have driven him away."

"If that were forbidden by God, I would make you say ten Hail Marys. As it is, I owe you ten guineas for making him quit the place."

Carnatus bellowed with laughter as Jeffries's whole body shook. Taking advantage of their distraction, Aventis bent close to me and brushed his lips to my hair.

"Margaret, I love you," he whispered. "I even love Megs!"

I put my arm on his shoulder.

"Stand and deliver!" I said.

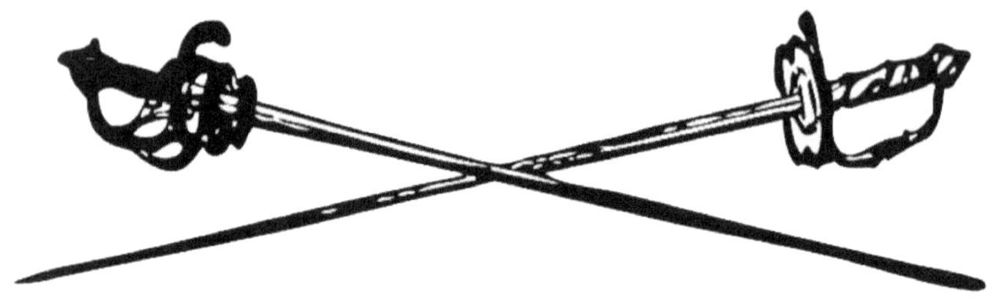

To download a FREE BOOK, go to:

https://amy-wolf.com/landing

www.ingramcontent.com/pod-product-compliance
Lightning Source LLC
Chambersburg PA
CBHW061018120726
47910CB00006B/2005

9781087846750